P9-DTD-031

GHOSTS *of* WEIRDWOOD

GHOSTS OF WEIRDWOOD

Thieves of Weirdwood 2

NEWBERY HONOR–WINNING AUTHOR
CHRISTIAN McKAY HEIDICKER

Illustrations by Anna Earley

A WILLIAM SHIVERING TALE

Henry Holt and Company
New York

Henry Holt and Company, *Publishers since 1866*
Henry Holt® is a registered trademark of Macmillan Publishing Group, LLC
120 Broadway, New York, NY 10271 · mackids.com

Copyright © 2021 by Wasabi Entertainment Inc.
All rights reserved.

Library of Congress Cataloging-in-Publication Data
Names: Heidicker, Christian McKay, author. | Earley, Anna, illustrator.
Title: Ghosts of Weirdwood / Christian McKay Heidicker. ; illustrated by Anna Earley.
Description: First edition. | New York : Henry Holt and Company, 2021. | Series: Thieves
of Weirdwood ; Book 2 | Audience: Ages 8–12. | Summary: Twelve-year-old reformed thieves
Arthur and Wally's determination to succeed as Novitiates of the Wardens of Weirdwood pits
them against the Order of Eldar and the ghosts they released for their own gain.
Identifiers: LCCN 2020022085 | ISBN 9781250302908 (hardcover)
Subjects: CYAC: Secret societies—Fiction. | Ghosts—Fiction. | Magic—Fiction. | Adventure
and adventurers—Fiction. | Fantasy.
Classification: LCC PZ7.1.H444 Gho 2021 | DDC [Fic]—dc23
LC record available at https://lccn.loc.gov/2020022085

Our books may be purchased in bulk for promotional, educational, or business use. Please
contact your local bookseller or the Macmillan Corporate and Premium Sales Department
at (800) 221-7945 ext. 5442 or by email at MacmillanSpecialMarkets@macmillan.com.

First edition, 2021 / Designed by Cindy De La Cruz
Printed in the United States of America by LSC Communications, Harrisonburg, Virginia
1   3   5   7   9   10   8   6   4   2

For Brian Geffen,
Boring Bits Exorcist, Cartographer Extraordinaire

"Practicing an art, no matter how well or badly,
is a way to make your soul grow."

—Kurt Vonnegut

GHOSTS *of* WEIRDWOOD

Wellsville, 1907

Jamie Hoxer's creature paintings were a smashing success.

"So *haunting*!" one person said of the flock of were-bats. "So realistic!"

"Wouldn't want to find one of *these* in my bathtub," said another of the copper spiders.

"This one looks like it could step right out of the canvas and sniff my hand!"

The woman was looking at the cloud fox. Jamie's favorite. She had sweated over its lightning bright eyes, its sleet teeth, over every hair on its nine tornado tails until the fox's portrait exuded a stormy *grandeur*.

"Oh! And look at this one! You could roast marshmallows on those horns!"

Jamie appreciated the praise buzzing through her art show. But she was starting to feel cramped in the crowded art gallery. So she stepped past her painting of the flaming bull and outside to get a breath of fresh air.

The evening was lit in pinks and oranges, the clouds rising like an eternal fire into the sky. Jamie was about to take a contented breath when something caught her eye across the street. Nailed to a telephone pole was a poster advertisement.

Come see! Come see!
Our ZOO OF MADNESS!
Creechers Unimaginationable!
Cheeper than a punch to the gut!
AT THE FAREGROUNDS

Jamie wasn't sure which part of the advertisement was worse—the spelling or the handwriting. But it struck her that it had been some time since she'd seen an actual animal. So she turned her fancy shoes down Main Street and headed toward the fairgrounds.

***

The zoo looked pasted together with spit and glue. The big top tent was ragged and patchwork, the cages lopsided and spotted with rust. Even the barker was rough around the edges.

"Letcherselves in, lovies and gents! Feast yer peepers on our *Zoo of Madness*! You'll swear yer dreams have sprung a leak!"

The man was tall with a round belly and an ill-fitting suit. His pant cuffs bunched at his ankles while his sleeves rode high on his arms. Scraggly gray hair hung greasy from under a frayed top hat, and his teeth were as brown and mottled as a tin can left beside a creek.

Jamie handed the barker a coin and then jerked back when a monkey shot out from under the man's top hat and, grinning, held out a ticket. Jamie smiled and took the ticket. Someone had sewn little gray wings onto the monkey's vest.

The barker grinned his rusted teeth. "Mind your hexpectations, Miss. They's about to be *reversified*."

Jamie joined a long queue of people, which slowly crept within the U of lopsided cages, circling the blood-colored tent. The visitors who'd seen the creatures had fallen completely silent, and Jamie couldn't tell if they were disappointed or awestruck.

Several minutes later, she reached the first cage and saw the unicorn. A rush of excitement bloomed in her chest but then quickly wilted away when she remembered that unicorns didn't exist. She squinted at the horn, which she assumed was made of tin, searching its base for signs of dried glue. She couldn't spot any, but the poor horse's head hung heavy, as if unable to bear the horn's weight.

Next came the goblin. It sat hunched in the corner of its cage, staring at the straw-strewn floor with slimy eyes as the zoo's visitors pointed and gawked. The goblin's chest and arms were dry and cracked, like someone had pasted dead frog skin to a malnourished child. This, thought Jamie, was in poor taste.

The third creature was meant to be some sort of basilisk. But clearly it was just three dead animals in one. Someone— that man with the awful teeth perhaps—had cut a rooster in half, glued a snake to its abdomen, and then stitched bat wings to its back. Finally, they'd arranged the body parts so that they resembled a single sleeping creature.

Jamie flinched when the basilisk seemed to *stir* in its sleep. But she excused the movement as the workings of an automaton, manipulated with cranks and gears by a remote operator. The only other possible explanation was that she'd been wrong about the glued horn and the pasted frog skin. That these creatures were actually . . .

But no. That was impossible.

Jamie reached the stifling heat of the last cage in the row and her face fell slack. She blinked at the thing, her pounding heart trying to decide whether to beat out of fear or excitement.

It was a flaming bull. No. It was *her* flaming bull, somehow escaped from her painting back at the art show. The bull's head swayed back and forth. Its molten eyes dripped tears of ember while its beard smoldered like a forest fire.

"Keep it moving!" a zoo-goer shouted. "My son wants to see the fire bison!"

Jamie blinked at the flaming bull several more times before snapping back to herself. She quickly left the line of zoo-goers and headed straight toward the ticket booth. But when she passed the scab-colored tent, a sound stopped her in her tracks. It was a mournful sound, and it echoed deep in the well of her memory. Trembling, she parted the tent's entrance flap and poked her head through.

Inside was a muscular woman with stone-gray skin. Her boulder-like biceps rippled as she tugged on a rope, which stretched taut into a giant *hole* that hung in the middle of the air. The hole was impossible. Like a tear in reality that looked onto an infinite cloudy sky.

The gray woman continued to grunt and pull on the rope until a net appeared in the hole. It seemed she had caught a cloud. Wait . . . It was too *fuzzy* to be a cloud. Jamie's heart sank when she saw the creature's scrunched tornado tails, its rainstorm eyes, its sleet teeth trying to chew through the netting . . .

It was her cloud fox.

You'll swear yer dreams have sprung a leak! the barker had said.

This hole seemed to be an entrance into Jamie's own imagination.

A hand smacked down on her shoulder, making Jamie jump and whirl around.

"Yer misplaced, Miss," the man with the rusted teeth said. He pointed a well-chewed thumb over his shoulder. "The beasties is *hindways* of ya."

Jamie noticed for the first time that the barker's eyes were almost entirely colorless. Like a shark's eyes.

She pointed a shaky finger toward her creation. "I . . . I don't know what's happening here, but that fox is *mine. I* painted it."

The man's eyebrows arched up his forehead. "Didja now?" He glanced at the gray-skinned woman. "Hear that, Astonishment? This here lady's the one we've got to thank for our current fount of wealthitude."

"I'm alerting the authorities," Jamie said, moving to step around the man with the rusted teeth.

The man matched her step, blocking her way. "Now, why would I let you leave when your imachination's so *valuating* to us?" He spoke so close, Jamie could smell the rot of his disintegrating teeth.

She looked over his shoulder and found the big gray woman blocking the way behind.

"*Silver Tongue!*" the man bellowed.

A moment later, a slight woman stepped into the tent. She was as thin as branches, and her skin was so pale, Jamie could see the blue of her veins showing. Her eyes were also colorless.

"Let's make our patron comfortified, shall we?" the man said.

"Sure thing, Rustmouth," Silver Tongue said in a voice as cracked and sugary as crème brûlée.

She pulled a flask from her belt and took a sip, a silvery

substance dribbling down her chin. *"Ah!"* the woman said, refreshed, then smiled liquidly at Jamie. *"Why doncha tie yourself up, cutie?"*

The words shrieked in Jamie's ears like metal scraping metal, and she found her hands involuntarily obeying the woman's commands, picking up the rope.

"Just think!" Rustmouth said. "With a bona fide *artiste* around, our humblish zoo can order up dreamity creatures on demand! Heh heh."

Jamie Hoxer continued to bind her own wrists and ankles against her will. And all the while, her cloud fox—somehow freed from canvas and paint—whimpered like a mournful summer storm.

1
THE THIEF AND THE NOVITIATE

Weirdwood Manor soared through the Fae like a lost balloon as the Novitiate tried and failed to tap into his magic.

Wally Cooper crouched behind a frozen bush, searching the courtyard for movement. Icicles dripped from the Manor's eaves while snow erased the sky. An icy wind froze the sweat on his arms and back. If the Manor didn't soar to a warmer pocket-world soon, he worried he might shiver to pieces.

Something caught Wally's eye—a wisp of steam coiling behind the stone fountain. Sekhmet might have been a master of hiding, but she couldn't keep her flaming swords from melting the snow.

Using his teeth, Wally tightened the straps on his gauntlets and then crept from behind the bush and through the howling flurries. Halfway to the fountain, the pressure in his ears shifted, and the blinding white of the sky disintegrated to murky green. The icicles dripped as the air grew thick, and the snow melted like butter in a hot pan.

Wally brushed the slush from his shoulders and loosened

his collar, adjusting to the swampy atmosphere. He sloshed the rest of the way to the fountain where he'd seen the coiling steam . . . but all he found was a single sword with a thorn-designed hilt lying on the ground.

"*Oh no,*" he said.

He heard the splash of a footstep behind him and whirled, raising his fists just as Sekhmet's other sword came slicing down. The blade sparked off of his gauntlets and deflected into a bush.

"Good!" Sekhmet said, rolling past him and scooping up her other trainer sword. "You made a mistake, believing I'd always have my weapons with me, but at least you stayed alert!"

Wally raised his gauntlets as she came at him again.

"Widen your stance!" she said, and struck—*Kling!* "But stay *flexible*." She struck again. *Clang!*

The last hit woke a sickening pain in Wally's left fist, but he swung with his right, trying to execute a sonic punch that would knock her flat. Sekhmet feinted back as smooth as smoke, throwing him off-balance.

"Remember, *creativity* fuels magic," she said. "Not strength." Before he could block, her left blade swept in and tapped his bicep. "It's not *here*." Her right blade tapped him on the temple. "It's *here*. Watch."

She closed her eyes and whirled her swords, sparking them together and sending out a flurry of flaming butterflies that Wally had to extinguish with his gauntlets before they singed his eyebrows.

"Hope that didn't tire you out!" Sekhmet said, and came at him again, giddy with the thrill of the fight.

As she drove him backward through the courtyard, the sky shifted again and again—from mossy green to swirling gray to salty blue. The air howled with wind, then roared with waves, then grew stale as a desert. In the brief silence, Wally tried tapping into his magic—arranging his stance and fists like Sekhmet had taught him and waiting for that *feeling* to come alive in his chest.

He swung again . . . only to feel his gauntlet whistle harmlessly through the air.

Sekhmet laughed. "Lady Weirdwood may as well have strapped *sponges* to your fists for all the good those gauntlets are doing you!"

They continued to fight as the sky curdled with clouds.

Thunder rumbled. Lightning struck one of the Manor's spires. After a downpour of rain so thick Wally could barely see his own swinging fists, the sky froze over again, encasing the courtyard in ice. The next time Sekhmet feinted back, Wally lunged forward as far as his feet would carry him, hoping to get in one measly shot. But his feet slipped on the ice and flew out from under him, his face smacking the frozen ground.

Wally rolled over and stared at the sky's shifting colors. A raw bruise spread across his cheek.

Sekhmet tapped his throat with her trainer sword. "*Dead.*" She clasped his arm and hauled him to his feet. "Final lesson of the day. Always pay attention to your environment."

Wally removed his gauntlets and flexed the ache out of his fingers. "The ground *froze* beneath my feet."

Sekhmet smirked. "I'll make sure to send a note to the Order of Eldar, requesting they never fight us anywhere *icy*."

"That's not what I meant."

"I'll tell them not to fight us anywhere *unpredictable*, then," she said, holstering her sword. "But that's going to eliminate most of the Fae."

Wally rubbed his bruised cheek to hide his embarrassment.

She pointed to his chest. "Before you even *think* about swinging, you've got to feel that magic rise up in you."

Wally touched his sternum. "What does it feel like again?"

Sekhmet shrugged. "The Wardens describe it all kinds of ways. A burning. A *tingling*. A fountain of stars. To me, it's like drinking a glass of iced tea on my grandma's back porch."

Wally had never felt anything like that. Not for the first

time, he wondered if Lady Weirdwood had made a mistake bringing him on as a Novitiate.

Before he had come to Weirdwood Manor, Wally had been a thief, taking from others in order to survive. But now the Wardens were giving him an opportunity to save people instead. To protect them against dangerous Fae-born that slipped into the Real through Rifts in the Veil—like murderous dolls or scythe-taloned birds or tentacles the size of ship masts.

Wally Cooper's life suddenly had purpose. And he didn't want to lose that.

"Don't worry," Sekhmet said, throwing her arm around his shoulder and guiding him back toward the Manor. "You and I have nothing but time to train until the staff figures out how to exterminate those Scarab larvae. You'll tap into your magic long before your first official mission."

It had been a month since the Manor's Abyssment had become infested with Golden Scarab larvae. The mechanical insects chewed on the roots, making Weirdwood hurtle from pocket-world to pocket-world—the Fae's many different realms. This was what made the weather in the courtyard about as predictable as a baby's temper.

"Focus on your drills," Sekhmet said, clapping Wally on the shoulder. "I'll see you out here tomorrow morning. Clock time, not sky time."

She vanished down the western passage, and Wally massaged his sore fists. The sky had finally settled, gleaming with crystalline branches that stretched toward purple stars.

He wondered how he could not feel magical in a place like this.

***

Arthur Benton was sitting so close to the courtyard's exit, he was nearly blocking the door. Wally's cheeks flushed with embarrassment. The only thing worse than being soundly beaten by Sekhmet was having an audience.

"You didn't see that, did you?" he asked.

"Hmm?" Arthur said, glancing up from his notebook. "Oh! Hello, Cooper! No, no, no. I just wanted a scenic window by which to work on my own magic." He gazed outside, where the colors shifted like a kaleidoscope. "Inspiring, isn't it?"

Arthur wasn't fooling anyone. The kid seemed to always be sitting right outside of Wally's magic classes, trying to absorb the lessons. After Arthur had behaved selfishly on their last adventure, Lady Weirdwood had refused to bring him on as a Novitiate. The only reason she hadn't dropped him off in Kingsport was because the Manor wouldn't hold still long enough.

Arthur saw this as an opportunity to change the old woman's mind about him.

"I'll tell ya, Cooper," he said, tapping his notebook with his pen. "This new spell is going to blow the wedding veil right off of Lady Weirdwood's head!"

"What's it do?" Wally asked.

Arthur smiled at his work. "It's a story about a *mean* case of insect cavities that erode the pincers of pesky Scarabs! Once this spell handles the Manor's current infestation problem,

Lady Weirdwood will probably skip that embarrassing Novitiate business and promote me directly to Wardenship!"

Arthur was also clearly working out of guilt. Wally wasn't sure whom he blamed more: his brother Graham for acquiring the pregnant Golden Scarab or Arthur for being gullible enough to sneak it into the Manor for him.

"Let's see this story, then," Wally said, trying to steal a peek.

"No!" Arthur said, snapping the notebook shut.

Beneath, Wally noticed the book Lady Weirdwood had given Arthur that told of their first adventure in the Manor. The book was called *Thieves of Weirdwood*.

Arthur blushed. "I mean, I wouldn't want to embarrass you with this spell, what with you struggling with your training and all."

"Kind of you," Wally said dully, and turned to leave.

"Wait!" Arthur leapt to his feet. "Where are you going?"

"Feasting hall. Fighting across half a dozen climates really works up an appetite."

Arthur rocked his head back and forth, then quickly followed after. "Oh, *why not*? Gotta fuel the old word burner, eh?"

Wally didn't point out that he hadn't invited him. But he was too hungry to care. When he'd passed the kitchen earlier, it had smelled like October—roasted chestnuts, pumpkin stew, apple sausage, and cider. He'd been dreaming of those flavors ever since.

As they descended the western staircase, the Manor bucked like a dropped dollhouse, nearly sending them sprawling down the stairs. A splintering sound echoed in the distance, like an entire wing was threatening to snap off.

"*Bloody Scarabs*," Arthur mumbled, using the bannister to pull himself upright.

An argument came storming up the stairs. Ludwig, the giant carpenter, stomped heavy, while Weston, his petite gardener twin, scrambled to keep up.

"Ve require *pesticides*!" Ludwig said. He held a black can marked with a skull between his giant forefinger and thumb. "Ze Scarabs vill overvhelm us ozervise! It vould be suicide not to bring zis!"

Weston jumped and snatched the poison can from his brother's giant fingers. "You spray enough of this stuff down there and it'll seep into the *roots*. You'll kill my imp locks!"

"And if ve don't handle zese Scarabs quick, my beautiful voodvork vill *crumble*." Ludwig plucked the poison can from his brother's hands as if stealing a toffee from a child.

Wally and Arthur made room as the twins passed between them and continued up the stairs.

"I don't get it," Arthur said. "Why doesn't Lady Weirdwood just squeeze insecticide out of the Manor's roots or something?"

"Lady Weirdwood may control every room and hallway in Weirdwood," Wally said, remembering one of his lessons, "but the Abyssment is a realm all its own."

He resisted a shudder. Weirdwood's basement was home to unspeakable horrors the Wardens had captured in the Real, but for one reason or another were unable to return to the Fae. Wally was just glad he was only a Novitiate and didn't have to join the staff as they descended into the pits beneath the Manor.

He and Arthur reached the first floor and stopped before

three doors, each carved with a different symbol: a heart, a star, and a set of balancing scales.

"Which one leads to the kitchen, again?" Wally asked.

Arthur shrugged. "You're the Novitiate."

Wally considered the three symbols. He'd never traveled to the feasting hall from the courtyard before, and some of the Manor's hallways could be dangerous if you were unfamiliar with how they worked.

"Star it is," he said, and opened the door onto a breathtaking passageway that shimmered with starlight and cricket song.

Its floor had collapsed.

Wally sighed. "Why did the Scarabs have to chew through the *nice* hallway?"

He tried the heart door next. It opened onto a passage that smelled of expensive perfume and trickled with waterfalls. But then dozens of stony eyes turned their way. An army of cupid statues drew stone bows, aiming heart-tipped arrows at the boys. Wally slammed the door moments before the arrows came piercing through.

"*That* one's turned on its defense systems," he said.

Finally, he tried the door with the balancing scales. Its oak panels and crimson rugs were stately lit and stuffy as a courtroom.

"Looks safe," Arthur said.

"There's a floor and no arrows," Wally admitted.

The two stepped carefully down the hallway.

"After I finish my story that eliminates those Scarabs," Arthur said, "I'll craft a spell that safely transports its reader from one side of the Manor to the other. Should be easy enou—"

He tripped, spilling his notebook and pen across the floor, then quickly collected them and stood up straight. "Darned Scarabs must be gnawing directly below here too."

In the dim light, Wally noticed the floorboards closing up right where Arthur had tripped.

They continued on.

"So, *Cooper*," Arthur said in a clearly rehearsed voice. "What has Sekhmet been teaching you? You know, besides how to punch stuff."

Wally tried to decide whether anything he'd learned would be dangerous in Arthur's hands.

"Nothing special," he said honestly. "Mostly that creativity fuels magic. She says that a lot."

"In that case, I've got magic up to my eyeball skins!" Arthur said.

And yet, you can't do any in front of me, Wally thought.

"This morning, Sekhmet said you can actually *feel* it when you've tapped into your magic," he said. "Like a *tingling*." He flexed his sore fingers. "My fists tingle every time her swords hit my gauntlets, but I think that's just because they're going numb."

Arthur scratched at the back of his neck. "Has she taught you any specific *magical spells*?"

Wally shook his head.

Arthur cleared his throat. "I only ask because I wanted to make sure she's teaching you the *right stuff*. I've discovered oodles of spells in my exploration of that sprawling library of wonder, the Bookcropolis, and considering I understood them all *perfectly*, I—*Augh!*"

The floorboards flew open beneath his feet. Wally's hand shot out, grabbing hold of Arthur's wrist and pulling him back up before the floor devoured him whole.

Arthur swallowed and straightened himself. "Good thing Sekhmet's been training your reflexes."

The boys stared through the parted floorboards into the boundless darkness of the Abyssment. A faint munching emanated from below as the Scarab larvae slowly gnawed away at the Manor's roots.

Wally doubted the metallic insects had caused the parting floorboards. He looked back toward the balancing scales on the door. "I think this hallway punishes lies, Arthur."

Arthur didn't say a word for the rest of the walk.

***

After a long journey of tilts and trembles and a detour around a caved-in ceiling, the feasting hall finally came into sight. The air grew spiced with apple, cinnamon, and pumpkin.

But before they made it to the entrance, Amelia stepped in their path, giving both of them a start.

"I checked the Slopping District of Mirror Kingsport," she said, her one blue eye fixed on Wally. "Your brother was nowhere to be seen."

"Oh," Wally said. "S-sorry about that."

Amelia narrowed her eye, as if she could glare his brother's whereabouts out of him. Weirdwood's head of staff was as intimidating as its most dangerous hallways.

"Wait," Arthur said, flipping open his notebook and preparing his pen. "How did you check Mirror Kingsport with the Manor on the fritz?"

Amelia shot him a look so withering she didn't have to remind him that he wasn't a Novitiate and therefore wasn't allowed that information.

Arthur quietly closed his notebook.

Amelia's gaze fell back on Wally. "Tell me where else your brother might be hiding."

Wally stared at the floor. "I honestly don't know, ma'am."

Up until a month ago, Wally had spent nearly every waking moment worrying about Graham. If he wasn't visiting his brother in Greyridge Mental Hospital, he was stealing money to pay the hospital bills. Now that Graham was free in the Fae, Wally could finally focus on himself.

"Mr. *Cooper*," Amelia said. "Your brother *attacked* this Manor with *mechanized Scarabs*. If you're hiding information regarding his whereabouts, then you are willfully assisting an *enemy*."

Graham the villain. The idea still didn't fit in Wally's head. It was true his brother wanted to bring down the Veil that separated the Real and the Fae—granting everyone and their great uncle Melvin access to magic and releasing chaos on the world. But Graham was Wally's only family.

He shrugged.

"You will let me know if you think of anything," Amelia said, and pushed past them down the hall.

"I hope you catch him, Amelia!" Arthur called after her.

"I mean, it is *Graham's* fault that this Manor is hurtling uncontrollably through the Fae, right?"

The door slammed shut, and Arthur sighed. "She'll like me someday."

They continued toward the feasting hall and its cornucopia of scents.

"*Wally!*" a voice called.

Wally whirled and raised his fists, ready to fight.

"At ease, soldier," Sekhmet said, smiling as she approached. "We've got a mission."

Wally slowly lowered his fists. "But—but the doors are still scrambled."

Sekhmet smirked. "Scrambled doors mean nothing to a Trackdragon."

"*Whoa.*" Arthur flipped open his notebook. "What's a *Trackdragon*?"

"Something you'll never have to worry about," Sekhmet said, and handed Wally a paper ticket.

It was printed with a steam-coiled *S* and the words *Shadowrail Company.*

"Lady Weirdwood spent the last month growing a Trackdragon platform in the northern passage. Now, while the staff handles the Scarab situation, you and I get to go sew up a *Rift*!"

Arthur took notes furiously. "Uh-huh, uh-huh. And what's causing this particular Rift?"

Sekhmet didn't bother looking at him this time. "It tore open somewhere in the countryside. The Order of Eldar is taking advantage of it by dragging fantastical creatures into the Real and selling tickets to humans."

Wally's muscles locked up. Would he have to fight the Order? He still hadn't tapped into his magic. His punches felt as harmless as kitten swipes.

Sekhmet was already backing down the hallway. "The Trackdragon will arrive at the Empress Archway in a half hour. We don't know when the Manor will be able to pick us up, so pack for three days, at least!"

"Should we pack for cold weather or hot?" Arthur called after her. "Dress or casual?"

"Not your problem, Arthur!" Sekhmet called back, and disappeared through the door.

Arthur seized Wally by the shirt. "Hide me in your luggage, Cooper. I *need* to go on this adventure!"

Wally shrugged him away. "Sorry, man. I gotta go pack."

He hustled down the hallway, only glancing back to get one last whiff of the October feast he would never get to try. Arthur stood, hands in his pockets, shoulders slumped. He tried to smile at Wally, but it faltered and died on his lips. It seemed it was finally sinking in. No matter how much Arthur boasted about his abilities, he simply wasn't Novitiate material.

Wally gave his friend a small guilty wave. Then he scaled the stairs to the Moon Tower.

***

Wally was packing as quickly as he could—gauntlets, boots, martial arts manuals—when an invisible force flopped into his bed.

"Wally, the Bookcropolis is *sooooo booooooring*," Breeth said. The ghost girl's face cascaded in the sheets off the side of his bed. "Lady Weirdwood gave me *research assignments*." She gagged the words. "Today, I had to possess a book about *Pesticides for Mechanical Insects*. I got so bored, the ink started to melt off the pages."

"Sorry to hear that," Wally said.

He was trying to keep his hands from shaking while coiling his belt. The sweat from that day's training hadn't even dried on his shirt yet. Bruises were still blooming all over his body. He needed to find some courage for the journey. But he couldn't pack something like that.

"When it's not boring, it's *gross*," Breeth said. "Yesterday, I was trying to find a book called *Tending to Your Living Manor* and instead found a book about tree people who read books made of human *skin*! Blech, right?"

Wally went to his bookshelf and grabbed a heavy volume that Weston had given to him—*Daydream Fae-born: 7,986th edition*—and placed it in his bag.

"But now your classes are finally done!" Breeth said, rippling up the sheets. "What are we doing today? Bush fencing? Staircase teeter-totter? And don't say *take a nap* again. Keeping the pillow fluffy is *not* fun."

Wally double-checked his bag, making sure he had everything he needed.

"Wait, whoa, are you *packing*?" Breeth said. She bounced the feather mattress like a toddler, nearly spilling Wally's duffel bag. "Are we going somewhere?" She gasped. "Is it the *Fae*?" She gasped louder. "A narwhal fencing match? Or, oh! *Centaur dressage*?"

Wally collapsed onto the bed. "I'm going on my first mission."

"*Yesssssssss!*" Breeth's sheet wrapped him up in a tight squeeze. "I am *so* ready to fight things again! Maybe I'll even possess another monster! Ha ha! *Wheeeee!*"

Wally sat up and squirmed until Breeth's sheet released him. She creaked out of his bed and into his wall shelf, which bent into a big, goofy grin.

"Um, Breeth?" Wally said, staring at his bruised hands. "I . . . think I need to do this one alone."

Breeth's shelf grin faltered, threatening to spill his candles and ink jars.

Wally quickly rescued the objects. "It's just that you helped so much against those monsters in Kingsport. And while I obviously appreciate it, I think it kept me from tapping into my magic." He set his ink jar on his desk. "If you come along, I'll just use you as a crutch."

Breeth smiled again, straining the shelf so much it was in danger of splitting in half.

"You okay?" he asked.

"Me? *Psh.* Of course I'm okay! I'll just go back to the Bookcropolis and read a *book* about an adventure instead. That's the same, right? Who doesn't love *books*?"

"*You* don't. You *just* told me that." He searched her knotted eyes. "Breeth, you can say if it's not all right. You can be mad."

Breeth smiled so hard the shelf actually cracked. "*I'm not mad.*"

Wally grabbed his duffel bag and went to the door. If he didn't get to the Trackdragon platform soon, Sekhmet would probably make him run drills the entire trip. "When I get back, we can do all those things you suggested. I promise."

"Heard *that* one before," the shelf creaked miserably.

Wally winced when he remembered all the promises to Breeth he'd broken. Like helping bring her killer to justice. Or getting her back to her parents in the afterlife. But he didn't know where to *begin* with those. And the more the ghost girl demanded he play with her, the more he felt like he was babysitting.

"Sorry, Breeth," Wally said. "My muscles are wrecked. It's all I can do not to crawl into this bed and sleep for a *week*. But instead I have to go on my first mission, and I haven't even tapped into my *magic* yet. I'm really scared."

He looked at his bookshelf, but it had returned to its normal wooden self. Breeth was gone. Creaked away into the Manor. Wally sighed and threw his duffel bag over his shoulder and started the long walk toward the Empress Archway. The image of Breeth's strained smile and Arthur's hopeless expression were burned into his memory. Wally wondered if he was making a terrible mistake, leaving behind the two people who'd kept him alive on the last adventure.

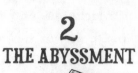

2
THE ABYSSMENT

B reeth was throwing a splinter fit.

She cruised around the Manor's walls at such a furious speed that she ripped the wallpaper, cracked the support beams, and frayed the floorboards like thorn bushes. Wally didn't want her on the adventure? *Fine.* She didn't want to go with him anyway. He was acting like a *grown-up*. And grown-ups were sad and serious and made you read boring books about algebra or how to exterminate mechanical *pests*.

She thundered through the upper attics, shaking shingles from the roof. What if this was her life from now on? What if as Wally grew older and older, he wanted to play less and less, while Breeth stayed exactly the same fun age until one day they were no longer friends?

The thought was so depressing it made her stop abruptly, sending a half dozen portraits clattering to the ground.

She heard a voice.

"All I know is that Lady Weirdwood said the staff would be as dead as dog meat without it."

Breeth pulled a U-turn, making the walls groan like a ship,

and arrived at the entrance to the Abyssment, where Arthur was animatedly speaking to the armored guard.

Arthur held a can, embossed with a skull and crossbones. "She told me to run downstairs, keeping my eyes on my shoes the whole time, hand this poison to Ludwig, Weston, and Amelia, and then sprint back up as quickly as my young legs can carry me. Her words, not mine."

"*Oy*," Breeth said in the walls.

She'd heard Arthur lie too many times to be taken in by his stories. Fortunately, the Abyssment's guard, a creaky suit of armor, also seemed immune to Arthur's charms. Its scalloped gloves angled its halberd to block the way as a haunted voice echoed within its helmet.

"*A thousand malodorous deaths await the thoughtless soul who would hazard to venture—*"

"Yeah, yeah," Arthur said. "I've read the same kind of warning in a hundred adventure books." He sighed, tapping the can of poison against his palm.

Breeth shifted in the walls. She wasn't convinced by Arthur's words. Not in the slightest. But she was worried about the staff, down there in the Fae-born infested darkness. Especially Weston, the small, hairy groundskeeper who'd once spared her life when she had possessed a mouse thing.

What if getting that poison did prevent the staff from getting eaten? Or fileted? Or *melted*? If Wally refused to let Breeth help on his mission, then she wanted to be able to do *something* good for Weirdwood that didn't involve reading *books*.

Breeth creaked into a nearby four-legged table, shook the lamp off her top, and then galloped toward the Abyssment door. Arthur leapt out of the way as Breeth clasped one of the table's clawed feet around the door handle and pulled. Before she could get it open, the suit of armor tackled her to the ground as if she were nothing but a naughty piece of furniture trying to escape.

After a lot of clanky wrestling and rolling around, Breeth managed to bend the table's four legs around the guard, binding his metal arms to his breast plate. Then she creaked into the floorboard, leaving the guard struggling in the oaken hug of the lifeless table.

"Sorry!" Breeth said, hoping it really was just a suit of armor and didn't feel pain. "All right, Arthur, let's get that poison to the sta—"

But Arthur was gone, having used the ghost girl's distraction to slip into the Abyssment. She got a bad feeling and creaked down the wooden railing of the stone staircase. Halfway to the bottom, she spotted the can of poison sitting on one of the steps.

"Ohhhhh crap," she said, and zipped down the bannister.

She didn't know what Arthur was up to, but she desperately hoped she wouldn't have to possess any of the Abyssment's nightmare Fae-born in order to save him. She had learned how to possess living things, but she had no idea how to escape them before they died. And she would prefer not to live an entire lifetime as some fanged and mucus-oozing *thing* in a bottomless pit.

Fortunately, Breeth caught up to Arthur before he reached the bottom of the steps.

"Gotcha!" she said, flexing her bannister to coil around his waist, spiraling him tight against the wall.

"Hello, Breeth," Arthur said, as if she were simply hugging him in greeting. "Thanks for distracting the guard for me."

"Where in bloody noses do you think you're going?" Breeth asked. She knew Arthur couldn't hear her, but she wasn't about to let that stop her from yelling at him. "Do you have any idea what's down there? *Rattledrakes! Katydidn'ts!* Mountain goats that are actually *mountain*-sized!" Her knotted eyes gazed down the dark steps. "Or at least that's what I *imagine* is down there. I've never actually been *batty* enough to check!"

Arthur sighed calmly. "Before you go thumping all over my idea, you should know something."

Breeth tapped her bannister impatiently, waiting for a typical grandiose speech filled with lies.

"I *really* want to be a Novitiate," he said.

"That is the worst reason *ever*!" *Thump thump thump thump thump!*

"It's my fault those Scarab larvae are skittering amok in the roots of this fine Manor," Arthur said soberly. "So I'm going to prove my worthiness by stopping them with my story magic."

"No!" *Thump!* "Bad!" *Thump!* "Death and loss of skin!" *Thump thump!* "Limbs torn from sockets and fingernails from fingers!"

Arthur ignored her thumping. "Breeth?"

Breeth froze. Something in his voice had changed.

"This is just between you and me," he said. "But I've been

working on my writing, and, well . . . my magic is disappointing, to say the least."

Breeth relaxed her grip a bit.

"Every time I try to breathe life into a story, it ends up as nothing more than ink on paper. I've never been able to tap into that *tingly* feeling the Wardens talk about." Arthur frowned at his shoes. "I've been so embarrassed about my lack of magic that I even *lied* to Wally about it. Of course, he believed me, innocent, gullible kid that he is."

Breeth tightened her bannister again.

"I've thought long and hard about it," he continued, "and I realized what my art's been missing: *danger*. When I inhabited Garnett Lacroix with Huamei's claw Quill, I was *terrified* that I was going to die. But it was that very fear that sharpened my writing skills and helped me save the day." He gazed into the darkness below. "What better way to reignite my latent ability than by hurling myself into a monster-infested basement?"

Arthur was *purposefully* trying to put himself in danger? Breeth was tempted to squeeze her railing even tighter. But that might kill him.

"I am in your hands, Breeth," Arthur said, then shifted uncomfortably. "Er, *bannister*. If you think this is a terrible idea, then you can roll me right back upstairs and turn me over to Lady Weirdwood." Arthur stared down the stairs. "*Or you can join me on my descent into this untapped well of adventure and help me redeem myself.*"

With that, Arthur leaned back against Breeth's railing, and he waited.

Breeth considered what Arthur had said. Something

dripped in the Abyssment. The armored guard clanged and struggled above. Her railing started to ache. Not a human ache but an ache of *boredom*. A boredom so complete she feared if she returned to the Bookcropolis and possessed one more book, she might turn into a book herself.

At least Arthur wasn't trying to act all grown up like Wally.

"*Fine*," she said as she slowly uncoiled the bannister, rolling Arthur down the stairs and plopping him at the bottom. "But if you die down there, I'll be so mad, I won't even talk to you when you haunt the Manor's walls."

Arthur didn't hear her, of course. He just patted her bannister like the head of an obedient dog, then pulled out his notebook so Breeth would have some organic matter to possess.

They continued down past the first-floor cells where Breeth had once freed Arthur and Wally, and then they descended into the fathomless depths of the Abyssment.

***

The Manor gave its last gasp of light as Arthur rounded the spiral staircase. A dark wind howled from below, but Breeth couldn't tell if it blew hot or cold. Arthur's sweat dripped on her notebook's pages while his fingers trembled against her spine.

To calm her nerves, Breeth counted the steps. After step seven hundred, the stairs started to *transform*—from wood to gleaming black diamonds. Like snakeskin.

"Boy, am I ever glad I don't have feet right now," she whispered.

Fortunately for Arthur, his eyes were trained on the expansive darkness ahead.

They reached the Abyssment's second floor where the air seemed to whisper with warning. Breeth widened her papery eyes and barely made out giant towers wavering in the darkness.

Arthur swallowed. "This is good," he said, voice trembling. "The more terrified I am, the better I'll write, and the faster we can get out of this place. Let's see . . . We could use some light."

He flipped open the notebook and closed his eyes for a moment as if trying to tap into something mystical. He opened his eyes and placed a trembling pen to paper. Breeth tried not to giggle as Arthur scribbled on her page:

The Abyssment filled with a light so bright and glorious that it frightened away any monstrous beings that would do harm to our valiant hero.

She squeaked when he stabbed a period with finality. They both gazed wide-eyed, blind and expectant.

"Any moment now . . . ," Arthur said.

The Abyssment remained as black as nothing.

Breeth sighed. "Guess this is *my* job."

She took a fluttery breath and leapt out of the notebook and into the darkness. She sensed squishy lumps on the ground and seeped into them. She was hoping to travel through the plant life to locate a wooden lamppost or something. But the moment she inhabited the squishy stuff, it tingled to life, emanating an electric blue light, which filled the dark space.

They were on the bottom of a vast, waterless sea. Towering strands of pale seaweed wavered under the movement of flitting skeleton fish. Giant albino crab shells skittered along the black sand around urchin carcasses that bulged as big as houses. A puffer fish the size of a blimp floated through the seaweed towers, searching with dead pearl eyes that beamed like spotlights. They were all dead. Ghosts of haunted depths that no longer needed water to float. Like an ocean of the underworld.

Arthur's eyes glittered in the blue light. "I *knew* I'd write well if I was in danger!"

"*I* did this!" Breeth said from the squishy lichen. "This is *bioluminescence*. My dad taught me about it. The plants light up when they're disturbed becaaauuuse—I just remembered you can't hear me."

She oozed through the lichen before his feet, lighting the ground electric blue, and Arthur strode past the seaweed skyscrapers, more confident than ever.

"Now to locate the Wardens . . . ," he said, scribbling something new in his notebook.

Breeth's lichen gurgled, annoyed. "Whatever you're doing, do it fast so I can do it better."

"*Our intrepid hero slash detective slash author extraordinaire noticed the devilishly subtle clues that led to the nest of the doomed Scarab larvae.*"

Breeth wasn't sure how to help with this one. But she extended her senses and found three sets of footprints pressed into the squishy ground. One giant. One dainty. And one Amelia's. She ruffled each indent, creating three sets of glow-in-the-dark footprints that led across the dead ocean floor.

Arthur laughed aloud at what he thought was his solution. "Benton, you literary *savant*! Come, Breeth! Nothing can harm us with my magic at hand!"

Breeth couldn't wait to tell Wally all about this so he could tease Arthur on her behalf. That was, if she decided to talk to Wally again . . . and Arthur didn't end up getting murdered by Fae-born.

The ghostly ocean floor ended at a jagged ledge, which fell away onto sandy stairs that looked like they belonged on a pyramid. The next floor resembled a starless desert.

"Hmm," Arthur said, squinting into the darkness.

Breeth located a dead bit of driftwood and rolled it into his path.

"Aha!" he said, snatching it up. "Excellent idea, Breeth! I *knew* you'd be of some value on this mission."

Breeth refrained from strangling him with his own shirt while he scooped up a clump of the bioluminescent matter and wrapped it around the top of the dead branch to make a blue glow torch, which Breeth seeped into.

They descended the sandy steps and landed on a giant slab of yellow stone that stretched to a sunless horizon. Arthur paused a moment, waiting to see what horrors awaited them. When nothing stirred, he lowered his blue torch and found the staff's footprints across the sandy stone. One giant. One small . . . And one limping.

Breeth gulped. Was Amelia hurt? The staff's footprints were crisscrossed with what appeared to be bird prints. But when Breeth squinted closer, she realized they were the impressions of tiny skeleton feet . . .

Then she noticed the great furrows that interlaced them and the scrapes in the stone itself. They seemed to have been carved by giant blades.

"Whoa, whoa, wait a minute," Breeth said.

But Arthur was writing again. *"Our intrepid hero found himself in a desert of destitution. Fortunately, he had remembered to wear his tan shirt and pants, perfectly camouflaging himself against the sandy backdrop so that no enemy could perceive him."*

Arthur held up his sleeve to the desert floor—which almost looked the same color under the blue light—and nodded with satisfaction.

"I can still see you!" Breeth yelled uselessly. "And so will whatever else is down here!"

Somewhere in the darkness, a voice whispered, as dry as a grasshopper carcass. *"Hepp?"* Shhhink! *"Hepp me?"* Shhhhhhhhhink. *"Hepp?"*

With the dry voice came a sound like swords dragging against stone. Something big was coming toward them. And it was desperate.

"Pease?" Shhhink! *"Hepp? Peeeeaaaaaaase? Hepp me?"* Shhhhhhhhhink.

Arthur's breath grew pinched. "We'd better get moving in case that thing gets a lucky shot in on my camouflage." He studied the staff's footprints in the sand. "This way!"

He moved quickly, but the scraping sound was gaining on him. *"Hepp? Pease?"*

Before the thing could catch up, Breeth leapt out of the

torch into the darkness behind them and soared through meters of emptiness. She located a dangling bit of something once living and possessed it.

Breeth was too horrified to scream.

She was inside a piece of dried skin. It hung from the jaw of a massive, desiccated creature, meat dripping from its bones. The creature walked on long scissor-like fingernails, which scraped against the sandstone. *Shhhhhink. Shhhhhink. Shhhhhink.* On its shoulder rode a mummified parrot that opened its cracked bill and spoke with the voice of a child. *"Hepp? Hepp me?"* Around its feet swarmed smaller desiccated creatures, hungry teeth clattering, empty eye-sockets searching, waiting for their mother to direct them to food. To *Arthur*.

"Arthur, *run*!" Breeth shouted helplessly. "You are *not* invisible, and you are going to *die*!"

Arthur didn't budge. Instead, he set down his torch to write in his notebook. The mummified skeleton creature broke into a lope, its fingernails shrieking against the stone. Breeth tugged back on its facial skin like reins, hoping to slow it, but the dead skin tore loose from its skull.

Breeth flopped helpless to the sandy floor. The thing galloped on its fingernails toward Arthur—*clink clink clink! clink clink clink!*—lifting its forelegs to slash him to ribbons so its children could feast.

Breeth gave her piece of skin a mighty push upward, shedding sand and flapping herself like a pair of wings. She flapped once and then again until she took flight. She watched in horror from the air as Arthur ducked to grab his torch at the exact same moment the creature slashed, shaving millimeters off the back of his hair. The thing lifted its other fingernails straight upward to skewer him just as Breeth swooped in and slapped herself over its empty eye sockets. The thing shrieked, trying to shake Breeth loose as Arthur quickly swiped up his torch and hustled deeper into the darkness.

The creature scraped the skin from its eyes, so Breeth spirited to the ropy meat that dangled from its skeletal limbs. She swung the meat in a wide arc again and again, round and round, wrapping it around the creature's fingernails and toenails that propped it up. They quickly bound together, and the creature collapsed, its brittle jaw crunching against the sandstone.

Breeth fluttered back into Arthur's notebook moments before the thing's skeletal children fell on their mother, chewing on her jerky skin.

"That you, Breeth?" Arthur asked his notebook pleasantly. "You just missed me crafting a brilliant sentence to stop whatever that thing was in its tracks! Good thing I write quick on my feet, eh?"

Breeth possessed his shirt and tried to pull him back toward the stairs. "We are going back. Right. *Now!*"

"Don't be silly," Arthur said, tugging his collar back in place. "We've made it this far and without a scratch on us!"

Breeth gave up pulling. Arthur's shirt wasn't strong enough to haul him all the way back up to the Manor. She returned to his notebook, helpless, as Arthur descended another set of stairs, which grew soft as mushrooms beneath his feet.

The Abyssment's third floor shimmered with dust, reflecting in the bioluminescent torch.

"The ground's getting weird," Arthur said, struggling to walk.

He lifted a shoe, pulling up a taffy strand of slime, and then held up his blue torch. The entire floor had been enveloped by a pulsing fungus. Its body was composed of nightmare Fae-born—goblins and demons and venomous fairies—absorbed into its mushroomy expanse. Squishy stems twined through the Fae-born's eyes and mouths, as if the fungus was *feeding* on them.

Arthur gulped. "Maybe we should turn back."

"*Y'think?*" Breeth said.

But before Arthur could turn to leave, something on the ceiling spotted him. A bloated, blue eye dangling from a mushroom stem. It blinked at Arthur, and then a dark wind moaned from the Abyssment's depths, wafting greenish spores from the fungus's gills. They whirled through the air just as Arthur gasped, drawing them into his lungs.

Arthur's face fell slack. He stared into the eye.

"Um, Arthur?" Breeth said. "We were just *leaving*?"

When he didn't move, she seeped into the blue torch and pulled it back, trying and guide him away. But Arthur simply let the torch fall to the squishy ground. He wouldn't stop staring at the eye.

Something squirmed out of the fungus. Slimy white threads stretched toward him like the growing hair of the dead, closer and closer to Arthur's legs. They wrapped around his ankles.

"*Arthur?*" Breeth said. "This is the moment when you kick that thing and *run*."

Arthur, of course, couldn't hear her. He just grinned at the big blue eye, his own eyes growing fuzzy with admiration. A cold horror seeped through Breeth's spirit when she saw that the green of his irises was slowly fading, leaving behind only white.

"Those spores got inside your brain!" she said. "You gotta sneeze them out!"

She possessed Arthur's collar and tried tickling his nostrils. But he merely brushed her away and lay down on the slimy soft ground, allowing the mushroom's threads to crawl up his chest.

"Arthur!" Breeth screamed. "Get up! *Please!* This thing's gonna *eat* you!"

She tugged his shirt as hard as she could, but the material started to tear. Arthur sighed, as contented as if he was lying in a sunny field instead of a nightmare basement. With each breath, he exhaled spores. With each blink, his eyes grew crustier white. The mushroom's threads had made it to his ears.

"Oh no, oh no, oh no."

Breeth stretched her ghostly senses toward the mushroom, hoping to possess it and stop it from eating Arthur. But the moment she touched its squishy skin, she was deafened by the souls of a thousand Fae-born screaming for release. She jerked back before her own soul became ensnared with them.

The threads were crawling into Arthur's mouth now.

"*Weston!*" Breeth screamed, swooping into the darkness toward the next level of the Abyssment. "Amelia! Ludwig! Arthur's getting eaten by a mushroom!"

The ghost girl's voice echoed silent through the Abyssment's depths.

3
THE MAD ZOO

The Trackdragon twined through a starry expanse like a train passing through a countryside. Wally and Sekhmet sat in a cozy compartment of vermillion and gold as star cluster cities, nightglow whales, and planet-sized statues of tentacle-mouthed beings swept past the window. Meteorites traced constellation creatures, while rainbow storms formed suns and planets at the speed of light. But at such great distances it seemed as slow as snowfall.

Wally decided he could remain on this train for months, chugging from one pocket-world to the next and admiring the endless night skies that lay between.

But then the journey was over.

With a final huff of steam, the Trackdragon snarled to a stop on the edge of a small country town in the Real. The door hissed open, and Wally and Sekhmet stepped onto a dead-grass field beneath a cream-yellow sky. Wally gazed back at the Trackdragon's sleek iron scales, its obsidian wheels, its black engine head and open throat burning with coal fire. Then it whipped forward like a thunderclap, its tail caboose vanishing into thin air.

"Let's get moving," Sekhmet said.

Wally's heart jerked. The galactic train ride had nearly made him forget the mission completely. He followed Sekhmet across the fields.

"Our top priority is to figure out how the Order is locating Rifts," she said. "The Wardens operate the only known Rift Detectors, but the Order has somehow found a way to reach holes in the Veil *days* before we do, tearing them wider with their misuse of magic." She looked over her shoulder and caught Wally's eyes. "Whatever happens today, we *cannot* let the Order escape without getting some answers."

"Sure thing," he said, hoping she couldn't hear the tremor in this voice.

A water tower rose up before them, and the air became tinged with the sounds and smells of animals. Wally and Sekhmet crouched in the high dead grasses. The zoo looked like any other. The cages were arranged in a boxy U shape and surrounded a big top tent the color of old blood. Hundreds of townspeople had gathered to gawk into the filthy cages, blocking Wally's view.

But then he caught a flash of something, bright and crackling. The crowd briefly parted, revealing a bull that seemed to be made of pure flames. A few cages down, he spotted a crusty-skinned goblin. And on the corner, a flock of what looked like *werewolf* bats.

"I don't recognize most of these creatures," Sekhmet said.

"And I've traveled all over the Fae. Which pocket-world did they come from?"

Just then the entrance to the big top tent parted and a large gray woman stepped out. She folded her arms, as if standing guard. The tent trembled even though the day was windless.

"The Rift must be in there," Sekhmet said. "Lucky for us, it hasn't started transforming the tent yet. Otherwise we'd really be in trouble."

Wally squinted at the tent's guard. "Is that woman's skin made of . . . *rocks*?" He scanned the zoo and noticed the carnival barker's brown, mottled smile. "And what's wrong with that guy's *teeth*?"

Sekhmet shook her head. "This doesn't make sense. The Order usually recruits *humans* because they tend to be greedier and will accept cash as payment. Money is useless to Faeborn." She studied the strange zookeepers. "Why would these creatures join?"

Wally already regretted leaving Breeth behind.

Sekhmet noticed his expression and squeezed his shoulder. "You'll be *fine*. We just have to get between the Order and the tent while they're still outside of it. We'll slap on some magma manacles, return the Fae-born to their pocket-worlds, sew up the Veil, and then head home."

"Well, when you say it that way . . . ," Wally said, feeling more than a little overwhelmed.

"I would make this a sneak attack, but I don't want to hurt any innocent bystanders," she said, drawing her swords. "I'll take out the stone lady and the gross one in the top hat. You guard the back of the tent. If anyone tries to escape through the Rift, knock them out with a sonic punch."

Wally slipped on his gauntlets. "But I still can't tap into my m—"

Sekhmet was already hustling down the hill.

Wally hurried after, nervously tightening his gauntlet strap with his teeth while his mentor walked around the U of cages toward the ticket booth.

"Sorry, everyone!" Sekhmet shouted. "This zoo is closed due to animal cruelty!"

The zoo-goers tore their eyes from the strange creatures to stare at the girl with the sword.

The carnival barker simply grinned his brown grin. "Seems our fantastral zoo's on brief hi*wait*us, lovies and gents!" His voice was so rough, it sounded like it was disintegrating. "But hold tight to them tickets! Reentry's half price! That's a Rustmouth guaranteeity!"

The crowd shuffled toward the exit, slightly confused, while Wally slipped into the U of cages and positioned himself behind the tent.

Once the last of the zoo-goers had departed, Sekhmet glared at the carnival barker. "Now that we're alone . . ." Her swords ignited.

Rustmouth chuckled, flames dancing in his colorless eyes. "The *Bore*dens're recruiting 'em young as tadpoles these days. Bring it on, girly-cue."

Wally watched from behind the tent as Sekhmet ran at the barker. She leapt, swords blazing, ready to bind him in magma manacles. But before she could reach him, the gray woman stepped in the way, deflecting the blow with her stony arm. A shower of sparks rained through the air.

Rustmouth laughed. "Funny thing about the Astonishment. She ain't so easy to slice!"

Sekhmet feinted back as the Astonishment took a swing at her, her rocky fist pounding a giant divot in the earth before drawing back to swing again. Sekhmet dodged once, then again and again before Rustmouth dove in from the side, trying to tackle Sekhmet's legs. Sekhmet jumped just in time, her whirling swords accidentally slicing the crown of his top hat clean off.

A cowering monkey with pigeon wings peeked out from Rustmouth's hat and then leapt to the ground and scampered away.

"You nearly uncapitated my li'l helper!" Rustmouth snarled. "And here I thought the Wardens was meant to be *compassionable*."

While Sekhmet glanced after the winged monkey to make sure it was okay, the Astonishment caught her in a bear hug and *squeezed*. Sekhmet struggled and strained in the stone woman's arms. Her flaming swords extinguished. Rustmouth seized her arm, twisting it so that one of her swords lay flat in front of his grinning mouth. He bit into the blade, his rusted teeth sinking through the steel as if it were made of butter.

Sekhmet's sword shattered.

Wally ran from behind from the tent, gauntlets raised to

save his mentor, but Sekhmet flashed her green eyes at him. "Keep guarding that Rift!"

Wally skidded to a stop as she bent her legs and kicked off of Rustmouth's belly, launching herself backward into the Astonishment's boulder chest. The momentum tipped the stone woman off-balance as Sekhmet curled her legs up and over her own head, kneeing the Astonishment in the face and toppling her to the ground like a fallen statue. Rustmouth roared and lunged at Sekhmet as she lifted her remaining sword . . .

Wally didn't see what happened next. A wheezing turned him around. Behind him stood a hunched woman with sallow skin and thinning hair. She was smiling. He lowered his gauntlets. The woman was unarmed and looked as harmless as an earthworm.

But then he felt a rush of fear as the woman removed a flask from her belt and tipped it to her lips. He raised a gauntlet to swat the flask out of her hand, but the woman hissed, *"Nuh-uh!"*

The word rang silvery in Wally's ears—painful, like it was injected into his brain by a needle. His gauntlet froze midair.

The woman smiled metallic, dripping teeth. *"Hit yourself."*

Wally's fist obeyed and came right back at him, smashing his nose and knocking him flat to the ground. His head rang. The sky blurred.

"Ditch them fancy gloves."

Wally's arms flopped at his sides, shaking the gauntlets from his hands.

The woman bent, greasy hair hanging, colorless eyes staring, and giggled.

"Y'know, sugar, I could tell you to beat yourself to death," she said, and coughed a fine spray of blood into her hand. "But you're cute, so . . ." She took another sip from the flask. "*Nap time.*"

And the world went dark.

THE MYCOPATH

Arthur found himself in a dark, cavernous space. He didn't remember how he'd come to be there. He blinked at his surroundings, looking for something. Anything. The darkness had a texture to it that he couldn't quite place: Was it . . . silky? . . . *fuzzy?*

"Well, if it isn't my biggest fan," a voice said.

Arthur spun in circles. The voice sounded exhausted . . . *Familiar.*

"Who are you?" Arthur asked the darkness. His throat felt tight.

A figure took shape before him. It was rotund with wisps of hair sticking off the top of his head. And it was covered in cobwebs.

"Come now, Arthur," the voice said dustily. "It hasn't been *that* long."

Arthur's eyes widened. *"Alfred Moore."*

The figure stepped into the light, the source of which Arthur could not see. There he was, the mad author: ink-

stained fingers, sagging pale face . . . Arthur couldn't see his bloodshot eyes. They were closed.

"Wh-what are you doing here?" Arthur asked.

Alfred Moore sneered, stretching the cobwebs around his mouth. "Why, *you* sent me here, of course. After you killed me."

Arthur took a step back. "I—I didn't kill you. I . . . *retired* you because you were causing all of that trouble in Kingsport."

Alfred Moore took a step forward. "You robbed me of my life, Arthur Benton. Just as you robbed Kingsport of new Garnett Lacroix adventures." He took another step toward Arthur and another. "You could have let me keep writing. You could have let the adventures continue."

Arthur stumbled backward. No one had been more disappointed to see the end of Garnett Lacroix's adventures than him. They had taught him how to be a gentleman and a thief.

"I didn't have a choice," Arthur said. "I had to save Kingsport. I—"

Moore lunged forward, his hands seizing Arthur's throat. His fingers were mushy soft but *strong*. Just as the mad author started to squeeze, Arthur managed to choke out, "*You're not even real!*"

Alfred Moore's lips drooped in a doughy frown. And with that, he and his cobwebs disintegrated in a cloud of spores.

Arthur touched his throat, massaging the bruises left behind by the author's strange fingers. He had never thought of what he'd done as murder. He was merely sending a troubled spirit to wherever all retired fictions go.

"*Boy*," a nasally voice said.

Arthur's spine straightened as another figure materialized in the darkness. This one wore a feathered cloak. A skeletal hand drew back the cowl, revealing a bald skull.

The Rook.

Arthur almost knelt on instinct. But his old boss wouldn't have been able to see the gesture through his closed eyes. The Rook was rotting. Flesh hung from his thin frame.

Arthur recoiled as the Rook twisted his scorpion rings around his skeleton fingers. "I could use you back in the Black Feathers, Arthur."

Arthur shook his head. He mouthed the word *No*, but his voice refused to cooperate. Something was stuck in his throat that he couldn't quite swallow.

The Rook was dead. Life in the Black Feathers was a fading nightmare. But if the Manor didn't accept Arthur as a Novitiate, he would have no choice but to return to Kingsport and rejoin his old gang. And he would wither under the dead Rook's feathered shadow until the day he too passed on to the Great Elsewhere.

The Rook smiled a skeletal smile. "Come closer, boy."

Arthur didn't move.

"You're a *killer* now, Arthur. You'll make *captain* with all the blood on your hands."

"I'm not a killer," Arthur said, but felt uneven on his feet.

The Rook raised his eyebrows, but he did not open his eyes. "No? Who was it, then, that made my daughter an orphan?"

Liza. Arthur's friend, who had also lost her mother to the

Pox. She became an orphan the day the Rook was devoured by that monster bird. Arthur hadn't considered that.

"That—" Arthur's voice caught in his throat. "That wasn't my fault. It was your Mirror counterpart. Yeah, I summoned it, but . . ." He had a flash of the shrieking black bill, the swoop of impossibly large wings. "I didn't know it would *kill* you."

The Rook tilted his bald head to one side. "Are you certain of that?"

Arthur opened his mouth to answer, but the Rook vanished in a shower of spores.

Arthur hugged himself, trying to find warmth in the cavernous space. He felt exposed. He felt like his mind was being washed down the drain. He hadn't felt any guilt when the Rook had died. But now it came crushing down around him.

The space was as quiet as the bottom of a well. Arthur looked left, then right, then behind him, searching the silky darkness for who came next. He had a terrible feeling he already knew.

"Hello, thief," said another voice. This one was young and rough with sea salt.

Arthur turned, heart pounding in his eyes. "I'm not a thief anymore."

Huamei, the dragon boy, formed out of nothingness. Every detail was in place. The swishing robes, the hair cue draped over his shoulder, the nose tilted upward with a royal air. His eyes were also closed, and his skin was cracked like porcelain.

"Oh, but you are a thief," Huamei said. "You *robbed* me of life. Killed me before I could return to my kingdom."

Arthur flinched. He tried to recall Sekhmet's words, so faint in his memory he wasn't certain she'd said them at all.

"Alfred Moore killed you. Not me."

"True." Huamei smirked. "But was it not your rash plan that put me in danger in the first place?"

"I—" Arthur's voice shook and then failed.

He had been reckless that day in the Mirror City. He'd tried to play hero, and the dragon boy had died because of it. But Arthur was trying to change. He had sworn never to put anyone's life in danger again.

He tried to speak these words aloud, but they came out in a whimper. Something was still caught in his throat, choking him, making it difficult to speak.

Huamei scowled, accentuating the cracks in his face. "You also robbed my mother of her only son."

The Duchess. The dragon Arthur had feared meeting since the day he'd heard of her.

"You stole *three* lives, thief," Huamei continued, spores twirling from his lips. "Alfred Moore. The Rook. *Me.* Can you find enough excuses as to why you weren't responsible for any of us?"

Arthur didn't have an answer to that.

Huamei removed his hands from his sleeves and held them out. They were dragon's claws, the scales cracked like porcelain. Huamei slithered toward Arthur, claws extended. This time, instead of retreating, Arthur stayed put. Huamei would have his revenge, and Arthur would pay his debt for the lives he took.

But before Huamei's dragon hands could reach his throat, another voice echoed from high above.

"*Arthur?*"

Huamei's cracked eyelids wrenched open, showing a fuzzy fungal white beneath. His mouth stretched impossibly wide, showing reptilian teeth, and he let out a deafening screech. Arthur plugged his ears as the dragon boy vanished in a puff of spores.

"*Arthur!*" the new voice said again.

Arthur unplugged his ears and stared up into the infinite blackness. "Amelia? I didn't kill you too . . . did I?"

"Not yet you didn't," she said.

Arthur felt a sharp pain as the thing lodged in his throat was ripped out.

Arthur blinked open his own eyes, which he hadn't realized were closed. His vision was fuzzy, as if he was staring through a layer of white moss. He was lying on the squishy ground of the Abyssment. A blue eye stared down at him. Little paper butterflies flapped a halo around Amelia's head, and she held mushroomy threads tight in her fist. The ones she had just pulled out of his mouth.

"Listen to me carefully, Arthur," Amelia said, snapping the appendage in half. "You've inhaled the Mycopath's spores."

"*Amelia*," Arthur said, feeling relief flood through his body. "How did you find me?"

"You have a very good ghost friend," Amelia said. "Breeth possessed Ludwig's origami butterflies and then used them to spell out the words: *Help! Arthur! Mushroom!*"

Amelia's leather whip coiled at her hip as if proud or embarrassed.

"But that's not important now," Amelia continued. "The Mycopath is a psychotic fungus. It haunts you with the guilt of your past, so you won't put up a fight as it consumes your soul."

Somewhere in the darkness, Alfred Moore chuckled. *You have no soul, Arthur Benton.*

You gave it away, the Rook said.

When you killed us, Huamei said.

Arthur's eyelids began to flutter shut, but Amelia slapped his face.

"You don't understand," Arthur said, rubbing the sting away. "I got Huamei *killed*."

And me, the Rook whispered.

And me.

"Whatever you're seeing," Amelia said, "it isn't him. The Mycopath summons images of people who have died. Just as mushrooms recycle dead things, the Mycopath recycles memories and brings them back to life in tainted form."

Behind her, the fungal expanse gurgled and squirted, quivering with rage. The Fae-born reached toward Amelia with their soft claws, but she drew her whip and struck them to pieces. The fungus's frills rippled and exhaled another cloud of spores, but Amelia's halo of paper butterflies flapped it away. Without its spores, the Mycopath was as helpless as a mushroom.

"*Look*, Arthur," Amelia said, pointing. "Look at all the Fae-born the Mycopath has consumed."

The other Fae-born moaned their spore-polluted breath, as if reliving memories of their own devouring.

"*You*"—she pointed toward his feet—"are next on the menu."

Arthur looked. The fungal floor had grown over his legs to his waist, slurping up his body, inch by inch. Part of him knew he should be afraid. But another part—a deeper part—wanted to give his body back to the earth. To make up for all the pain he'd caused . . .

So I can finally rest, Alfred Moore said.

So my daughter— the Rook said.

And my mother— Huamei said.

Will have retribution, all three said simultaneously.

The whispers of the dead seeped all the energy out of Arthur's limbs until even lifting a pinky finger seemed impossible.

Amelia's sleeves suddenly ruffled to life and lifted her arms, forcing her to reach out.

The Warden made her hands into fists. "I can't *force* him, Breeth. The Mycopath has a grasp on his soul. If I pull him out now, it would shuck him like an ear of corn, pulling away a husk of a body while leaving Arthur, the *real* Arthur, behind—trapped for eternity with a thousand nightmare Fae-born."

The invisible force released Amelia's sleeves.

Arthur blinked some of the fuzziness from his eyes. Breeth was still trying to save him? Even after how reckless he'd been by venturing into the Abyssment?

"*Arthur*," Amelia said, seeing the clarity in his eyes. "I need you to stand up of your own will. It's the only way to keep your spirit intact."

Arthur felt a faint warmth in his muscles. They considered obeying. Considered getting up and returning to Kingsport and a life of petty thievery. Considered soldiering on while knowing somewhere in the Real a girl was missing her dad and somewhere in the Fae a dragon duchess was missing her son. Considered living his life when he knew he'd caused so much pain.

Arthur's vision grew fuzzy white with mold again.

Amelia grabbed Arthur by the suspenders and shook him. "If you've actually wronged someone, Arthur, then being eaten by a mushroom won't do them any good. Who do you need to apologize to?"

An apology won't bring the adventures back, Alfred Moore whispered.

It won't give my daughter her father, the Rook whispered.

Or my mother her son, whispered Huamei.

"*Who*, Arthur?" Amelia demanded.

"*Liza.*" Arthur hiccupped a cloud of spores. "I need to apologize to Liza. I . . . I made her an *orphan*. And . . . Huamei's mom. I accidentally killed her son. But I've never even met her."

Amelia nodded. "Then break free from the Mycopath so you can return to the surface and make amends. *That*—not your death—will rid you of your guilt."

Liza burned to life in the Stormcrow Pub of Arthur's memory. The dragon duchess, whom Arthur had never met, remained obscured. Mold crawled across his brain like a fuzzy blanket.

"I can't," he whimpered. "I can't face them."

Amelia huffed. "Don't you have someone waiting for you back in Kingsport? You have a father, correct? Do you want to rob him of his only son after he lost your mother?"

Arthur imagined Harry sitting at home all alone, picking at his fingernails like he did when he didn't know what to do with his feelings. This image made Arthur's eyes sting with tears, which washed some of the fuzzy white away. He gazed through the fog of spores to the pulsing expanse of the Mycopath. He saw the fungus-entombed Fae-born with protrusions coming out of their mouths and eyes. He saw the frilly mouth that had whispered to him with three different voices.

Then Arthur looked at his legs, half-swallowed in the mushroom floor. A wet horror gripped his heart.

"It's . . . *eating* me," he said.

"Thought you'd never notice," Amelia said dryly.

He wriggled free from the Mycopath, suddenly unable to get away from the thing fast enough. The Fae-born screamed, thickening the air with spores, as the fungus slipped from his legs as easy as bedsheets and Amelia yanked him upright.

Arthur frowned at his feet. His shoes were gone. As were the toes of his socks.

"You're lucky you didn't lose more than that, kid," Amelia said.

"Right," Arthur said as feeling flooded back into his limbs. "Right."

How had Amelia known which words would free him from that mental prison? Had she lost another staff member to the evil mushroom? He looked up at the ceiling and found the single bloated eye staring down at them. It was bright blue. Just like Amelia's remaining one.

Arthur straightened himself. "Thank you for saving my life, Amelia. When I get home, I swear to make amends with those I've mistreated."

Amelia wasn't listening. She cracked her whip, shredding the fungus that had grown over the next set of stairs.

"Where are we going?" Arthur said, then smacked his lips to get the mushroom taste out of his mouth. "Can I catch my breath first?"

"I must return to the roots," Amelia said, continuing to crack her whip. "I left Weston and Ludwig behind to battle the Scarabs alone so I could come rescue *you*."

Arthur winced. Once again, he'd endangered others' lives.

"I can make it up to you!" he said. He located his notebook on the ground and snatched it up.

Amelia rotated and in one smooth motion, cracked the notebook out of his hands, making it explode in a hundred bits of paper. She gave him a look more withering than any she had given him before. "Now that you're safe, I can tell you what an impossibly *selfish* child you are."

Arthur crossed his arms over his chest.

"You don't *have* any magic in you, Arthur," she continued, blue eye burning. "You proved that tonight. The only reason you were helpful on our mission to stop Alfred Moore is because you *stole* a dragon-bone Quill and just happened to be a hopeless *fanboy* for a particular fictional *Gentleman Thief*." She sneered at him. "Unfortunately for you, there won't be a *Garnett Lacroix* wherever the Wardens go."

With that, Amelia whistled sharply through her teeth, and her paper butterfly crown flapped straight toward Arthur. Before he could so much as gasp, they plucked up his clothing with their tiny paper feet and then hefted him off the ground, whisking him back up the pyramid steps.

The last thing Arthur heard was "Come, Breeth. Unlike Arthur, you might actually be of *use* in this fight"—before he was carried back up three stories of the Abyssment and to the Throne Room, where Lady Weirdwood was waiting for him.

5
THE FIRST PUPPET

Light blurred watery and bright through Wally's eyelashes.

He blinked open his eyes and found he was lying in a field beneath a yellow cream sky. On the edge of the field was a fence. A puppet hung from one of the posts. Before Wally could focus on the puppet, his nose throbbed sharply. He touched it and felt blood drying there.

Wally sat up as quickly as his pounding head would allow. He was still in the zoo behind the scab-colored tent. Things had gone quiet, save the otherworldly animal noises of the caged Fae-born.

Wally picked himself up and limped around the tent, holding his throbbing head. He found Sekhmet, sword sheathed, standing over Rustmouth, whose wrists were bound in magma manacles.

"How did the Order know about this Rift?" Sekhmet asked him.

Rustmouth grinned brownly. "A little birdy twittered it in my ear."

"What was this little birdy's name?"

"That's between me and the birdy," Rustmouth said, and spit an orange wad at Sekhmet's feet.

She gazed around the miserable zoo. The sputtering flames of the bull. The dried-out skin of the goblin. The withered wings of the werebats. "Fae-born creatures are not your playthings. They need to return to their unnatural environments."

"Y'know?" Rustmouth said. "Perhaps yer right, Missy. Perhaps I *should* liberize 'em." He bellowed toward the cages. "A'right, then, the lot of ya, *shoo!* Away with ya! Yer evicticated, ya hear? Yer free! *FREE*, I said!"

The Fae-born lay miserable in their cages.

"Huh." Rusmouth shrugged, that foul grin forever plastered to his lips. "Guess they prefers my brand o' hopsitality." He spotted Wally approaching. "And who's this one? His face's *familiarating*."

Sekhmet turned around and frowned at Wally's bruised nose. "Sonic punch didn't work, huh?"

Wally recounted what had happened with the woman and the flask filled with silver.

"The Order must have harvested that liquid from the Mercury Mines," Sekhmet said. "It's pure language. If someone drinks it, their words are unable to be ignored." She smiled at Wally. "You're forgiven for punching yourself in the face and letting the rest of the Order escape."

"Thank you?" Wally said.

Sekhmet turned to Rustmouth. "You're not hiding any more of that silver stuff, are you?"

"Just try and search me," he said, grinning. "See that I don't chew off those pretty fingers."

Even though Wally hadn't stood a chance against the frail woman and her flask of silver liquid, he still wanted to make things up to his mentor. With Rustmouth's attention fixed on Sekhmet, Wally quietly stepped behind the carnival barker.

Sekhmet studied the man and his rusted teeth. "I've been trying to figure out why Fae-born would join the Order of Eldar . . . But you're *human*, aren't you?"

Rustmouth's grin faltered slightly.

"Yeah," Sekhmet said. "You're human. And I think I've figured out the Order's new tactics."

Rustmouth glared at her.

"My guess is that the Order is using unnatural resources from the Fae to give normal people extraordinary powers. Pure language from the Mercury Mines, a rust flower from the Garden of Steel . . . maybe a stone biscuit from some obscure pocket-world?" Sekhmet drew her remaining sword and placed its tip on one of Rustmouth's buttons, making him grunt in discomfort. "You've turned yourselves into human guinea pigs for magical products. Disintegrating your teeth and, from the sounds of your silver-tongued friend, lungs, as well. The question is . . . why?"

Rustmouth sniffed. "Saved me and my friend from gettin' sliced by that murderfying jabber o' yers, didn't it?"

Sekhmet's mouth twitched.

"*Aww*," Rustmouth said, noticing the expression on her

face. "Was that witto toothpick I crunched to bits *special*? If it's any comfortation, it tasted *delicious*."

While Sekhmet stared daggers at the man, Wally knelt behind Rustmouth and gave his magma manacles a wiggle. Rustmouth rounded with a grunt and flashed his colorless eyes at him.

"Just checking you're secure," Wally said, and then quickly rejoined Sekhmet.

"Your solutioning our plans ain't gonna stop us from building our maddening zoos," Rustmouth said. "They's our most *profitizable*. 'Sides"—his stained grin returned—"the *Eraser* tidies up after all our messes."

The moment Rustmouth spoke the name, Wally felt an emptiness inside. Almost like he hadn't eaten in days. *The Eraser.* Was that the Order's leader?

"Who's the Eraser?" Sekhmet asked. "What's his real name?"

"The Eraser ain't a *his*," Rustmouth said with admiration, "'cause it ain't an *anybody*. Wherever it goes, it don't leave a trace."

Wally tried to wrap his mind around what that could possibly mean. He held up the scroll he'd just pickpocketed from Rustmouth's jacket. "Maybe this will have some answers."

"You little *weasel*!" Rustmouth shouted, struggling to escape his binds.

"Nice thieving, Wally," Sekhmet said as she unrolled the scroll. It was a map, wrapped around an empty inkpot. Fear touched her eyes. "This is my mom's." Her sword flashed to Rustmouth's throat. "What did you do to her?"

"I didn't do nuffin'," Rustmouth said, "save steal that map so's we could escape them knotty Mines. Me, Silver Tongue, and the Astonishment got so bemuddled that we had to leave our deary Steel Fingers behind."

"And leave the Wardens trapped," Sekhmet said, trying to contain the tremor in her voice.

Rustmouth licked his teeth. "Collateral damnages."

Wally stared at Sekhmet's mother's inkpot. Something about family members and important objects stirred a memory: a puppet seen through woozy eyes.

"I'll be right back," he told Sekhmet. "I, um, forgot my gauntlets."

He ran around the tent to the fence he'd seen when he'd first regained consciousness and plucked the puppet from the post. It was a Punch puppet. Its nose and chin were pointed and long, while its eyes and smile were dull and wicked. It held a tiny wooden finger to its lips, as if it wanted Wally to keep a secret.

Punch wasn't holding his signature slapstick. Instead he held a tiny message:

"Farewell, dear brother!" cried Mr. Punch.
Time to put down the fists and rely on your hunch.
When flames are spreading across the plain,
What are the chances that it could rain?

Wally turned in a circle, searching the fairground. His brother, Graham, had been there. He'd left this message for

Wally. But where was he now? And what did this riddle mean? Wally gazed into the open sky. There wasn't a cloud in sight. The chances of rain were . . . zero.

A metallic sound shrieked on the other side of the tent, and Rustmouth started to cackle. *"What a loyal boy have I!"*

"Wally!" Sekhmet cried.

Wally dropped the puppet and sprinted back around the tent, scooping up his gauntlets on the way. The first thing he saw was the flaming bull. It was out of its cage. Its beard crackled like a wildfire. Its coal glow hoofs charred the grass. On either side of the bull was the screeching basilisk and the sneering goblin, which rubbed its slimy hands together.

Rustmouth's winged monkey sat beside him, holding a key and grinning whisker to whisker.

"Free!" Rustmouth said. "Set the creatures *free*, my little helper did! Just as his master commandered."

Laughing, he struggled to his feet and, hands still bound in magma manacles, sprinted toward the tent. Sekhmet moved to catch him but was quickly blocked by a cloud of howling werebats.

Sekhmet grimaced, then lifted her sword. She nodded toward Wally. "Hope you're ready for a real fight."

Wally quickly slid on his gauntlets as the bull lowered its molten horns and charged.

6
LUDWIG

Amelia ran through the Abyssment, and Breeth spirited after. The ghost girl propelled herself along whatever organic matter she could find—the stamen fangs of a bloodthirsty flower, the mossy tail of a stone mermaid, and the fingernail of a solitary crawling finger.

They reached the heart of the Abyssment and found total chaos.

A vast mud pit descended like a telescope into untold depths. Massive roots extended out of the mud, thousands of feet up to the foundation of the Manor. Both the pit and the roots were swarming with giant insects. Their pincers were as wide as bear traps, their shells as dark as gun metal. By feasting on the Manor's sap, the Scarab larvae had grown up.

Now they were the size of oil drums.

On one side of the pit, Weston had collapsed in the mud. He weakly blew his command whistle, making one of the roots stand at attention like a loyal soldier to shake off the giant Scarabs before crushing them in an explosion of springs and metal plates. But sap ran down the root like blood. It was growing weak.

On the pit's other side, Breeth spotted a large mound, lying in the mud. *Ludwig.* The Scarabs had chewed off one of his arms and were gnawing on his massive legs. The giant trembled as he tried to fold paper butterflies with his remaining hand.

Breeth was furious with Arthur. Amelia had left the fight to save him, and now Ludwig would be missing an arm for the rest of his life.

"Zat poison vould certainly be useful now, ja?" Ludwig bellowed to his twin, across the chasm.

Weston grunted, helplessly kicking at a Scarab that the root had failed to smash. "Only if you're too weak to fight 'em off!"

"Vell, of course I'm *veak*!" Ludwig cried. *"Zey ate my arm!"*

"Ah, stop whining!" Weston called back. "It'll grow back, ya big softy!"

"Wait, what?" Breeth asked Amelia. "Did he just say Ludwig would regrow his *arm*?"

Amelia didn't hear her, of course. She coiled her whip around a root and swung across the pit to the opposite mudbank. As she landed, she whipped a nearby Scarab, cracking open its carapace in one brutal stroke. Breeth followed behind, skipping along bits of fossilized shell in the mud.

Amelia's whip lashed forward once again, breaking open another Scarab's wings, and a dozen of Ludwig's butterflies fluttered inside, sacrificing themselves between its oily gears. The Scarab rolled its clockwork eyes as its pincers stuttered to a screeching halt. It keeled onto its side, and its six legs folded into its abdomen.

"One down!" Amelia said. "A *swarm* to go."

"Zey ate my folding finger!" Ludwig cried, holding his injured hand up and away from the gnawing pincers of the Scarabs.

"Breeth?" Amelia cried into the darkness. "I need you to possess Ludwig's paper butterflies, like you did when you wrote us that message! I'll whip open the Scarab's wings and you fly into the gears!"

"Got it!" Breeth said.

She swept around the chasm, collecting whatever bits of paper she could find. But they were all too shredded or too oily, and no amount of flapping would make them airborne. Then she noticed the loose sheets twirling out of Ludwig's pocket.

Breeth possessed one and then hesitated. She'd always been terrible at folding paper airplanes. Whenever she threw one of her own creations, it immediately nosedived and scrunched on the ground a few inches in front of her.

On the other side of the chasm, Weston was screaming, "*Take this, you glorified pests!*" He kicked at the Scarabs, as if trying to squish them, but his small feet did nothing against their metal-plated armor. "*Gah!*" Soon he was surrounded by pincers too.

Breeth couldn't even see Ludwig among the gnashing pincers anymore.

In a fluttery panic, she tried curling two corners of her paper to the center before folding it in half. But this was about as simple as touching her toes with the top of her head before folding in half so her ears connected.

Sharp sounds echoed through the chasm as Amelia whipped open Scarab wings left and right, exposing the Scarabs' gears. But with no paper butterflies to fly inside and bring them to a halt, the Scarabs continued their gnawing.

"*Breeth?*" Amelia cried. "I could use some help here!"

"I'm *trying*!" Breeth called back soundlessly.

She folded herself again, trying to match the paper's corners. But she couldn't get them to align. She couldn't get the seam to fold flat. She crumpled herself in frustration and let the ball of paper tumble into the pit.

She cruised around the chasm, searching for something, *anything* else she could possess. And that's when she found the big mound of dead plant matter in the mud. Breeth gasped. It was Ludwig. He had died from his injuries.

"*Amelia?*" the giant suddenly shouted, nearly scaring Breeth into a second death. "I do not have much body left! Zese Scarabs are going to consume me!"

Breeth's soul fluttered. How was Ludwig talking when he was *dead*? There was only one explanation: He'd been dead all along. A giant made of fleshy plant matter that somehow walked around the Manor. She'd never thought to poke at Ludwig's mind because she didn't think it would do anything. But now . . .

Too desperate to worry about getting trapped in Ludwig's mind, Breeth splashed into his giant, sloshy brain. She felt his veins hum with water, his skin ache for sunlight, and the place where his arm had been squeal in pain.

Beneath all of this was a pure, pulsing fear. The giant was strong, but he was terrified—all wilted leaves and shrinking vines. And who could blame him? Scarabs chew plants to bits.

Despite the giant's plant panic, Breeth felt the strength of forests in his limbs.

"Hiya, Ludwig!" she said into Ludwig's thoughts.

The giant screamed aloud. "Augh! Who is zere?"

"It's Breeth! The ghost girl that haunts the Manor. Sorry I let myself into your head without knocking. You're made of *plants*? Congratulations!"

Ludwig gave a giant gulp. "Ja."

"Listen, it'd be a real shame to waste all of this plant strength. Mind if I take over for a bit?"

"Vill . . . vill it hurt?"

"I dunno! I've never asked anything I've possessed before! But considering your only other option is to get eaten by a bunch of Scarabs, I think you should let me try. If I can't unpossess you afterward, we'll be brain roommates for life!"

Ludwig considered a moment. "Vhat do I do?"

"Um, just . . . hand the controls over to me and—I dunno—take a nap in the back of your mind!"

Ludwig nodded like a scared child, and then he relaxed. Breeth felt herself spread through the giant's green veins and corpuscles all the way to his rooty toes. She curled her giant vine-like fingers and then punched her massive fist right into a Scarab's pincered kisser.

Next, she hefted her giant leg and brought it hurtling down like a tree stump, smashing through another's back, then punted yet another, breaking its head in half before punching two more to pieces. Once she had cleared the armored insects around her, she stomped across the mud and laid waste to the Scarabs attacking Weston.

"You're welcome!" she said in a booming voice, and then smiled Ludwig's giant smile.

"Ludwig?" Weston said, staring at his twin in disbelief. "What happened to your accent?"

"*Oh!* You are *velcome*," Breeth said, trying to imitate the giant's voice. "*Is zat better?*" She picked Weston up with one hand and set him on his feet.

Amelia whipped open more wings while Breeth used her rootlike fingers to rip the gears from out of the carapaces. Ludwig's leaf-thin skin sliced open and bled green, but Breeth could feel his plant juice rushing to the cuts to seal them up. Her giant belly rumbled for sugar.

Breeth continued to smash every last Scarab infesting the pit. She felt good. Large and powerful. With real legs and . . . arm to swing.

In fact, for the first time since she'd died three years before, Breeth felt almost . . . human.

***

Upstairs, the shifting light slowed in the Manor's window, settling on a single blushing pink.

Lady Weirdwood sat on her waxen throne, stroking her snake.

Arthur did a double-take. Was the snake . . . dead? It certainly looked that way, lying completely still, its mouth partially open, the color faded from its scales. Still, Lady Weirdwood stroked the serpent, as if trying to resurrect it with her fingertips.

The Lady smiled sadly at Arthur. "Well, Mr. Benton. It looks like it's time we take you home."

7
WILD FAE-BORN

Three feet before the flaming bull gored Wally, Sekhmet spun her sword, creating a whirlwind that diverted the bull's trajectory. It tore circles around the tent, horns blazing, beard crackling, leaving behind a smoldering trail of burnt grass.

"That spell won't last long," she said. "We need to handle the other Fae-born fast before it wears off." She nodded at him. "Sorry you didn't get more time to train."

Wally swallowed. "Me too."

She and Wally scanned the zoo through rising ash. The basilisk screeched near the ticket booth, whirling its reptilian tail. A swarm of giant copper spiders slurped the juices from a dead unicorn.

"You handle the basilisk!" Sekhmet screamed to Wally as she swept toward the spiders.

Wally ran toward the ticket booth, clacking his gauntlets together and frightening the hissing creature back into its cage, which he quickly bolted shut. On the other side of the tent, Sekhmet managed to herd the skittering arachnids back into their cage. The unicorn was drained beyond saving.

Once she'd locked up the spiders, Sekhmet cried out to Wally again. "Find that goblin! Rustmouth said it drinks memories! I'll handle the flaming b—*Aaauuggghhh!*"

She screamed as the flock of werebats descended on her like a fuzzy cloud. They dove and ripped at her long hair, trying to sink their fangs into her skin. Sekhmet thrashed at them, as if a single bite would be fatal.

Wally, knowing his mentor could take care of herself, searched the fairgrounds, sweat pouring down his forehead in the cool air. He spotted the goblin sneaking toward the town and sprinted after it. The little beasty was sluggish from being in captivity, so Wally quickly caught up. Shaking the gauntlets from his hands, he dove and snagged the goblin's frog-like arm and dragged it screeching and wriggling back toward its empty cage.

But before Wally could toss the goblin inside, he heard a huff behind him, as powerful as a geyser. Wally slowly turned. Sekhmet's whirlwind spell had worn off, and the bull had spotted him with its eyes of melted iron. It snorted embers as it padded the grass to ashes. Then it lowered its blinding horns and charged toward him like a flaming train.

Wally dodged behind an open cage door the moment before the bull's horns seared through the wire in a wave of blistering heat. It reared up, ripping the door from its hinges and hurling Wally into the air. He hit the ground hard, and then rolled across the grass, extinguishing his sizzling shirt.

He leapt up, ready to dodge another charge, but the cage

door was stuck on the bull's horns. It bucked and reared, trying to shake it loose. Wally took the distraction to press his stinging palms into the grass to soothe the crosshatched burns.

"*Wally?*"

On the other side of the tent, Sekhmet was using her sword to spin up a tornado to try and wrangle the werebats. She flashed him a concerned look, and for a moment he thought she might be checking on him after he was nearly gored by a bull made of *lava* . . . but then she pointed behind him.

"The *goblin?*"

Wally made an exhausted sigh and pushed to his feet. He searched the zoo and found the goblin had scaled the U of cages and was careening back toward the town. Wally sprinted and reached the last cage just as the goblin hopped, managing to snatch it out of the air by its slimy foot. The goblin hissed and pressed its sticky suction-cup fingers to his forehead.

A memory flashed in Wally's mind.

His mother. Pouring pancakes on a Sunday morning. The sun warm and bright in the window behind her . . .

The memory began to wilt like a dying flower.

Wally hurled the goblin away from him before the memory faded completely. The goblin tumbled across the ground but landed on its knuckles and feet. It didn't make another break for the town. Instead, it stared at Wally's forehead and licked its lips. Something in its swampy eyes had changed. It *wanted* that memory.

Wally backed away. His mother had died. He would never watch her make pancakes again.

By the tent, the bull managed to shake the wire door from

its horns. It found Wally with its burning eyes. Wally shifted his retreat, keeping one eye on the approaching goblin and the other on the pawing, huffing bull. How was he supposed to catch the goblin if he couldn't even touch it? How was he supposed to tame a bull made of flames before it skewered and roasted him like a barbecue?

"Taste tornado, you shrieky monstrosities!" Sekhmet screamed, still occupied with the werebats.

The bull charged again. Wally somersaulted behind one of the cages, which collapsed under the bull's horns as if it were made of paperclips. The goblin was momentarily frightened away, but then came loping back through the ashen trail toward Wally.

The bull rounded and pawed again. Wally considered retrieving his gauntlets, but he didn't know how to summon that tingling feeling, and a normal punch would only make the bull angrier.

Time to put down the fists . . .

That was how Graham's riddle began. But what should Wally do instead? Hadn't the rhyme mentioned something about rain? Why did Graham's riddles have to be so frustratingly cryptic?

Wally unfocused his eyes and took in the whole of the fairgrounds: the cages and the tent and the ticket booth. The lines of colored flags that connected them all . . .

And the water tower.

When flames are spreading across the plain
What are the chances that it could rain?

"Let's see how you handle a waterfall," Wally whispered to the bull.

He plucked up a support pole from the demolished cage and jabbed it at the goblin to keep it at a distance. With one eye on the pawing bull, he worked his way to a drooping line of flags and leapt, snagging a red one from the string before tying it to one of the support pole's ends. He held the pole like a lance, using its back flagged end to draw the huffing bull's attention while prodding the front end at the goblin, guiding them both outside the U of cages toward the water tower.

The goblin soon grew tired of being poked, and with a frustrated gurgle, scaled one of the water tower's legs.

"Good goblin," Wally said, breathless.

He waved the flag high in the air until the bull's flames seethed, burning as bright as a collapsed star. It shook its beard and huffed fire and pawed the earth to cinders. It burned so bright, the grass caught fire, enveloping the zoo in swirling ash.

Wally's heart beat in his throat. There were no cages between him and the bull to deflect the blow this time.

"*Come on*," he whispered, rocking from foot to foot. "I'm ready for ya."

The bull came at him like a meteorite. Wally continued to wave the flag, ready to dive out of the way at the last second so its horns would strike the water tower, buckling its leg, and pouring the reservoir down like a waterfall, extinguishing the hellish beast.

But halfway to Wally, the bull stopped charging and started

to *prance* toward him. Its roaring flames dwindled before snuffing out completely, leaving behind steaming coal skin. Wally was so shocked that he just stood there as the bull romped right up and gave his face a lick, leaving behind a streak of sooty saliva.

Wally pulled away, disgusted and confused as the swirling ash dissipated, revealing a bright blue sky. The bull's charcoal lips stretched into the same goofy smile Wally had seen on the bookshelf in his room.

"*Breeth?*" Wally said.

The bull wagged its tail and rolled onto its back, showing a charred black belly. The tension left Wally's shoulders. It wasn't relief he felt, but disappointment. He'd almost won. He'd thrown himself into an impossible fight against wild Faeborn. With Graham's riddle, he'd been *this close* to succeeding.

The charcoal bull writhed on the grass, waiting for its belly to be rubbed.

Wally threw down the pole. "Breeth, what are you *doing* here?"

The bull rolled onto its stomach and cowered like a scolded puppy.

"I told you I didn't want your help!" he said.

The bull gave him an imploring look. He knew she had just been trying to prevent him from being gored to death, but he couldn't shake his disappointment.

Wally wiped gray saliva from his cheek. "And now you're *stuck* inside this thing. I don't think we can even squeeze it in the Manor like we did the tentacle monster."

The bull shook its head and wagged its tail, but Wally

couldn't understand what Breeth was trying to tell him. In fact, he didn't care right then.

"Out of the way, Wally!" Sekhmet screamed, running up, sword drawn to bind the bull in magma chains.

Wally held up a hand, stopping her. "It's Breeth."

"Oh," Sekhmet said, slowing. "Well, that's good news. The Manor must have exterminated the Scarabs."

Breeth's tail started to wag while Sekhmet spun up another whirlwind to pluck the goblin off the water tower and deposit it into the cage beside the werebats.

Sekhmet clapped Wally on the shoulder. "We need to work on your stance. A sonic punch would've sent this guy *flying*." She ruffled the charcoal bull's ears. "Good thing Breeth was here to save the day."

Wally stared at the ground, humiliated. He would have saved the day all by himself. He squeezed Graham's riddle in his pocket. Well, *almost* by himself.

The Breeth bull was trying to catch Wally's eye, but he refused to look at her.

"Where's the Manor, Breeth?" Sekhmet asked.

Breeth trotted to the edge of the fairgrounds, leading them to an old outhouse. It didn't smell foul but was twined with the forest scents of the Manor. Amelia was already stepping out of the moon-cut door, uncoiling her whip, ready to fight.

"The Fae-born are secure," Sekhmet said.

"And the Order?" Amelia asked.

Sekhmet gazed back at the zoo and her cheeks reddened. Rustmouth, the Astonishment, and Silver Tongue were nowhere in sight.

"They, um, escaped," Sekhmet said.

Amelia scowled and holstered her whip. "At least the Fae-born are secure."

Sekhmet took out her mother's map and inkpot. "The Order fled the Mercury Mines by stealing my mom's map and inkpot. Now she and the other Wardens are trapped there."

"But how did the Order locate the Rift before *we* did?" Amelia said, seemingly unconcerned about the Wardens' safety.

"One of the Order members said he heard it from a *little birdy*," Sekhmet said.

Amelia considered that a moment and then turned to Wally. "Anything to report, Cooper?"

Wally's head jerked up. "No, ma'am," he said, removing his hand from his pocket so she wouldn't hear the crinkling of Graham's riddle.

As dangerous as his brother's actions were, the thought of turning him over to the Wardens made Wally's stomach squirm. Graham was Wally's only family.

Amelia leaned back into the Manor and called out, "*Pyra?*" Then she nodded toward the zoo. "Judging by the diversity of creatures, there will be more Rifts beyond the one in that tent. We need to get these Fae-born back where they belong and then seal those Rifts before this entire countryside and all the people in it are dragged into a Daymare."

A moment later, Weirdwood's green-haired chef stepped out of the outhouse.

"Pyra," Amelia said, pointing to the cages, "make these

Fae-born docile so we can get them back to their pocket-worlds. And for heaven's sake, don't *cook* any of them like the last time."

"*Grrmph*," Pyra said, and set to work over her cauldron.

"How did the staff defeat the Scarabs?" Sekhmet asked.

Amelia told them the story. How Arthur had tried to play hero and nearly gotten his soul eaten by some giant, evil mushroom. And how Breeth had saved the day by possessing Ludwig and using his tree-trunk limbs to pound the mechanical monstrosities to smithereens.

"Seems like Breeth's saving everyone's day," Sekhmet said.

Wally ignored this. "Is Arthur okay? Can I see him?"

"Mr. Benton is gone, Mr. Cooper," Amelia said. "We dropped him back in Kingsport the moment the Manor stopped flying through the Fae."

"Oh."

Wally thought he would feel relieved, no longer having to worry about Arthur moping around and spying on his classes. But instead his heart broke to think of his friend returning to a life of petty thievery, trying to survive in that cruel port city. The adventures were over for Arthur Benton.

The bull nuzzled Amelia's arm.

"Got yourself caught in another one, hm, Breeth?" Amelia asked.

Breeth sheepishly nodded her giant charcoal head.

Amelia huffed. "Let's see if my lesson stuck." She grabbed Breeth's extinguished horns. "*Let go*," she said, tersely. "The fear, the anger of being murdered. *Let it go*."

The bull squeezed its eyes shut as if fighting off an ice-cream headache.

Amelia swatted her charcoal snout. "Not like that. You're *clenching*. You have to *relax* out of it. Like waking from a dream."

The bull's eyes unwrinkled a fraction, but nothing happened. Wally bit his lip. Amelia was taking the worst possible approach. Breeth did not like being told what to do.

"*Fine*," Amelia said. "I'll do it for you. *Again*. But tomorrow I'm going to make you possess something simple, like an earthworm. If you can't find a way to escape it as easily as you do a floorboard, you can wriggle around and eat dirt until you figure it out."

She looped her whip around the bull's horns and gave it a quick yank. The bull's head jerked down, leaving behind an afterimage of itself, and then it folded its hoofs under its chest, laid its head on the grass, and fell asleep.

Breeth's face swirled to life in the wood grain of the outhouse door. "Sorry I saved your life, Wally."

"You know that's not why I'm mad," Wally said. "I had it handled, Breeth."

Breeth's face grew long with sadness down the door's whorls.

"Excuse me?" someone called across the fairgrounds. "Um, *excuse me*? Is someone out there?"

Amelia, Sekhmet, and Wally followed the voice to a corner cage. There was a woman inside, hidden among the many tails of a fox that seemed to be made of cloud fluff. Amelia nodded at Wally, who quickly picked open the lock. After the last adventure, he hadn't gone anywhere without his lock picks.

Amelia stared at the woman, uncoiling her whip. "Who are you? Do you work for the Order?"

"My name's Jamie," the woman said. "And do you mean those weird people made out of *stone and rust*?"

Amelia holstered her whip.

The woman, Jamie, wrung her hands as she gazed at the caged Fae-born. "Those people *locked* me in here after I told them that these were *my* creatures. I *painted* them." She held up a piece of paper and a pencil. "They told me I had to stay in this cage and sketch horrifying things. I refused."

Amelia unlocked the cage, keeping her blue eye fixed on the cloud fox, which seemed quite tame.

Jamie made a beeline for the zoo's exit. "I need to get back to my art show. People are probably worried sick—"

"Wait." Amelia caught her by the arm. "I need to ask you a few questions. Sekhmet?" She nodded toward the scab-colored big top tent that was flapping and trembling under a storm that only it seemed to feel. "Handle that."

"What about my paren—the other Wardens?"

Amelia sighed. "After you've dropped the Fae-born in their pocket-worlds, head to the Mercury Mines. I'll question this woman, then open a door into the Mines where we originally dropped off the Wardens."

Amelia guided Jamie toward the outhouse. Pyra finished dosing the zoo's Fae-born with a bubbly purple liquid and then arranged them in a straight line to the scab-colored tent, like an otherworldly ark. Even the pigeon-winged monkey was there.

"Breeth?" Sekhmet said vaguely into the air.

Breeth ruffled the charred grass. "Yeah?"

"We could use your help in case there are more Fae-born on the other side of that Rift. You up for it?"

"I dunno," Breeth said, flashing an ashen scowl at Wally. "I wouldn't want to be too *helpful*."

"She said she'll do it," Wally said.

Breeth coiled herself into a rope and drew open the tent flap, unveiling the first Rift Wally had ever seen. It was like a rip in the air. Its frayed edges swooped up and up, gently sucking at the top of the tent like a vacuum. Strange things were happening to the area around the Rift. The grass at its bottom shivered a brilliant gold, while the top of the tent was slowly transforming into a silky rainbow material.

The Rift itself looked out onto a stormy sky, ribboned with a path of starlight. Beyond that was another Rift that showed a dense shadow swamp and then another that opened onto a hairy forest.

"Stay in that rope, Breeth," Sekhmet said. "I'm not sure there's anything to possess in the Mercury Mines."

Breeth whipped herself around Sekhmet's shoulder as she stepped onto the starlit path. Wally clacked his gauntlets together to get the line of Fae-born walking. Once the last of the werebats had flapped through, Sekhmet used her sword to draw a Ward in the air, stitching the Rift shut behind them.

8
THE GRIM ORATOR

"Gather 'round, lovers of wonder, to hear a spine-tingling tale of how one boy single-handedly saved Kingsport from nightmares beyond belief!"

Arthur stood atop an apple crate in the center of Market Square, desperately trying to be heard over the bustle of shoppers.

"*Who* was this valiant boy who saved our fair city, you ask? Why, it was none other than a young rogue of quick wit and even quicker charm!"

The shoppers shuffled past, avoiding eye contact.

"Was this hero a figure of legend?" Arthur said, trying to catch someone's—anyone's—attention. "A prince? A magical spirit?" He nodded to his new cap, one of Harry's old ones, which lay upside down on the cobblestones. "This hero's identity shall only be revealed once my hat is overflowing with coins!"

A woman paused in front of him and, for one enthralling moment, Arthur thought she'd stopped to listen to his story. But the woman simply sneezed and continued on.

"Very well!" Arthur called out to the others. "If it will get you to stop and listen, I'll tell you that your hero stands before you on this very apple crate! It's me! Arthur Benton!"

He bowed.

The market shoppers continued about their business, choosing to spend their hard-earned money on overpriced, mushy turnips rather than hear a story that was certain to make them collapse to their knees in gratitude.

Arthur stood straight and cleared his throat. "You know, if it weren't for *yours truly* and a certain magical Quill composed of *dragon bone*, *no one* would be enjoying the Square on this lovely morning! Every last one of you would've been hauled into the air by evil crows or dragged into the sea by giant tentacles!"

Still, no one looked his way. Arthur slumped onto his apple crate. The Wardens of Weirdwood may not have recognized his magical abilities, but there was no denying that he was a hero to his fellow Kingsport citizens. If only they would stop and listen long enough for him to convince them.

After Arthur had stepped out of the charred door of Hazelrigg back onto the streets of Kingsport, he had avoided the Stormcrow Pub—his old gang's hideout—like the Pox. The Black Feathers wouldn't look kindly on the kid who had caused their gang leader's death.

Besides, Arthur couldn't face Liza. Not yet.

Instead, he had returned to the tenements, where he found his dad arguing with the landlady about rent. Apparently, the Black Feathers had abandoned the thieving business altogether, leaving Harry unemployed.

So Arthur had set off to Market Square to earn rent money by telling harrowing tales drawn from his true-life adventures. But Harry's cap lay crumpled and empty.

A handsome couple walked past, and Arthur hopped back onto his crate.

"Good afternoon, sir!" Arthur shouted a little too loudly. "Care for a story that will chill your wife's bones so deep, she'll snuggle close come nightfall? I promise it will be the finest adventure you've laid ear on since the tales of Garnett Lacroix!"

"Who?" the man said.

Arthur's arms flopped to his sides. "You're *kidding*."

The couple looked at each other and shook their heads.

Arthur was aghast. "*Everyone* knows who Garnett Lacroix is. You can check in any bookshop. Or better yet, I'll show you . . ."

He patted his vest pockets and a wave of devastation swept over him. He'd been so bereft when he'd left the Manor that he'd forgotten to bring the copy of *Thieves of Weirdwood* Lady Weirdwood had given him.

Arthur scowled at the couple. "If you don't know the gentleman thief, you don't know *anything*."

The man took his wife's arm and they hurried past.

"Marriages grow stale without a little adventure!" Arthur yelled after them. "*Good luck keeping the romance alive!*"

"Allll right," a gruff voice said behind him. "Move it along, son."

Arthur turned around and found an Oaker patting his nightstick against his palm. Arthur relaxed. He'd avoided arrest *dozens* of times in the past. And this time he wasn't doing anything wrong.

"Morning, officer," he said. "I have the right to be here, same as anyone else."

"Sure ya do," the Oaker said, scratching under his cap. "'Cept for that *trifling* detail that you're disturbing the peace."

The smile faded on Arthur's lips. "I *make* peace!" he said, staring down at the Oaker from his apple crate. "This city wouldn't *exist* if it weren't for me!" He leaned in so he was nose-to-nose with the man. "My deeds have done more for this city than all of the Oakers and your pathetic little sticks ever have."

The Oaker chuckled his sweetly foul breath and gave his baton a spin. "Tell ya what. We'll pit your story against this here little stick of mine, and we'll see who comes out on top."

Arthur cleared his throat and stepped down from the apple crate. "I'd love to stay, but I don't want you to have to control my adoring crowd," he said, swiping up his empty hat. "You might strain yourself and end up splitting your pants."

The Oaker raised his baton, and Arthur ran, leaving the people of Market Square ignorant of the real hero whose actions had allowed them to shop on that lovely Sunday morning.

✳✳✳

Arthur slumped back toward the tenements. He needed to work on his pitch. The story itself was alive and bright in his mind, but actually getting people to listen was another thing altogether. He turned down Center Street and entered the Wretch.

An old woman sat on a stoop, crying into her hands.

Arthur's imagination swirled to life. *This woman's cat was abducted by sewer crocodiles. Her purse got hooked by the stern of a pirate ship. She manages an orphanage, but it's currently sinking into the muck of an ancient graveyard no one knew it had been built on.* If he could solve this woman's problem, whatever it was, then she could tell the people of this city that he was a bona fide hero, and they would have to listen every time he spoke.

"Ma'am?" Arthur said, approaching the woman and removing his hat. "Is everything all right? Has someone wronged you? I just happen to be in the business of avenging ladies of any age."

The woman sniffed and looked up. "My husband passed away this morning."

"Oh." Arthur bowed his head. "I'm . . . I'm sorry to hear that."

The woman studied the veins in her hands. "The last thing I said to Joe as he walked out the door was to not waste our money on those butterscotches he was so fond of." Her eyes welled with tears. "How could I say such a horrible thing?"

Arthur nodded sadly. He couldn't remember the last thing he'd said to his mom before she'd died. He never thought he'd have to keep track.

"How did old Joe make his living?" Arthur asked.

The old woman sniffed. "He was a cobbler. He made shoes for children. They loved him. Said his shoes made them feel like they were walking on clouds."

Arthur remembered his time in the hospital, after the Battle of the Barrows between the old gangs of Kingsport. He and Wally had been the only ones there whose parents hadn't visited. Arthur had tried to make Wally feel better the only way he knew how. By spinning stories.

Arthur looked at the sky. "Well, Joe is in the *Great Elsewhere* now. And there are plenty of kids there in need of shoes. Only up there it's the other way around. See, the floor is made of *clouds*. Kids keep sinking through and tumbling back to earth where they become ghosts, haunting the schools and playgrounds with their lonely wails. But Joe makes shoes that allow the kids to walk across the clouds without falling. They're so grateful, they pay him in butterscotch."

The woman stared at Arthur with shining eyes. She seemed to really see him then. His frayed suspenders. His hand-me-down hat. His split shoes. She reached into her purse, pulled out a coin, and held it out to him.

"Oh, I couldn't possibly—" Arthur began, but stopped when she pressed the coin into his palm.

"*Take it.* You made my day a little brighter, and I want to do the same for you."

She frowned at Arthur's shoes, a pair of Harry's old ones, which were far too big but were Arthur's only option after his other pair had been taken by the Mycopath.

"I wish I could give you a pair of Joe's shoes, but—" The old woman shrugged sadly.

Arthur took the coin, if only to make her feel better.

She placed her hands on her knees and stood creakily. "It's time for me to sort through Joe's things." She smiled down at

Arthur. "You're a good boy. I hope fortune finds a way to lift you out of your current lot in life."

And with that she left.

Arthur stayed on the stoop a while. He spun the coin over his knuckles, thinking.

***

"Sir, your daughter is cycling around the Great Elsewhere like a shooting star. A bicycle made of starlight was waiting for her the moment she arrived. Had it not been for the lessons you gave her, she wouldn't have been able to pedal from earth to the moon, let alone the farthest reaches of the galaxy. She only wishes she hadn't grown ill before she learned how to ride the streets of Kingsport. She wants you to watch her pedal across the sky."

The man cleared a lump from his throat. "Thank you." He opened his pocketbook and stared at the last bill inside. "I've been struggling lately. Maddie's funeral expenses were considerable. But I would be remiss if I didn't—"

Arthur closed the man's pocketbook with the bill still inside. "My payment can be you teaching Maddie's younger siblings how to ride their bikes."

The man nodded gratefully. "I'll tell everyone what you did for me."

"Remember," Arthur said, "whenever you miss Maddie, just look up. You'll see her shimmering in the rain or beaming through the cloud-shine."

The man gave a ghost of a smile and then walked down the street, head tilted toward the sky.

Arthur had turned down a lot of money from impoverished souls that afternoon, but his hat was still spilling over with bills and coins. Word had gotten out about the boy who spun tales for the dearly departed, and people who had lost family members as far back as the Pox came to him for a bit of comfort. His tales had become so popular, he'd even overheard strangers talking about the Great Elsewhere, filling it with stories of their own lost loved ones.

Arthur's crate sat near the funeral parlor now, tastefully set a half block away. He'd used the old woman's coin to purchase a bit of black cloth to cover the crate and he'd made a sign:

TALES OF COMFORT
DURING TIMES OF GRIEF
(DONATIONS ACCEPTED BUT NOT ENCOURAGED)

In a single afternoon, Arthur had comforted the widows of several miners, who had perished in a collapse, by telling them there was no underground in the Great Elsewhere. He'd comforted a man whose wife had died of a tooth infection by telling him that her pain had ceased because rotten teeth were immediately removed up there. And he had comforted a woman whose grandfather had lost his hearing shortly before he'd passed away, assuring her that her final *I love you*, which he hadn't heard, was written in the clouds so he could look on it every day.

Arthur had comforted these people and many others. And he'd ended each of them with an encouragement to *Just look up*.

It felt different, telling these stories. More quiet and hopeful than the adventuresome kind. But after the trauma of seeing the Mycopath's reflections of Huamei and the Rook, he felt compelled to *comfort* people with the ghosts of their past instead of haunt them.

All morning, his skin had tingled with the feeling of performing good deeds.

A strange man in a top hat approached the crate. His limbs were long, his suit ill-fitting.

"Good afternoon, sir," Arthur said. "What comfort can I bring you today?"

The man grinned reddish-brown teeth. "Oh, I ain't griefin'. Not in the funerary sense, anyway. I'm lookin' for an object."

"Caskets and flowers are around the corner," Arthur said, pointing.

"Nah, nothing like that," the man said, still grinning. Arthur noticed the brown had burrowed holes through his teeth. "Though it is an object of the *grim* variety. See, I'm searching for a bone. A bone what's been transformicated into a *quill*."

Huamei's claw Quill.

Arthur's heart started to race. He tried not to let it show on his face.

"Pen and ink shop is your best bet," he said.

"I think you know exactly what I'm talking about," the man said, stepping close. "In fact, I'd be surprised if that quill weren't hiding on your person this very *mo*. Now be a mouse and hand it over to yer dear old Rustmouth so's I can bring it back to the Order victorious-like."

Arthur's mind worked quickly. Wally and the Wardens must have gone to the Fae-born zoo and sewn up the Rift, disrupting the Order's moneymaking scheme. Now the Order was sniffing after bigger prey. If they got their hands on the dragon-bone Quill, they wouldn't have to wait until a Rift opened to do their dirty work. With a few scribbles, they could simply write fantastical creatures into the Real themselves. Dozens of Fae-born zoos would pop up across the world, and Rifts would rent the sky, destroying the Veil and causing a worldwide Daymare.

Fortunately, Arthur had no idea where the Quill was. It had vanished from his hand after he'd been knocked unconscious in the Stormcrow's basement.

He smiled at the stranger. "No quills on me." He turned out his pockets. "See?"

"Funny," Rustmouth said. "And here you've been screaming your throat raw in public spaces, talking about how you used this particular *boned* instrument to save this verity city." The man clasped Arthur's suspenders and pulled him so close, Arthur was afraid he was going to chew his nose off with those rusted teeth. "I has it on *good authority* that you was the one who last had possession of the sorcerical pen."

"Who told you that?" Arthur asked, discretely unsnapping his suspenders from his pants.

The man grinned. "A little birdy."

Arthur nodded. "Speaking of little birdies . . ." And he sprinted down the street, leaving his suspenders, his money, and his father's hat behind.

The man came after him on his long legs. Arthur's oversized

shoes slowed him down, but he knew Kingsport better than anyone. He dodged in and out of crowds, losing the man briefly on Willow Street before squeezing down an alleyway and exiting onto Paradise Lane. He sprinted toward the docks to hide inside a salt barrel when a massive hand caught him by the throat.

"Well, look who it is," said Charlie, the Rook's bodyguard. "You just saved me the trouble of scouring the city. Boss wants to see ya."

"*Boss?*" Arthur said, the word coming out strangled. "But the Rook is . . ."

Charlie smirked. "New boss."

Rustmouth exited the alley, panting raggedly. He saw Arthur and the bodyguard, built like a marble slab. He cracked his knuckles, looking as if he was about to attack. But then his colorless eyes fell on the copper bowie knife on Charlie's belt, and he sneered his rusted teeth.

Rustmouth composed himself. "If it ain't no perturberance, I gots business with that slipperish urchin." He nodded at Arthur and then took out a purse and jangled it. "I'd be willing to pay pretty-like."

Charlie made a *tch* sound. "You'd need a whole lot more purses to match what my boss pays. Now shove off before I toss you in the drink."

"Very well." Rustmouth smiled his brown teeth at Charlie. As he departed, he winked at Arthur. "You'll keep that brick of a man close, if you catch my measuring."

Charlie dragged Arthur toward the Stormcrow.

"It's good to see you, Charlie!" Arthur said. "Glad you survived that monster bird attack. I barely made it out myself.

Where do you think that thing came from? My money's on the lab of some mad scientist."

Charlie, in his usual manner, didn't respond. A cold fear gripped Arthur's heart.

"Level with me, Charlie," he said. "Am I about to die?"

"Guess you'll find out in a minute," Charlie said.

Arthur only hoped someone would write a tale about him in the Great Elsewhere as good as one he'd spin for himself.

***

Only a month had passed since the Stormcrow had been destroyed by the scythe-like talons of the Mirror Rook, but the pub had been rebuilt anew with a fresh sign and everything. Now it was the StormCrow.

"You capitalized the *C*," Arthur said. "I like it."

Charlie hauled him inside.

The windows were transparent now, allowing sunlight to gleam off the bronze-lined bar, the redwood tables and chairs, slick with polish. The fireplace had been renovated and crackled pleasantly.

The patrons were no longer scarred and toothless lowlife thieves, but regular people with aboveboard jobs come in to wet their whistles. None of them looked at Arthur as Charlie guided him directly to the back door, whose picture of a rook had been painted over with a single feather. The door opened and then shut, and once again, Arthur was locked inside the Rook's office.

A woman sat behind the desk. Arthur's mouth fell open. Not a woman. *Liza.* He'd barely recognized her. Her hair was shorter and dyed black. And she looked older. Almost like a grown-up.

Arthur felt a knot in his throat when he realized losing both of her parents had matured her beyond her thirteen years.

"*So*," Liza said, leaning back in her father's chair. "Arthur Benton lives."

Arthur shifted from one foot to the other. "For the time being."

He tried to read her dark brown eyes. She'd been there that fateful night when Arthur had written the word that killed her father. But she'd been sweeping up glass in the pub. Did she know that Arthur was responsible? More importantly, did she know her father's death had been an accident? By summoning the Mirror Rook with the claw Quill, Arthur had only been trying to create a distraction so he could escape the pub and save his city from destruction. He hadn't known that the spell would kill the Rook.

Arthur flinched as Liza stood from her chair and stepped around the desk. He started to back away as she approached him . . . But Liza swept him into a hug.

"I thought those tentacles got you," she said, holding him close. "I was afraid Charlie was going to return with the remains of your suspenders that he found in some gutter."

Arthur lifted his numb arms and hugged Liza back. He glanced at Charlie over her shoulder. The bodyguard was as stone-faced as ever. He had been in this very office. He'd seen Arthur scribble the word that had killed the Rook. But Charlie couldn't *read*. Could Arthur really be that lucky?

Arthur pulled back and smiled at Liza so big he worried his teeth might shatter. "Heh. You think I'd die knowing there's someone out there who's read more books than me?"

Liza smirked. She sat back in her chair and gestured to the chair opposite, which Arthur took uneasily.

"Liza," he said, speaking in the same tone he'd used with Kingsport's bereaved. "I'm sorry about the Roo—I mean, your *dad*. You, um, doing okay?"

Liza's smile faltered. "Charlie, would you mind giving us a minute?"

The bodyguard let himself out, shutting the door with a definite *click*.

Liza opened a drawer while Arthur squirmed in his chair. This was it. The moment when Liza revealed that she knew what he'd done. She would pull out a knife and she would plunge it into Arthur's heart, avenging her father.

But instead of a knife, Liza pulled out a bone quill, veined red. Arthur's eyebrows nearly leapt up his forehead, but he stopped them just in time. It was *Liza* who'd stolen the claw Quill from the cellar that night.

"Do you know what this is?" Liza asked.

Arthur leaned in and squinted. "It looks like a quill. That's a strange handle, though. I don't think I've ever seen anything like it."

"*Arthur*," Liza said.

"Okay," Arthur said, sitting back defeated. "I know what it is."

"And do you know how to use it?"

He wasn't sure how to answer that. He had written three spells in his life. The first he'd messed up by writing the word *magical* before Kingsport, landing him and Wally in the Mirror

City, which was full of monsters. The second had acciden-tally brought down the Rook. His only successful spell had been when he possessed Garnett Lacroix like a puppet. But as Amelia had so cruelly pointed out, Arthur had only suc-ceeded because he knew the Gentleman Thief's adventures inside and out. Garnett Lacroix would not be in any future adventures.

Arthur rocked his head side to side. "I might know how to use it. Why?"

Liza knelt and opened a secret compartment in her father's desk and pulled out an old leather journal, which she thunked down before Arthur. It was made from golden-scaled skin and bursting with sheaves of yellowed paper. It looked like a book for warlocks.

Liza opened it. "I think you know that my father was trying to find a way to bring my mother back from the dead."

Arthur remembered the waxen woman in the corner of the Rook's office, waiting for a soul to inhabit it. Thankfully the frightful thing had been removed.

"That's what he was working on before he died," Liza continued, "searching for answers in this world and others." She flipped through the pages of the tattered book. "I've been studying my father's notes for a solid month. I've even tried making my own journeys into the pocket-worlds. None of them have worked." She fixed her eyes on Arthur. "I need someone with a flair for storytelling who knows how to use the Wardens' magic."

Arthur's heart started to race. He knew what came next.

"Arthur," Liza said. "Will you help me find the afterlife and bring back my mom?"

Arthur bit his lip. Dragon-bone Quills were temperamental things in the best of situations, and he would think twice—no, a *dozen* times—before he scribbled so much as an apostrophe with one. The Fae was a dangerous place, and one wrong move could be deadly. It could even kill a dragon.

But then he remembered the horrible things the Mycopath had made him see. The dead he'd spoken to may not have been real, but they had been right. He had made an orphan of Liza. This was his chance to make amends.

Arthur swallowed and then smiled. "You're talking to the right person. The Wardens taught me absolutely everything there is to know about magic."

9
THE MERCURY MINES

After dropping off Fae-born in several pocket-worlds—the shadow swamp, the fiery plain, the hairy forest—Wally, Sekhmet, and ropey Breeth arrived at a Rift that sloped into a network of tunnels made of reflective silver.

The Mercury Mines were slippery underfoot. The path before them split in two and each of those split again and then again. But these splits were temporary. The liquid silver walls slowly dripped and melted into each other, making and unmaking new passages every minute.

"Is it just me," Breeth asked from her rope, "or does it feel like we're being digested by a metallic monster?"

"Not helpful, Breeth," Wally said.

"Oh, and standing there looking terrified is?"

Wally ignored her. His reflection bent and warped along the tunnel's walls. "Isn't mercury poisonous?"

"You're thinking of the stuff in thermometers," Sekhmet said. "This stuff descends from *the* Mercury, god of communication. The Wardens came here to stop the Order from harvesting pure language." She nodded to Wally's broken nose. "You can understand why."

Still, Wally kept his distance from the ever-changing walls. "Silver Tongue coughed up *blood* after she drank this stuff."

"Well, let's be sure not to drink any then," Sekhmet said. She gazed down the tunnel. "Some say this mine is bottomless. Every tunnel represents a word that branched from old words that came before it. Only the greatest linguamancers are able to find their way through. Fortunately, we've got my mom's Mimic Map."

She took out the map. The ink shifted around the paper, perfectly copying the tunnels' movement, maintaining an accurate picture of the mines.

Sekhmet tapped five stick figures in the inky tangle of tunnels. "These must be the Wardens." She found another lone figure nearby. "And this must be Steel Fingers."

A pit opened in Wally's stomach. He wasn't sure he'd survive another fight. He imagined Arthur sipping apple cider back at the Stormcrow Pub and wished he was there next to him.

Sekhmet ignited her remaining sword. Its flames danced along the reflective walls as they descended into the dark tunnel, Breeth's slithering rope leading the way.

The liquid mines continued to split and combine, swallowing and opening dark passageways around them. When the tunnel they were heading down vanished, Sekhmet slashed at the wall with a wet *skish*, sending silver droplets twirling through the air before they rejoined the floor and ceiling. She had created a shortcut.

Wally snorted. "Aren't you supposed to *talk* your way through these tunnels?"

"Sure," Sekhmet said. "If you're not awesome with swords."

They continued deeper and deeper, and Breeth's rope stretched longer and longer.

"Wally, for the record, I'm still mad at you for being mad at me for saving your life," she said. "But I need you to please tell Sekhmet that I've never been *unspooled* before, and it feels *wild*. The air at the top of the mines is tickling my tails while the rest of me is getting pinched in the closing tunnels! It's like all of me is trapped in one of those finger-trap things. But I definitely don't hate it!"

Wally chose not to repeat this. Breeth had embarrassed him enough that day.

Breeth slithered ahead, sad and silent.

The tunnel closed again, and Sekhmet created another hole in three slashes. "This would go a lot faster if Rustmouth hadn't *eaten* my other sword."

"I thought you said the magic wasn't in the weapon," Wally said.

Sekhmet sighed. "It isn't. It's just . . . Rose forged these swords for me."

Wally knew the story. Rose had been Weirdwood's black-smith and Sekhmet's mentor. On Sekhmet's first mission as a Novitiate, her mentor had brought her to the Neon Pastures. Sekhmet had grown overly confident and ventured off to cap-ture her first Fae-born, leaving her mentor's back unguarded. A demon lamb had attacked and killed Rose. Sekhmet still hadn't forgiven herself.

"Rose was the one who told me that bonding with my swords was a bad idea," Sekhmet continued. "If you believe your art is inside your weapon instead of you, and the weapon breaks on the battlefield, then you might lose touch with your magic. She taught me to learn to let go." Sekhmet sighed. "Little did she realize that advice would apply to losing her."

Many slashes later, the liquid tunnels started to solidify. They no longer shined bright and reflective but grew dull like iron that hadn't been cleaned in centuries.

"We've reached the dead languages," Sekhmet said, checking the map. "The mines will stop shifting, but I can't slice through them anymore."

Sounds echoed from the depths. War drums. Steel on steel. A scream.

A battle raged in the heart of the Mercury Mines.

Sekhmet quickened her steps. "*Mom! Dad!*"

They reached a fork in the mines. Sekhmet broke down the left tunnel, sword flaming, shadow stretching wild against the silvery walls. Wally hurried after her, heart pounding, tightening his gauntlets. Who could the Wardens be fighting down there? Was Steel Fingers powerful enough to take on *all* of the Wardens?

Breeth's rope slithered up beside him. "*Whoa, wait, wait, whoa, Wally, stop!*"

Wally kept running. "I don't have time for your jokes, Breeth!"

Breeth coiled the rope around his ankles and gave a sharp tug, making him trip and hit the hard metal floor.

"*Ow!*" he said as the rope dragged him back up the tunnel. "Breeth, what are you *doing*? I need to help Sekhmet!"

Breeth hauled him back to the fork, then rolled his body so he was facing the tunnel to the right. She pointed the rope's end like a finger. "*Look!*"

Far down the tunnel was a little girl. She held a candle that flickered on auburn hair, brown overalls, and big, moony eyes. The little girl glanced back at Wally before disappearing around a bend. The sight gave him a sinking feeling. What was a little girl doing in the Mercury Mines? And why did she look *familiar*?

"Wally," Breeth said, barely able to talk. "Wally, Wally, Wally, Wally, Wally."

The threads of her rope prickled like hairs on the back of a neck.

"Breeth," he said. "Take a breath or whatever it is you do. What is it?"

"Wally . . . ," Breeth said. "That was . . . *me.*"

Wally watched the little girl's candle fade into the darkness. "*What?*"

"It. Was. *Me!*" Breeth said. "I'd recognize me anywhere! Yeah, I look a little bit older, but that's *my* body running around these mines. *Without* me inside it! I have no idea what that means, but we have to go talk to her! *Right now!*"

Wally stared down the tunnel where the little girl had vanished. What Breeth was saying was impossible. She was *dead*. Killed by the Rook as an experiment to try and locate his wife's spirit in the Fae.

Breeth gave the rope a whip. "Get up! She—I mean, *I'm* getting away!"

Wally shifted his gaze down the left tunnel toward Sekhmet, whose fiery sword had nearly faded in the distance. The drums continued to beat. The metal continued to shriek. The shadows continued to war with one another.

If Wally followed Breeth now, he would be abandoning his duties as Novitiate. He could lose his place in the Manor forever.

"Breeth, listen to me. There's no *way* that was you."

"Oh, so you'll talk to a ghost-possessed rope, but you won't believe *this*?" Breeth said. "How will you feel if that really is my body, and it gets away, and I stay dead forever? *Huh?*"

Wally gazed toward Sekhmet. He had no idea what she was running toward. She could get hurt. She could die like Huamei.

"*Wally,*" Breeth said, gently turning his head with her rope so he could look into her coiled eyes. "The day we met, you promised you'd help me find a way to get back to my parents. And so far, you haven't done anything. But that's my *body* down there. You finally have a chance to help me."

Wally stared down the right tunnel. The little girl's candle had faded, and the mines had fallen black as pitch. They would no longer have Sekhmet's sword to light the way. He remembered what his mentor had said about the impossibility of navigating tunnels as twisted and expansive as language itself. Even the Wardens had become lost down here.

"We'll be going in blind," Wally said, hoping this would deter Breeth.

But Breeth uncoiled her rope from his ankles and into his hand. "I'll lead you."

Wally gave one last look down the left tunnel where the battle was growing louder and more intense. Then he grabbed hold of Breeth's rope and followed it deep into the mines, toward the strange little girl.

10
THE FIVE FACES

The StormCrow Pub was closed for the night. Fog licked the windowpanes. Flames crackled in the fireplace. Charlie sat sleeping at the bar. The only sounds were the bodyguard's snores, the pop of burning wood, and the shuffling of pages.

Liza had laid her father's research across the pub's tables, having organized them into notes, maps, and charcoal etchings. She grabbed a map from one of the tables and laid it in front of Arthur. The map showed a city whose layout seemed to be modeled after a galaxy. The ink even *moved*, spiraling the city around the page like a tide pool.

Arthur's eyes widened. "Is *this* the afterlife?"

"Not quite," Liza said. "It's called the *Whirling City*. My father found a passage in an old alchemy book that claims this city has gateways that lead to every pocket-world in the Fae. Including, he hoped, the afterlife. Few people have set foot in the Whirling City, and it's questionable whether any of them got out alive."

"Guess we'll be the first, then," Arthur said. "How do we get there?"

"The caster must have access to a great magical source." Liza pulled out Huamei's claw Quill. "That's why my father stole this." She rolled the Quill between her fingers, inspecting it in the low firelight. "I think he would have found my mom if those Wardens hadn't killed him."

"*Wardens*," Arthur said with feigned disgust.

He wondered what Lady Weirdwood would say if she knew he was about to use magic again. After all, a single word written with a dragon-bone quill could release a nightmare into the world.

But Arthur had experienced some trial and error with the Quill now, and he would carefully consider each word before he dotted any eyeballs or crossed any T. rexes.

"We'll pick up where my father left off," Liza said, lifting a page from the sketches table. It was old and delicate and looked like it could disintegrate in her fingertips. "This is the culmination of his work, rubbed from the walls of the Inverted Temple. It's a puzzle of sorts. And, according to his notes, the only way to enter the Whirling City. They don't want humans just strolling in, even if they do manage to get their hands on a dragon-bone quill."

"*Psh*," Arthur said. "Puzzles *solve themselves* when they see me comin'."

Liza handed him the paper and rested her hand on his shoulder. He felt a tingle of the old days when the pub had been a place to relax and flirt with his favorite server. He got comfortable in his chair, took a sip of apple cider, and examined the page. He was ready to unscramble words, untangle double meanings, to step outside of the box of his own mind and consider the puzzle from every angle . . .

But there were no words on the page. Instead, five charcoal-etched faces stared back at him with exaggerated expressions. One laughed. Another sobbed. One screamed in terror, while another gritted its teeth. The last face simply winked.

Arthur's brain scrambled for answers. He had told Liza he was the master of magic and riddles. But these drawings looked less like a puzzle and more like portraits of the patients in Greyridge Mental Hospital.

"Anything?" Liza asked.

"*Shh!*" Arthur said. "I think I've almost got it."

He wrinkled his forehead in a thinking manner and took another sip of his cider, trying to buy more time.

"The one thing I learned with the Wardens," he said, stealing a line from Wally, "is that all magic is based on *art*."

"Obviously," Liza said. "How does that help us here?"

Arthur bit his lip and studied the facial expressions. When they still refused to give up their secrets, he subtly imitated each one, trying to get a sense of what it represented. When he reached the screaming face, his open mouth froze. It reminded him of the people's expressions in Kingsport when everyone thought they were going to be killed by ravens and tentacles.

Arthur plonked his cider down, sloshing some on the table. "So *that's* why your dad had Alfred Moore summon monsters to Kingsport! *Fear!*"

"Huh?" Liza said.

"He just hadn't started incorporating comedy or tragedy or the others. Or maybe he hadn't connected the dots . . ."

Liza gave him a quizzical look.

Arthur turned the paper toward her. "Art is meant to make people *react*, right?"

"So?"

"*So.* What if these faces are part of some artistic spell? Like brewing a magical potion, except all of the ingredients are *creative* elements." He pointed to the laughing and crying faces. "Making your audience roll in the aisles or pull out their handkerchiefs." Next he pointed to the faces with gritted teeth and a screaming mouth. "Bringing them to the edge of their seats or making them shrink back in fear." Finally, he tapped the winking face. "Add a dash of romance, and you have the perfect adventure story."

Liza took the page of faces from Arthur. "So you're saying when my dad summoned monsters into Kingsport . . . he was trying to fulfill the *fear* part of the formula?"

"Exactly," Arthur said. "And if we create a piece of art that captures all of these elements—*comedy*, *tragedy*, *suspense*, *horror*, *romance*—it might transport us to the Whirling City." He kicked his feet up on the table, satisfied with himself.

"That solves getting us there," Liza said, then looked toward the bodyguard still snoozing at the bar. "We just have to hope Charlie can keep us protected from the dragons."

Arthur's feet slipped off the table and thumped the floor. "What?"

"According to my dad's notes, dragons reign over the Whirling City." She flipped to the back of her father's warlock book. "Their magic is so powerful that they can access every pocket-world in existence. If anyone knows where the entrance to the afterlife is, it's them."

Arthur put his hands in his lap so Liza wouldn't see them shaking. "*Dragons*, huh?" Huamei's mom was a Duchess in the dragon kingdom. "That's"—he tried not to gulp—"awesome."

Liza grabbed the picture of the faces. "Which one should we do first?"

"W-we're starting *now*?"

Liza smirked. "You have somewhere to be?"

Arthur stared out the window into the misty night. This was his last chance to return to the tenements and live out a safe and boring life with Harry. To replace a magical adventure with the promise of never being eaten by a dragon . . .

Then again, it was also his last chance to make things up to Liza.

Arthur breathed deep, summoning his Gentleman Thief bravery. "And miss out on the adventure? Just try and hold me back."

Liza walked to the pub's windows and closed the shutters. "We'll keep our creations within the confines of this pub so we can control them." Next, she went to the back office and retrieved a notebook and a fresh bottle of ink and then sat at the center table. "Where do we start?"

Arthur picked up the page of faces and saw them anew. They looked less ridiculous now and more like lit sticks of dynamite.

He cleared his throat. "A little comedy never hurt anyone, right?"

He held his hand out for Huamei's claw Quill, but Liza gripped it tight.

"I'll hold on to this, if you don't mind."

Arthur pulled his hand back. For a brief moment, he thought he'd seen black feathers ruffling in her hair.

"Right," he said. "Your handwriting is probably better than mine anyway."

Liza dipped the Quill and then stared at him, waiting.

Arthur circled the tables, nose lifted, trying to give off a creative air and pretending wasn't terrified. "Comedy . . . comedy . . . comedy . . ."

He saw the bar and felt a touch of inspiration. "Our journey begins . . . in a pub."

Liza glanced left, then right. "Where *do* you come up with these brilliant ideas, Arthur?"

Arthur's smile didn't falter. He was starting to feel that sweeping sense of adventure. He could finally make his imagination come to life again. No more waiting for that magical tingling in his chest that never arrived. The dragon-bone Quill would handle it all.

He sat next to Liza, brimming with excitement. "This is a *different* kind of pub. It's called the Roasted Parrot, and it's exclusively for that dastardliest of scallywags, the *pirate*. In fact, before we transport to this place, you might want to give us some cloaks and eye patches."

Liza wrote the words, and cloaks spilled over their shoulders and down their backs like water. She gave Arthur an eye patch, opting for a grim scar along her cheek, but she absolutely refused to give him a curled mustache for what he referred to as *comedic effect*.

"The Roasted Parrot was—sorry, *is* the last resort for outcasts of the sea," Arthur began. "Tucked in the armpit of the poorest port city, upstanding citizens avoid walking past the foul pub's doors, let alone pointing their noses in its general direction, lest they catch a whiff of the pungent stench of *evil*."

Arthur spoke, Liza wrote, and the Pub began to change. The air itself rippled, replacing oaken panels with moldy stone walls, polished tables with lopsided benches, and lighting fixtures with dangling knives, hung for decoration . . . or emergencies. Next came the stench—a musk of gas-heavy bellies, crevice sweat, and breath that had dined for decades on whatever tuna, anchovies, and scallops were too spoiled to sell. Finally, the owners of these scents materialized in every open space—the kind of crooked, haggard, cuss-mouthed outcasts that every mother had nightmares about.

A heavily scarred bartender plonked a frothing stein on the worm-infested bar next to Charlie, who was still fast asleep. And thus, the StormCrow Pub became the Roasted Parrot.

Arthur searched the foul pub with his uncovered eye, peeking past splintered peg legs and grimy hooks and between lewdly tattooed arms. He nodded toward the corner where a frail figure sat as slack as a scarecrow. "That's our guy."

Keeping their noses down, Arthur and Liza made their way through the boisterous crowd—bumped by scabby elbows, sloshed by sour ale, and tripped by still bodies that may or may not have been breathing.

Liza pulled her hood farther over her face. "What exactly makes this a *comedy*?"

"Witty banter," Arthur whispered. "And a happy ending, of course. But first? Banter."

"I have to be *funny*?"

"Leave it to me," Arthur said. "Just call me Doctor Feather."

"Um, why?"

"Because I tickle funny bones."

Liza didn't so much as crack a smile.

"Well, I can't help you if your funny bone is *missing*."

They reached the hunched figure in the corner. The man

was ancient and bug-eyed. With his patchwork beard and thinning hair, he resembled a plucked rooster.

The elderly man squinted cataract milky eyes at Arthur. "I'd sit elsewhere, *boy*," he wheezed, curdling his lips. "Unless you want that face of yours *peeled* off your skull like an orange skin."

Liza . . . *snorted*. Arthur flashed her a look of warning.

Sure, it was funny to hear such murderous words from the withered lips of what appeared to be a helpless old man. But this was *Alabaster Fringehead*—the cruelest, skeeviest, most bloodthirsty pirate in all imagination. He just happened to be elderly now.

Fortunately for Liza, Fringehead was hard of hearing these days and did not hear her snort. Fortunate for her *face*, that was.

When Arthur and Liza didn't budge, the old man coughed into his hand and wiped a streak of yellow phlegm across the table. "What do ye want?"

"*Arrgh*," Arthur said in his best pirate impression. "Just thought you might like to hear a joke."

"Feh," Fringehead said, like Arthur had offered to spit in his face.

Normally, Arthur would steer clear of Fringehead and his milky glare. But the old pirate had the coordinates to the most valuable treasure on the seven seas: a ship whose stern functioned as a compass needle for *gold*. He was just too old now to seek it out himself.

Arthur had dictated every detail to Liza. A while back, Alabaster Fringehead had promised everyone in the Roasted Parrot that he would share the coordinates with any soul who could give him something no one else could: He wanted to *laugh*.

"Go on, then," Fringehead wheezed. "Let's hear this *joke*." He slapped a mold-spotted hand axe on the table. "And if I don't like what I hear, I'll cut you up so proper, your own mother won't be able to distinguish you from a bowl of *blood pudding*."

Arthur felt like he'd swallowed a jellyfish. He didn't think Alabaster was capable of something that strenuous. Not anymore. But Arthur suddenly wasn't sure he wanted to test it. He wished he'd put more thought into this scene before they'd gotten started. Things never felt this hair-raising on the page.

"*Arr*," Arthur snarled, trying to steady himself. "What did the old pirate say on his birthday?"

Fringehead smiled like a demon. "Tell me, sonny. What *did* the old pirate say on his birthday?"

Arthur opened his mouth to answer, then closed it again when he realized his mistake. Gus from the Merry Rogues had told this joke as easy as a breeze. Then again, Gus was getting up in years, so it sounded charming coming from him.

Still, it was too late for Arthur to turn back now.

"He said . . . *Aye, matey*."

Fringehead tightened his gnarled fingers around the handle of his axe.

"Get it?" Arthur said, ready to turn and run. "*Aye, matey? I'm . . . eighty?*"

Before he knew what was happening, Fringehead's hand shot out and flipped Arthur onto the table. The old man lifted the axe high over Arthur's forehead and—

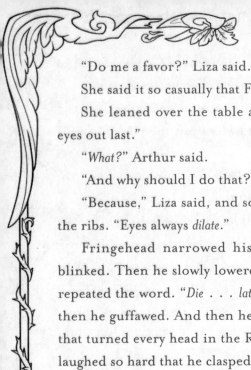

"Do me a favor?" Liza said.

She said it so casually that Fringehead froze in place.

She leaned over the table and studied Arthur. "Cut his eyes out last."

"*What?*" Arthur said.

"And why should I do that?" Fringehead asked.

"Because," Liza said, and softly elbowed the old pirate in the ribs. "Eyes always *dilate*."

Fringehead narrowed his own eyes at her. Then he blinked. Then he slowly lowered the axe as his withered lips repeated the word. "*Die . . . late.*" Fringehead chuckled. And then he guffawed. And then he burst into explosive laughter that turned every head in the Roasted Parrot. The old pirate laughed so hard that he clasped a hand to his chest, fell to the floor, and died.

Arthur rolled upright and stared in disbelief at the axe that had nearly chopped him into blood pudding. "Liza . . . that was *incredible*. How did you come up with that?"

"Read it in a joke book once," she said. "And *you* were trying too hard. Comedy should come naturally."

She smiled down at Fringehead's dead body, his lips contorted in eternal laughter. Then she flipped open the notebook and with a slash and a swirl, crossed out the description of the Roasted Parrot. The pirate pub snapped shut like a threatened clamshell, leaving only the StormCrow behind.

"Wait!" Arthur said. "We never got the coordinates to the treasure!"

"It doesn't matter," Liza said, and held up the charcoal rubbing. The laughing face had shut its eyes and closed its mouth and now wore no expression at all. Almost like it was satisfied with the comedic scene. She waggled the claw Quill. "Who needs coordinates when we can just make up what happens next?"

"I *guess*," Arthur said. "If you don't care about *internal story logic*." He sighed. "And the next part of the story *is* boring."

"What do you mean, *next part*?" Liza asked. "Aren't you making this up as you go?"

"Hmm? Oh. Yes. Of course I am." He nodded at the expression with clenched teeth. "We can jump right to the *suspenseful* bit."

Something bumped the pub's front door. Arthur and Liza jumped, then stared as the doorknob slowly turned this way, then that.

Arthur crept to the window, peeked through the shutters, and gazed into the coiling mist of the evening. Three figures stood in the street.

"I think we've got company," Arthur said.

"Probably just patrons looking for a late-night drink," Liza said.

Arthur studied the figures—one slight and hunched, one built like a marble slab, and one with a top hat. "I don't think those are patrons."

Liza went to Charlie and patted his broad shoulder. The bodyguard snorted awake and then rubbed his eyes, staring at the bar, which was still slightly worm-eaten.

"There's trouble outside," Liza said. "Be a dear and fetch a bludgeon."

Charlie rubbed the tired from his face, then trundled to the back room and returned with a steel baton, which he carried outside. Liza closed the door behind him, and she and Arthur stood silent and listened. There was a crunching sound. Then a shatter. Then a heavy thunk, followed by a sound like a body hitting the cobblestones.

Liza quickly locked the door.

"What are you doing?" Arthur asked. "We have to get him back in here! He's our *bodyguard*."

"Exactly," Liza said, double bolting the door. "Taking hits is his *job*." She collected the Quill and notebook. "If my father worried after the health of every single gang member, he never would've gotten anything done."

Arthur wanted to say something but bit his lip. He had hoped that Liza hadn't inherited the Rook's more brutal traits.

Liza tapped the Quill against the notebook. "Let's get suspenseful."

Arthur gave one last glance at the window, gulped, and cleared his throat. "Right. Next. We're kidnapped by the Pirates of Penultimate Pier. Naturally."

He gave her the details, Liza scribbled the words, and the floor suddenly heaved beneath their feet. The hanging lamps swayed. Glasses slid back and forth across the bar while tables scudded toward the bar, then back toward the windows. There came a great roaring sound above as water splashed through the cracks in the ceiling and splashed on the floor, smelling of brine.

Arthur's heart began to thrum.

"Are we in the hull of a ship?" Liza asked, hand to her stomach. Her face was turning the slightest shade of green.

"Not just *any* ship!" Arthur said.

He ran to the ladder behind the bar and scaled it to the pub's roof, throwing wide the trapdoor . . . onto the deck of the most resplendent ship in the imaginary seas. Kingsport was gone—replaced with sparkling, cerulean waves that stretched to the horizon beneath a wide, salt spray sky. Liza climbed up beside him.

"The *Treasure Bolt*," Arthur said with bursting admiration.

On deck, three rogues were in the middle of a swashbuckling battle against a fiendish gang of pirates. One grabbed a rope on the forecastle and swung across the deck, knocking over a group of pirates like bowling pins.

"Hey, Mim!" Tuck said, landing with grace. "How do you make a pirate mad?"

"You mean besides kicking 'em like you just done?"

"You take away the *P*! Get it? *Irate*?"

Mim rolled her eyes. "Hasn't anyone told you that pirate puns are deader than a doornail?"

"I thought they were deader than a dead man's chest!" Tuck said.

"Keep up those lousy puns," Mim said, "and I'll start fighting you instead of these pirates!"

Gus, meanwhile, was fencing two pirates at the same time. "Give it up, ya filthy rat! We'll give your captain an offer he can't refuse!"

"Wrong puns, Gus!" Tuck said.

Mim shook her head. "Poor sod's got his adventures crossed."

Arthur beamed. It was the *Merry Rogues*! Skin and muscle back on their bones where it belonged. He was about to call out to them when Liza tackled him to the deck a split second before an errant knife twanged into the mast right where his head had been.

Arthur checked his hair. "Close one. Thanks, Liza."

They quickly crawled behind some barrels and peeked over the tops.

"*You* came up with all this?" Liza said, examining the many details of the scene.

"Well . . . ," Arthur said, blushing. "I *might* have stolen some of the details from *Garnett Lacroix and the Pirates of Penultimate Pier.* Like the pub. And this ship and everything on it. And the story's entire premise. That Doctor Feather joke was mine though!"

Liza, at last, chuckled.

Arthur breathed the sea air, but then his chest deflated. "Wait, where's Garnett Lacroix?"

The Gentleman Thief was nowhere to be seen. Arthur hadn't expected any *new* adventures from his favorite fictional hero, but he did expect him to make appearance in one of his *old* stories. Wherever the Gentleman Thief had disappeared to when he had walked into the sunset, it seemed he'd *stayed* there.

"Who?" Liza said.

The wind of adventure flagged in Arthur's soul. "No one. It doesn't matter."

"Okay . . . When does the suspense start?"

Arthur looked down at the charcoal etching, whose teeth still ground with anxiety.

"Oh . . . ," Arthur said, remembering the next part of the story. "Oh no."

"What's wrong?"

Without Garnett Lacroix's pinpoint precision, how would the Merry Rogues possibly survive the Pirates of Penultimate Pier? How would Arthur and Liza?

"*Liza*," he said, breathless. "You need to write us out of here. *Now.*"

"I'm not wasting ink, Arthur."

A harsh cackle drew their eyes toward the entrance to the ship's cabin. The imposing pirate captain made his dramatic entrance, kicking over a barrel and scattering black powder across the deck. He pulled a single match from behind his ear.

"All right, you scummy pile of so-called *heroes*," the pirate captain cried to the Merry Rogues. "If you don't mosey off that plank in the next five seconds, I'll light up this ship and everyone on it. Savvy?"

"Easy, now," Tuck said, holding up his hands.

"You'll blow us all to smithereens!" Mim said.

Gus gulped. "Ain't no one comes back from smithereens."

"What's happening?" Liza whispered to Arthur.

"That's Luckless Chuck," Arthur said. "He's obsessed with gold. He'd rather die and let this treasure-tracking ship sink to the bottom of the ocean than let anyone else have it."

"You're bluffing!" Gus yelled to the pirate captain.

"*He's not*," Arthur whispered to Liza.

"We'd say you're a liar, liar pants on fire," Tuck shouted.

"But we know you ain't got the guts to actually light your pants on fire!" screamed Mim.

Luckless Chuck grinned. "Let the countdown begin then." He scratched the match on his golden tooth, and then held the flame over the gunpowder. "*FIVE!*"

"We shouldn't have called his bluff," Gus said.

"Boy is my face red," Tuck said.

"Not as red as it's about to be," said Mim.

"I can think of something else suspenseful!" Arthur hissed at Liza. "Um, um, roulette tables are pretty suspenseful. As are Ferris wheels . . . *Why aren't you writing this down?*"

"*FOUR!*"

Liza eyed the spilled gunpowder. "How did these rogues escape in the story?"

"The Rogues don't do *anything*!" Arthur said, unable to tear his eyes from the burning match. "At the last possible second, *Garnett Lacroix* throws his dagger with such accuracy that he extinguishes the flame a split second before it hits the gunpowder. Except, I'm not sure if you noticed this . . . *Garnett isn't here!*"

"*THREE!*"

Even Luckless Chuck's men were starting to look nervous.

"Is that his last match?" Liza asked.

"Yes!" Arthur said. "But it's enough! If you won't use the Quill to get us out of here, then write a shark jumping on board and eating Luckless Chuck!"

"*Quiet,*" Liza said. "I'm thinking."

"*TWO!*" Luckless Chuck screamed.

Some of the pirates decided right then would be a good time to walk the plank themselves.

"It's been an honor," Tuck said.

"It's been a yawner," Mim said.

"We're goners," said Gus.

"LIZA!"

Arthur tried to grab the Quill from her hand, but she shoved him away, then coiled her foot through a rope connected to the boom that held the billowing sail.

"*ONE!*"

Liza gave her foot a jerk, pulling the rope taut, and sweeping the boom overhead. Luckless Chuck released the match just as the sail caught the crosswind, making the ship turn sharply and the deck dip steeply beneath their feet.

A split second before the match touched the gunpowder, the breeze extinguished it.

There was a quiet moment of ocean waves and shrieking seagulls.

Gus slowly peeked between his fingers. "Is this . . . heaven?"

Mim frowned at the pirates. "I expected something nicer."

"It don't get much nicer than being alive!" Tuck said. "*Attack!*"

And the Merry Rogues returned to dueling the pirates.

Arthur blinked. "Liza. That . . . was . . . *genius!*" He wiped the sweat from his forehead. "But also a *really* close call! Why didn't you just use the dragon bone to transform the gunpowder into dirt or something?"

"Because," Liza said, lifting the paper. The face with gritted teeth had fallen placid as a puddle. "That wouldn't have been very *suspenseful*, would it?"

Arthur realized his jaw was hanging open and quickly shut it. "I guess not."

While the Merry Rogues tied up the pirates, he and Liza descended back into the hull and the StormCrow Pub.

"Two down, three to go," Liza said, studying the charcoal etching. She pointed to the face with collapsed eyebrows and a downward curving mouth. "Tragedy's next."

"The story I chose already has us covered," Arthur said with a smile. "While Mim's tying up Luckless Chuck, she accidentally drops her knife and chops off her pinky toe."

He cupped his ear toward the ceiling just as a scream rang out on the above ship deck.

"Aaaaauuuuugggggghhhhhhh!"

Arthur smiled. "Luckless Chuck regains control of the ship while the Merry Rogues rush Mim to the hospital where the doctor quickly sews it back on. And *that's* where they meet a mysterious bandage-wrapped figure, who leads them to the next part of the adventure."

"Losing a toe isn't particularly *tragic*."

"It is for Mim!" Arthur said.

He described the hospital he'd imagined in the story. Liza sighed and wrote the words. With a low moan, the pub's windows began to stretch skyward. The fireplace and bar extended out on either side like the ends of an accordion, flipping the floorboards into white marble tiles and the tables into clean, crisp beds.

Arthur and Liza found themselves standing in the grand hallway of an endless hospital.

Liza searched the beds. "Where's Mim?"

Arthur couldn't answer. His jaw had locked up.

This wasn't the hospital from the Garnett Lacroix story.

It was the hospital Arthur's mother had died in.

11
THE LOST GIRL

The Mercury Mines had gone liquid again. Wally could hear his footsteps rippling up the tunnel walls while Breeth slithered ahead of him. He held her rope, walking slow and uncertain, eyes straining in the complete darkness.

"See anything?" he whispered.

"Just 'cause I'm a ghost doesn't mean I have *glow-in-the-dark eyes*," Breeth said.

The farther they journeyed away from Sekhmet, the more uneasy Wally became. What if following Breeth and neglecting his duties put his Novitiateship in jeopardy? He couldn't return to his old life with the Black Feathers. It felt so heartless now.

"Are you *sure* that little girl was you, Breeth?" he said. "How is your body still running around?"

"If I knew that, I would have insisted we come down here ages ago!"

Wally sighed. "Fair enough."

A few steps later, he ran chest-first into a fork in the tunnel and paused. His head spun with the infinite tangled possibilities of the twisting mines. The little girl could have taken one of a hundred different pathways.

Far behind them, the battle raged on. Beating drums. Metal on metal. Bursts of flame.

Wally's throat tightened. "Breeth, what if I follow the rope back up to the fight? I'll come back with Sekhmet and the map as soon as I can. Then we'll find your body—or whoever that was—together."

The rope bristled. "Go ahead."

"Breeth . . ."

"Breeth *what*?" she said, jerking the rope painfully from his hands. "Breeth, be reasonable? Breeth, don't be excited about finding your body and maybe not being *dead* anymore? Breeth, please forget all the times I promised you I'd help out and then didn't? Is that what you were going to say?"

Wally was at a loss for words.

"You're *real* good at following orders, Wally," Breeth said. "You followed that gang leader guy for years. You know, the one who *murdered me*? You didn't argue with the doctors when they treated your brother like human garbage. And now you jump whenever the Wardens say jump and hurl yourself at a freaking *fire buffalo* when they tell you to do that. But if your best ghost friend in the entire world asks you *nicely* to help get her *body* back, then you're all excuses. I guess my feelings can't be hurt because there are no *grown-ups* here telling you what to do."

Wally was shocked into silence. He'd never thought of himself as a naive follower. He had just done what he had to do

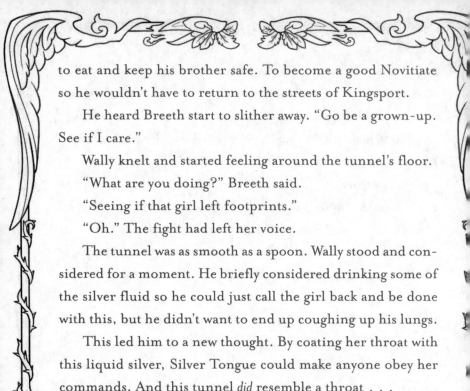

to eat and keep his brother safe. To become a good Novitiate so he wouldn't have to return to the streets of Kingsport.

He heard Breeth start to slither away. "Go be a grown-up. See if I care."

Wally knelt and started feeling around the tunnel's floor.

"What are you doing?" Breeth said.

"Seeing if that girl left footprints."

"Oh." The fight had left her voice.

The tunnel was as smooth as a spoon. Wally stood and considered for a moment. He briefly considered drinking some of the silver fluid so he could just call the girl back and be done with this, but he didn't want to end up coughing up his lungs.

This led him to a new thought. By coating her throat with this liquid silver, Silver Tongue could make anyone obey her commands. And this tunnel *did* resemble a throat . . .

Wally felt inside his gauntlets. They were lined with wool.

"Breeth, possess my gauntlets," he said.

"Ew, no," Breeth said. "Too sweaty."

"Do you want to catch that little girl or not?"

"Ugh, *fine*."

The gauntlets' wool ruffled to life with Breeth's presence, and Wally pressed his gauntlets into the tunnel wall.

"Say, *Come back, little girl!*" Wally said.

"Um, *Come back, little girl?*"

Breeth's voice vibrated the metal gauntlets, which reverberated against the tunnel, and rippled into the darkness.

They waited a moment in breathless silence. And then they heard footsteps.

The air tinged with smoke. A light ached to life. The little girl rounded the tunnel, her candle flame shimmering against the silver walls.

Wally finally got a good look at her. Her blue eyes and sickly brown hair. Her pudgy nose and knobby knees. Other than the scowl on her face, she looked *exactly* like an older version of his friend—only without wood for skin.

"*Give me back my body, kid!*" Breeth screamed.

The girl didn't budge, somehow unaffected by Breeth's silvery words. The bristle left Wally's gauntlets right before the rope reared to life and struck at the girl like a cobra. The girl turned to run, but the rope whipped around her ankles, yanking her to the ground and spilling the candle, still lit, across the floor. The little girl grunted and thrashed, feet stomping, hands slapping the walls, helpless prey to Breeth's serpentine rope.

"I don't remember being this *strong*!" Breeth shouted in a strained voice. "Gonna have to do this the old-fashioned way!"

The rope fell limp, and the girl was knocked back by a powerful force. She continued to thrash as if fighting something invisible or *something inside her own head*. Wally watched in shock as Breeth tried to *repossess* her own body.

After several moments of struggle, the rope coiled to life again. "*Uck!*" Breeth said, coughing. "Whoever's in there punched me in the ghost throat!"

Before Wally could work out how a ghost could be *punched*, Breeth's rope struck again. But this time, the girl managed to draw a knife with a thorn-designed hilt from an ankle holster. Every time Breeth struck, the girl slashed, severing another piece of the rope, which grew shorter and shorter.

"I'm running out of rope, Wally!" Breeth screamed. "Quick! Use your fists and knock her out!"

"I'm not punching a little girl in the face!" Wally said.

"It's *my* face, Wally!" Breeth said. "I give you permission!"

The little girl thrashed and grunted. The tunnel filled with frayed bits of rope.

Wally searched the area and found the candle flickering nearby on the tunnel floor. He placed his foot on top of the candle and took careful aim. He gave it a push, rolling the candle right underneath the girl's foot. The girl slipped on it, slamming hard to the ground.

Before she could recover, Breeth spun her rope around the girl like a boa constrictor and squeezed until she stopped struggling.

Wally kicked the knife away and retrieved the candle. He looked at the girl, all trussed up and glowering. Her familiar face was contorted by an anger he'd never seen on his ghost friend. The girl's eyes glittered cruelly while her chest heaved and spit foamed at the corners of her lips.

"Who are you?" he asked.

The girl sniffed. "I ain't telling you *nuffin'*."

She even sounded like Breeth. But the energy behind the voice was different. *Rougher.*

"Who gave you permission to talk like that with *my* vocal cords?" Breeth asked, squeezing the girl until her forehead turned cherry red.

"You owe my friend an explanation," Wally said.

"What *friend*?" the girl spat.

"Her name's Breeth," Wally said. "That's her body you're in."

The girl's scowl melted.

Breeth squeezed the rope even tighter. "Tell her if she painted my toenails, I'll string her up by her *ankles*."

"Ease up, Breeth," Wally said.

Breeth grumbled to herself, but the rope loosened.

The red left the girl's face. "Yer friend's *here*? Yer talking to her now?"

"She's possessing that rope," Wally said.

The girl's muscles loosened. She was done trying to escape.

Breeth yanked the girl to her feet and gave the rope a whip. "*Mush!*"

The girl grunted in pain and started to walk.

"*Gentle*, Breeth," Wally said.

"Oh, that's rich," Breeth said. "Be gentle. With *me*. Don't tell *my* feet where to walk. Don't tell you not to punch me in the face. Don't tell myself that I *hate* the haircut I gave me. *Psh.*"

✳✳✳

They returned to the fork where they'd separated from Sekhmet and hurried down the other tunnel, leading Breeth's bound impostor behind. The clash of metal and bursts of flame had ceased.

Wally slowed as they approached the intersection of several tunnels. Four figures surrounded a man who sat on the floor, hands bound behind his back. His face was beaten to a pulp. Wally recognized him from when he'd first entered the Manor. It was Linus. *Sekhmet's dad.*

Wally raised his gauntlets. Were the others Order members? Which one of them was Steel Fingers? One of the figures turned around and saw Wally and smiled, her teeth covered in blood. Wally prepared to run, to scream at Breeth to trip these people with her rope if they came after them. But then he noticed that the smiling woman looked very much like Sekhmet. In fact, Sekhmet stood behind her, standing over her beaten father, her own ear pouring blood.

It was only then that Wally noticed that Sekhmet's dad's wrists were bound in magma manacles. And that he too was smiling.

Linus's arms jerked at the manacles as if they had a mind of their own. "It's a good thing the others wore me out," he told his daughter. "Otherwise you'd never have bound me."

"I'm missing a sword, and I *still* beat you, old man," Sekhmet said.

He smiled proudly at his daughter. "Sorry for kicking you in the ear, honey."

Wally understood then. Before Silver Tongue fled the Mercury Mines, she must have commanded Sekhmet's dad to attack the other Wardens. Maybe even kill them.

"Everyone okay?" Wally asked, stepping into the opening.

"Wilberforce!" Sekhmet's dad said. "I hear you're a Novitiate now! Quite the meteoric rise for a young thief, eh?"

"Sekhmet?" her mother said. "Aren't you going to introduce us to your ward?"

Sekhmet was clearly not as pleased as her parents were to see Wally. "Wally, these are my parents, Ahura and Linus." She nodded to a hairless, albino drummer and a woman with furry wings like a moth—*Fae-born* Wardens. "And this is Cadence and Willa. Where have you *been*?"

Wally didn't know where to begin. So he stepped aside, revealing Breeth's bound impostor.

Sekhmet gave him a horrified look. "Wally, why did you tie up this child?"

"That *child* is a member of the Order of Eldar," Cadence, the drummer, said.

"She *is*?" Wally said.

"No, whoever's *inside* me is," Breeth said. "Tell them I'd never join losers like that."

"Steel Fingers," Willa, the woman with the moth wings, said. "Their weapons master. She's also been welding the cages that hold the Fae-born."

Wally shook his head, trying to connect the various puzzle pieces. *This* was Steel Fingers?

"According to Breeth, this girl is *her*," he said. "Or . . . her *body*, anyway." He studied the impostor's scowling face. "Someone else's spirit seems to have possessed it."

Sekhmet's father chuckled. "Well, that explains how the Order found such a cruel little girl."

Sekhmet stared at the girl, as if she too recognized her. But the girl refused to look her in the eye. Wally realized the girl hadn't said a word since they'd found the Wardens.

"I'm surprised they left such a valuable asset behind," Sekhmet's father said. "It seemed the Order couldn't escape the Mines fast enough."

"They were heading toward a new Rift to collect Fae-born for their zoo," Sekhmet said. "The question is how they knew about it."

"I saw a figure," Willa said. "It appeared in the tunnels and spoke to the one who calls himself Rustmouth. I didn't catch the figure's face, but whoever it was talked like this." She lifted her hand and moved her fingers up and down like she was speaking with a sock puppet.

The tunnel floor seemed to sag beneath Wally's feet. *Graham.* Graham was the little birdy who told the Order where the Rifts were located. Of course. Who else would know where Rifts were opening besides an oracle? And Wally knew exactly why his brother did it. The Order would misuse magic, tearing the Rift until it was sky high and bringing the Veil crashing down, giving magic to everyone.

But killing a whole lot of people in the process.

"Do we have any guesses who this mysterious hand-speaking figure might be?" Sekhmet's mother asked.

The Wardens considered. Words weighed heavy on Wally's tongue. Graham posed a threat to the Balance between the Real and the Fae. But Wally couldn't make himself believe that Graham would ever intentionally hurt a soul. And the thought of turning his only family over to the Wardens made him nauseous.

"Let's get back to the Manor and regroup," Cadence said. "Then we can check the Rift Detector and see where the Order's headed next."

Sekhmet pulled out the Mimic Map while Ahura helped Linus, still bound, to his feet.

"After five weeks of fighting," Ahura said, "the Order escaped with several gallons of mercury. And all because *you* refused let me drink any."

"It's *poisonous*, dear," Linus said.

"So is *losing*."

Sekhmet located a drawing of a door on the map and pointed. "That way."

She led the Wardens up a rising tunnel, Ahura guiding Linus by his magma manacles and Willa guiding the impostor on a Breeth-possessed leash.

"Working for Weirdwood," Linus said pleasantly, "it never gets dull, does it?"

On the ascent, one of Wally's gauntlets came loose from his belt and slipped down a gently sloping side tunnel. He went to fetch it . . . and found another puppet dangling from the ceiling. It was Judy—Punch's wife—with an equally exaggerated nose and chin. Her eyes were kinder though. She held a flower in one hand and a scroll in the other.

The scroll held another riddle.

When lost in the woods full of surprises,
Remember what a forest despises.
What once was extinguished now you stoke.
What once was exterminated now is woke.

Wally gazed down the bottomless throat of the tunnel, searching for signs of his brother. Did this mean more danger was on its way? Graham's last riddle hadn't actually helped. For some reason, Wally's oracle brother hadn't foreseen Breeth's interference. Still, that didn't mean this one wouldn't come in handy.

He felt a sharp prick on his thumb and sucked through his teeth. He didn't realize he'd been squeezing, nor that the rose Judy held was covered in thorns. Wally sucked the blood from his thumb while ditching the puppet and stuffing the riddle into his pocket. He scooped up his gauntlets and ran to catch up with the Wardens.

12
THE DAPPLEWOOD

The endless hospital stretched to the vanishing point in both directions, leaving zero trace of the StormCrow Pub.

"*Fascinating*," Liza said. "Tragedy tends to make everything else vanish."

Arthur was less fascinated and more crushingly overwhelmed. The hospital's walls were lined with countless white-dressed beds. The beds were filled with children. Nurses floated like angels down the corridor, and the arched ceiling echoed with whispers as they broke bad news to the children. The kids' faces crumpled when they realized their parents were gone and were never coming back.

Arthur felt as if he was suddenly eight years old again, visiting his mom in the hospital. The brightness of the place made his eyes ache. The scent of antiseptic burned his nose. The high ceiling made him feel like he was going to start falling and never stop. He remembered his mother's pale face, her cracked lips, her fragile touch as the Pox slowly gobbled away her breath.

Arthur collapsed to the floor.

"Come on, Arthur," Liza said, nudging him with her foot. "You're letting your personal life interfere with the spell." She showed him the page with the faces. "This feeling will go away as soon as you come up with something horrific."

The checkerboard floor wavered in Arthur's eyes. His bones felt like sponges.

He crawled to one of the many beds, slipped under its snow-white blanket, and pulled it over his head.

He felt Liza's weight on the bed's edge. She rested a hand on his side. "I know how you're feeling. I went through the same thing last month when I lost my dad."

A wave of guilt sank him deeper beneath the sheets.

"But I found reasons to get out of bed," Liza said. "When my father brought that waxen thing that was supposed to be my mom to life, it gave me this cold, wet hug. I can still *feel* it on my skin. Whenever my real mom hugged me, she always held me too tight and rocked me back and forth a little. Even after I was too old for it. I've needed a hug from her ever since. That's what keeps me going." She squeezed Arthur's side. "Who knows? Maybe we'll find your mom too."

Arthur felt numb. He hadn't given the chance of seeing his mom much thought because the chance of it not happening was too much to handle. He wondered how Liza could be so confident.

"How did you pull yourself out of the dark place after you lost her?" Liza asked.

The answer was he hadn't. Not for many months. Getting out of bed had felt like climbing an impossibly steep mountain peak. He'd spent years learning to guard against this feeling, using the tragic memories of his mom as a part of his hero myth, propelling himself higher and higher through the Black Feathers.

But in this endless hospital, he didn't think he could ever escape his grief.

"It's been *four years*, Arthur," Liza said. "For me it's been a month. If I can keep going, so can you."

Arthur remembered the Mycopath, the Rook's mushroom-white lips whispering, *Who was it then that made my daughter an orphan?*

Arthur lowered the blanket from his face. "Liza, I need to tell you something."

"What?"

I killed your dad, Arthur thought.

"I—" The words caught in his throat. "I can't go to the Whirling City."

"Why not?"

"Because I accidentally caused the death of the Duchess's son."

Liza stared into his eyes, as if she was searching for something. As if she knew that wasn't what he was going to tell her.

"Well, well, well," said a rusted voice. "We chase ya through a scum-packed pub and across the choppity sea only to find ya *here*, wrapped like a pig in a blanket, ready to be gutted."

Liza leapt off the bed as Arthur sat bolt upright. Three figures had stepped into the endless corridor: a man with a top hat and rusted teeth, a large woman with stone skin, and a frail-looking woman with a flask at her hip.

Arthur pieced together what had happened. Rustmouth

must have followed him back to the StormCrow. They had attacked Charlie outside, then broken into the pub and covertly pursued Arthur and Liza, waiting until they were at their most vulnerable before attacking.

"That bodyguard o' yers gave us a bit of a brawltercation," Rustmouth said, "but turns out a man what's built like a brick is easily crushed by a woman o' *stone*."

Liza moved to run down the corridor, but Rustmouth blocked her way. Arthur felt pathetic and ashamed. He'd let his emotions get the best of him, and now it was too late.

Rustmouth held out his hand. "Hand over that Quill, girlie, and we'll all mosey out of here peaceable-like."

Liza's hand tightened around the Quill.

The rusted man clicked his tongue. "It's always conflictions with the young ones, ain't it?" He gestured to the frail woman. "Miss Silver Tongue?"

The woman took a sip from her flask and smiled at Liza. *"Toss us the Quill, girlie."*

Liza's arm cranked back as if it didn't belong to her. In the split second before she threw the Quill, Arthur reached out and plucked it out of her hand. He scribbled *Attack!* on the bed sheets, which billowed to life and whipped at Silver Tongue, slapping the flask out of her hands and spilling it across the marble. The woman fell to her knees, trying to lick the silver fluid from the floor.

Rustmouth clicked his brown tongue. "Astonishment? Pop their skulls."

The gray woman cracked her stone knuckles and came at them.

Liza and Arthur scrambled over the beds and then down the endless corridor as the Astonishment stomped after them, leaving craters in the marble floor.

Liza pulled out the piece of paper. The tragic face had grown serene. "Horror's next!"

"Um um um . . ." Arthur's thoughts felt like molasses.

An image flashed in his mind: the last time he'd been in this hospital, after the Battle of the Barrows, cheering up Wally and himself with tales about the Great Elsewhere. But that was no use right now. He remembered the next part of the Garnett Lacroix story. But it didn't feel particularly horrifying compared to being chased by a woman made of *boulders*.

"Well, you can't have a scary story without *atmosphere*," Arthur said, out of breath. "Storm clouds and the like."

Liza wrote as she ran.

THUNK THUNK THUNK!

The Astonishment's rocky feet stomped cracks in the marble, which spread up the walls and to the ceiling. A cataclysmic rupture split the hospital in two and the hallway before them fell away like a snapped branch.

Arthur and Liza skidded to a stop on the edge of a jagged precipice. The floor gave way to open air that continued down, miles and miles, toward a vast storm cloud city. The buildings were white whirls of precipitation. Strange beings made of falling rain walked the thundering streets. Somewhere, church music played.

"I didn't write an entire city," Liza said, studying the notebook. "Is this one of yours?"

Arthur shook his head. But something about the place did

feel familiar. "We must have broken into another part of the Fae."

THUNK THUNK THUNK!

The Astonishment had nearly caught up to them. Liza got down on her belly and slid over the floor's edge, descending the hospital's broken water pipes like rungs. Arthur did the same just as the Astonishment reached the precipice, followed closely by Rustmouth.

"Wouldja look at this *breathquaking* sight?" Rustmouth said, gazing down over the cloud city. "Them precipitatious persons could sell a *lot* more tickets than boring old beasties. Intarresting."

Arthur and Liza descended frantically. But they quickly ran out of pipes.

"Astonishment?" Rustmouth said. "Snag that Quill and snap them kids. Silver Tongue? That there below might be nothin' but a mere-raj. Use your persuasioning and nab us some *insurance*. I'm gonna see what this storm cloud capital's all about!"

The Astonishment crawled over the precipice's edge and started to descend, her massive fists crumpling the broken pipes like flower stems. Arthur and Liza desperately searched for an escape. There was nowhere to go.

"Let's drop down to that city!" Arthur shouted.

"The streets are made of clouds!" Liza said. "We could fall forever, and I can't write while falling!"

The Astonishment dangled from one of the pipes and made a grab for them with her rocky fist. Arthur's sweaty grip on the pipe loosened. He stared down hundreds of feet to the cloud city below. Liza desperately organized the flapping pages so she could write on them.

"*Arthur?*" Liza said, urgent. "I need an idea. *Any* idea. *Fast.*"

Arthur squeezed his eyes shut and saw his mom's smiling face. He remembered her voice, reading him adventure stories. But the Gentleman Thief was gone now. He needed to dig deeper.

The Astonishment's boulder fist swooped overhead as the stone woman made another swipe at them.

"*Arthur!*" Liza screamed.

Arthur yelled the first thing that came to mind, Liza wrote, and they released the pipes. They went into a freefall, limbs spinning, hair whipping, hurtling toward the city of storms. The moment before they struck the ground, the clouds dissipated, revealing a quaint village.

Arthur and Liza crashed through a thatched roof and landed on a pile of something soft and clean smelling. They lay there a moment, breathing heavy. Arthur patted his arms and chest and found that he was still in one piece. Liza was also unscathed.

She felt around the pile of laundry that had broken their fall and picked up a tiny bonnet. "Where have you brought us, Arthur? A clothier for *babies*?"

Arthur looked through a small high window and saw watercolor clouds against a golden apple sky. A warm breeze passed through his soul. "*The Dapplewood.* My mom used to read me these stories when I was a kid."

Liza stuck her fingers through two slits in the bonnet and wiggled them. "Well, it's the *opposite* of horrifying."

Arthur made himself comfortable, the despair he'd felt in the endless hospital quickly fading in his mind. "If you're trying to thank me for saving us from falling to our deaths, then you're *welcome*."

"A-*hem*."

Arthur and Liza sat up. A ferret had entered the laundry room. The creature walked on two legs and wore a sensible yellow dress. It considered them with its beady, caramel eyes, then tilted its nose toward the hole in the ceiling.

"*Well*," the ferret said in a gentle accent. "The weather forecast's always wrong about somethin', ain't it?"

A shudder ran through Arthur's bones. Ever since the Pox, he had hated rodents more than anything in the world. And if ferrets weren't rodents, he didn't care. This one came up to his shoulder, outweighing all of the Pox rats he'd ever caught combined. Its translucent claws were as long as daggers, its sugar-white teeth as sharp as nails. The fact that it was in a dress somehow made it *worse*.

The ferret held out a paw. "My name's Audrey. I'm a seamstress. That's my laundry you're soilin' up with your shoes." She glanced up. "And that was my roof."

Liza shook the ferret's paw, while Arthur's hands sought shelter in his armpits. The ferret extended her paw toward him, but he could only stare at it in disgust until Liza elbowed him in the side. He put out his trembling hand, and Audrey shook it. Her pads squished against his palm, her fur tickled his fingers, her claws pinched his flesh. When the ferret finally let go, Arthur tried to wipe away the creepy feeling on the laundry.

"Pleasure to make your acquaintance," Audrey said as she

turned to the door. "I'll go make the tea while you two remove
any splinters from your fall and get ready."

"Um, excuse me?" Liza said. "Ready for what exactly?"

Audrey smiled her sharp teeth. "Why, to fix that hole in
my ceiling, of course. You don't go making holes in other
people's lives without fixing 'em before you leave."

"Actually," Liza said, opening her notebook, "I can take
care of that for you right now."

She lifted her Quill to write a new roof but then noticed
that the ink bottle had missed the laundry and shattered across

the floor. Whatever ink was inside the Quill was all they had left to reach the Whirling City. Liza would need to preserve as much ink as possible.

Audrey frowned at the ink stain on her floor. "I'll scare up a mop too. Y'all will need to pay a visit to Mr. Beaver. He can lend you some wood for the roof."

The moment Audrey stepped into the hallway, Liza grabbed Arthur's arm and pulled him toward the laundry room's small window. "*Come on.*"

"*Good idea,*" he whispered.

They had just figured out how to get the tiny window open when Audrey reentered, holding a tray of tea. "Just my luck, the teapot was already bubblin'!" The ferret saw them trying to escape and froze. Her smile didn't change, but her eyes did, making her teeth look more ferocious. "Whatcha all doin'?"

Arthur's skin rippled from his scalp straight to the soles of his feet.

"We, um," Liza said, "were just going to look at the damages from outside?"

"See?" Audrey said, gently setting down her tea tray. "I was bein' *polite* before. Clearly it wasn't *your* fault that you fell from some great height right through my poor little roof. That's why I was willing to work it out *civil*-like instead of turn you over to the Badgers with Badges." The ferret narrowed her eyes. "But the thought of you trying to skedaddle without fixing the damage you done, well"—she smiled sharply—"it's all I can do not to maul y'all's faces."

Arthur went pale. "Please don't."

Before Audrey could so much as take a step, Liza threw

a fistful of laundry in the ferret's face. Audrey flinched, dropping her tea tray as Liza lunged forward, shoving her into an armoire before slamming the door and locking it. The armoire rocked back and forth as the ferret snarled and thrashed inside.

Arthur couldn't get out the window fast enough.

***

Liza and Arthur hustled down the cobbled streets of the Dapplewood, past watercolor shopfronts and animal townsfolk—hedgehogs, ducks, frogs, and mice—who skittered and waddled about their business.

"G'morning!" a blind mole said in a nasally voice.

"Hullo!" squeaked a mouse.

"What a pleasant day we're having, hmm?" quacked a duck.

"Couldn't be pleasanter!" Arthur said with a forced grin.

He kept glancing over his shoulder, in case the Badgers with Badges were on their way to arrest them. But the town remained as cozy as a picture book. The only thing that seemed amiss was the sky, which was cracked with the lines of floor-boards, yellow lightbulbs shining through. This pocket-world must have opened in the StormCrow's cellar.

"Who were those *terrifying* people chasing us?" Liza asked.

"Oh, them?" Arthur said. "They, um, want the Quill."

She shot him a scalding look. "And how do they know I *have* the Quill, Arthur?"

"I have no idea!" Arthur said, throwing up his hands innocently. "That guy with the rusted teeth said a *little birdy* told them." He nodded to a handsomely dressed chickadee, who whistled down the lane. "And I'm guessing he didn't mean him."

Liza sighed and gazed down the cobbled road behind them. "Well, whoever those people were, I think we lost them. Lucky for us, that Rustmouth guy was distracted by that storm cloud pocket-world."

"And also thanks to my escape tactics."

Liza ignored this and considered the cracked-floorboard sky. "We need to get somewhere high. I don't want to cross out the Dapplewood and find ourselves *buried in the earth* beneath the StormCrow's cellar. *You* think of something horrifying."

They found an abandoned barn that had once been a recovery home for lost chickens. They slipped through the door and then climbed a rickety ladder toward the hayloft. As they climbed, Arthur brainstormed. This story had really gone off the rails back in the endless hospital, but if anyone could get it back on track, it was him. Without the fear of being chased, he easily recalled a perfectly chilling scene from a Garnett adventure.

They reached the hayloft, and Arthur spoke in a haunted voice. "This scene takes place in a graveyard, set against a misty, crooked nightscape. The neglected headstones are bathed in bloody moonlight. And from the frozen earth grow scraggled weeds that look like skeleton fingers waiting for an unsuspecting soul to step—"

There was a commotion outside. A squawking. A squealing. The ruffle of feathers and the scrabble of clawed feet. Arthur peeked through the slats of barn, and the warm breeze in his soul turned icy cold.

The watercolor sky was *vanishing*, as if absorbed into the

white paper on which it was painted. The Dapplewood continued to erupt with sounds of a barnyard fire as its storybook colors faded away. Beneath all of the squawking and squeaking and scrabbling, Arthur heard something strange. Something like . . . *silvery whispers*.

"*Look*," Liza said, holding up the etched faces.

The screaming face had grown calm.

Arthur stared back through the slats at the blank sky. "Maybe we should go help the critters. It sounds like they're being *attacked*."

"They're not real, Arthur. Remember? The moment we leave here, things will go right back to normal. Like turning a page in a picture book. Now, are you coming or what?"

Arthur stared into Liza's eyes and not for the first time that day thought he saw more of her father in them than he was comfortable with. But he nodded. Whatever was happening outside, he knew he didn't have the magic to help. Not without the Quill.

Liza and Arthur pushed open the trapdoor to the barn's roof . . . but wound up in her father's office. Liza swept into the pub, as if undisturbed by the sounds they'd just heard behind them. Arthur couldn't stop staring into the barn cellar, wondering what had just happened . . . and if it was his fault.

As the barn itself started to vanish, bleaching away to nothingness, he quickly slammed the cellar shut and joined Liza in the pub.

She had laid the face etchings on the table. "One more left."

"*Already?*" Arthur said.

Each pocket-world had felt all-consuming. His heart had

been ripped from the murky menace of the Roasted Parrot to the soaring adventure of the high seas to the bottomless despair of the endless hospital. But now that it was nearly over, the adventure felt like it had passed by in a flash.

"Which one's left?" Arthur asked, peeking at the page.

He saw the winky face—*romance*—and his heart started pumping blood into his cheeks. He was certain Liza had noticed him turning the color of a cooked crab, and his cheeks grew redder still.

He turned his face away. "So I guess all that's left now is . . ."

"Yyyyep," Liza said.

His stomach fluttered nauseously as he remembered the mushy parts in Garnett Lacroix's stories. The parts Arthur had skipped over until he'd turned eleven and decided he *might* start tolerating them to see what the fuss was about. The Gentleman Thief plucking flowers from the upside-down garden for his lady love. The skin-crawling, page-long smooch at the end of *The Cliffs of Innocence* . . .

But Arthur couldn't just *kiss* someone. How could anybody?

A small smile curled Liza's lips.

"What?" Arthur said, taking a step back. "What is it?"

His stomach felt the same as it had when they were both tumbling through the air.

Liza wrote in her notebook. She dotted her sentence with a final period then threw open the StormCrow's shutters.

Two figures were dancing in the misty streets. One spun the other around their fingers before dipping them low toward the cobbles.

Arthur squinted. "Is that . . . ?"

"Uh-*huh*," Liza said, delighted. "Didn't you see those rogues on the ship? You could have cut that tension with a *sword*."

Arthur watched as Gus and Tuck continued to twirl down the street like they were in some great ballroom. He was about to argue that the only romance in those adventures was between Garnett Lacroix and Lusty Lizbeth and that you couldn't just *wedge in* a relationship long after the book was published. But then Liza held up the piece of paper with the charcoal etchings. The winking face had stopped smirking and closed its other eye.

This was it. They were going to the Whirling City where the dragons dwelled. This was Arthur's last chance to run out of the pub, to return to Harry and some sort of normalcy. But then Arthur saw the expression on Liza's face. For the first time since he'd met her, there was *hope* in her eyes.

He gazed around the pub. He saw the sea spray dripping through the ceiling from the ship deck roof. He saw the gloomy light of the endless hospital beaming from the clouds upon the two new lovers. And he saw a blank-page whiteness shining up through the floor slats from the cellar. Everything he'd experienced over the last few hours—comedy, tragedy, suspense, horror, romance—came flooding into his chest.

The pub and all its pocket-worlds started to spin like a roulette table, spiraling around him and blurring together in a constant stream of color and scents. It spun and spun until Arthur thought he might come apart at the seams. He squeezed his eyes shut just as Liza grabbed tight to his shoulders.

The pub began to swallow itself.

13
THORNS

With the Wardens returned from the Mercury Mines, the Manor thrummed with activity. What had once felt like a peaceful forest now felt like a military training ground. The war room rang with clashing swords as Linus and Sekhmet dueled. The courtyard echoed with Cadence's drums, while the Bookcropolis rustled with Ahura's maps as she searched for any sign of the Order. Willa fluttered down the many hallways, trailing her intricate battle kites.

The staff, meanwhile, was playing catch-up. Weston repaired the weather damage to the plants in the courtyard while Ludwig sang opera to himself in the healing room. Pyra's kitchen was in full bubble, and Amelia kept a burning blue eye on the Rift Detector.

But Wally was getting a break from all of the activity. He stood in the quiet of the Throne Room where Lady Weirdwood and Breeth's impostor were engaged in what had to be the strangest hostage situation in history.

The impostor stood before the waxen throne, unbound and scowling. She hadn't tried to escape, as if she knew that the old architect had the power to close every one of the Manor's doors in her face.

Lady Weirdwood sat in her waxen throne. Her snake hung lifeless as a scarf around her shoulders. She studied the impostor. "Who *are* you? Who's hiding in there?"

The impostor folded her arms.

"Who *cares* who she is?" Breeth, the ghost version, said from the ceiling. "Tell her to get out of my body or I'll collapse the whole roof on her head and *force* her out! My bones will heal eventually!"

Wally looked up at her and held a finger to his lips.

"Don't shush me!" Breeth said. "*I'll crush you too!*"

When they'd first arrived back at the Manor, Amelia had used her lasso trick on the impostor, trying to oust the spirit just as she had freed Breeth from the flaming bull. But the spirit was as stubborn as a walnut, refusing to exit Breeth's body. It seemed in order for Amelia's trick to work, the spirit had to depart willingly.

"When did you join the Order of Eldar?" Lady Weirdwood asked.

The impostor's lips remained sealed.

"How long have you been making weapons?"

The impostor scowled.

"*Rrrrrgggggggg.*" The ceiling strained under Breeth's rage, and the impostor glanced up, her grumpy demeanor briefly giving way to fear. "I swear, Wally," Breeth said, "if she doesn't start giving us answers, I am going to bust a *beam*."

Asking questions wasn't getting them anywhere. They might have to solve this themselves. But who could have possibly possessed Breeth? She'd died roughly three years ago, around the time the Rook had been ejected from the Manor . . .

Wally had a chilled moment, wondering whether it was the Rook possessing his friend. But no. He'd died just six weeks ago. Besides, the little girl's expression wasn't crafty like the Rook's. It was more *clueless*.

"How did you possess this girl's body?" Lady Weirdwood asked.

The impostor snorted, as if challenging the old architect to ask questions until the apocalypse.

"Oh, that is *it*!" Breeth said.

She rippled down the wall, thundered through the floor, and then heaved up the carpet like a tidal wave, knocking the impostor flat. The impostor rolled across the floor, thrashing at nothing before managing to fling Breeth's spirit across the room, knocking over an expensive-looking lamp. The impostor used this opportunity to run from the Throne Room, slamming the door behind her. Breeth rocketed after, knocking the door off its hinges.

Wally was about to follow when Lady Weirdwood stopped him with a lift of her hand. "Let them fight it out a while," she said. "Perhaps Breeth will tire out whoever's in there and we'll be able to get some answers. We have something to discuss, you and I."

The fight echoed down the hallway.

Wally was anxious to check on his friend. But he stepped before the waxen throne and clasped his hands in front of him, waiting to be reprimanded for not following Sekhmet's orders in the Mines.

Lady Weirdwood reached behind her and pulled out the Punch puppet Wally had found in the fairgrounds. Wally's body went cold.

"Did your brother convey a message to you?" Lady Weirdwood asked.

Wally's tongue froze in his mouth. He swallowed to get it working again. "I, um, saw that puppet right before the Faeborn broke loose. The fight began, so I didn't get a good look at it."

"Why didn't you tell me about this sooner?" Lady Weirdwood asked.

"Um," Wally said. It was hard to concentrate while just outside the door Breeth continued to war with herself, screaming with two voices—one from a human throat, another from a ghostly one. He wished he could be out there helping his friend instead of in here being interrogated. "With so much happening, I just . . . forgot."

"You didn't see Graham?" Lady Weirdwood asked. "He didn't speak to you?"

"No," Wally said honestly.

He shifted and swore he could hear the crinkle of his brother's second riddle in his pocket. If he handed it over to Lady Weirdwood, would Graham stop sending him helpful hints? Would Wally fail his future missions? Would the Wardens kick him out of the Manor for being an inept Novitiate?

"If your brother really can see the future," Lady Weirdwood said, "he holds far more power than my Manor's humble Rift Detector. If you have any information about him whatsoever . . ."

My brother is helping the Order find Rifts, he thought.

But he couldn't get his lips to say the words. He couldn't betray his brother.

"What did your brother say to you when you saw him in Mirror Kingsport?" Lady Weirdwood asked.

Wally remembered the Slopping District where Graham had placed a hand on Wally's shoulder and told him that he, *Wally*, would help bring about the fall of the Veil. But Wally couldn't imagine anything that would make him do something so foolish. He knew how dangerous bringing down the Veil would be. Wild Fae-born would run rampant through the streets. The flaming bull would gore innocents with its molten horns, and the goblin would drink the survivors' memories through its slimy fingertips.

Wally looked straight into Lady Weirdwood's eyes. "He told me a riddle about graham crackers, ma'am."

The old architect wrinkled her eyes, as if trying to read his thoughts. Wally was saved from explaining further when Sekhmet and Amelia entered the Throne Room.

Amelia pointed a thumb over her shoulder. "There's a little girl beating herself up in the hallway."

"I'm aware," Lady Weirdwood said. "Has Ahura located the Order yet?"

Amelia shook her head. "We believe they fled to an uncharted pocket-world."

Lady Weirdwood sighed. "Things can never be simple, can they? Sekhmet? Tell me everything Rustmouth told you about this . . . Eraser."

"He didn't say much, Lady," Sekhmet said. "Only that

he was nobody and that wherever he goes, he doesn't leave a trace."

Lady Weirdwood stroked her blind snake, which looked oddly *limp* to Wally. "There are Voids that walk the earth. They're one of the rarer problems the Wardens have to deal with. And one of the most challenging. A Void appears whenever a being is forcefully torn out of the Fae. Like when a mass book burning erases a character from existence."

Wally tried to wrap his mind around that. Was the Eraser one of these characters?

"This *absence* leaves behind a vacuum that tries to fill itself by absorbing everything around it," Lady Weirdwood continued. "Usually, the Manor travels to the pocket-world where the character disappeared, and we use Wards to close the Void, to soothe it, both in the Fae and the Real. People suffer when a beloved character is destroyed."

Wally hoped he would learn that power someday. To fill the holes on the other side of the Veil and heal the minds that once held them.

"But in all my years in this Manor," Lady Weirdwood said, "I have never heard of a Void with *sentience*. In fact, I've never seen one move from its original spot, let alone *organize*. That's like a hole in the ground deciding to join the army. How we even *begin* to stop a hole like that, I have no idea. The question is why a Void would align itself with the Order? Better yet, why would they want it?"

No one, not even Amelia, had an answer to that.

"*Well*," Lady Weirdwood said. "We'll address that problem when we come to it. How's Ludwig's arm coming along?"

"Still twiggy," Amelia said. "It refuses to grow back straight, so Weston is trimming and shaping it with wires, like a bonsai tree."

In the ensuing discussion, Wally's eyes landed on the puppet, hanging from the arm of the waxen throne. He still had to solve Graham's next riddle. But he couldn't remember a single verse. The words had fled his mind the moment he'd pricked his finger on the thorn of that flower . . .

Wally's eyes went wide. He remembered the impostor's dagger, whose hilt had the same design as Sekhmet's sword. Of *course*. *Steel Fingers*. The Order's *metalworker*. No wonder the imposter hadn't spoken in front of the Wardens or Lady Weirdwood.

While Amelia and Lady Weirdwood continued to plan the Wardens' next steps, Wally crept over to Sekhmet and whispered his theory.

Sekhmet's eyes went wider than his. "Are you sure?"

Wally shrugged.

"Ma'am?" Sekhmet said to Lady Weirdwood. "Sorry to interrupt, but permission to bring in the impostor?"

Lady Weirdwood gave her a questioning look, but then nodded to Amelia, who drew her whip, cracked it into the hallway, and dragged the impostor grunting and kicking back into the Throne Room.

"This is *impossible*!" Breeth said, creaking in after her. "It's like trying to get a can of beans open without a can opener. I'm hungry for beans, Wally. And by that I mean I want my body back."

Sekhmet approached the impostor, who still refused to look at her . . . until Sekhmet drew her sword.

"Whoa, whoa, *wait a minute!*" Breeth said. "I don't want me *stabbed!* Even if it gets the spirit out!"

Sekhmet kept approaching. The impostor clenched her jaw.

Amelia took a step forward. "Sekhmet, what are you—"

Sekhmet swung her sword, and the impostor faded back, as smooth as smoke.

"*Whoa,*" Breeth said.

Sekhmet stared into the impostor's eyes and beyond to the spirit within.

"Hello, Rose," she said.

The impostor sniffed. "Hullo, Sekhmet."

Everyone in the Throne Room went silent. Except Breeth. Who screamed.

"*Aaauuuggghhhh!* Wait . . . who's Rose again?"

Sekhmet's jaw trembled as she stared at her former mentor.

A woman she'd thought was dead and gone.

14
THE WHIRLING CITY

When Arthur opened his eyes again, the StormCrow Pub was gone—replaced with an island.

But not just any island. It wasn't surrounded by water but *air*. It bloomed with chrysanthemums and floated across a green sky, which was occasionally split by flashes of purple lightning. More islands circled around them—massive chunks of earth held up by nothing at all. One cascaded with waterfalls. Another held a temple crowned with a statue of a green phoenix. Miles below churned a blood-pink sea.

"We did it," Liza whispered, marveling at the impossible sight before them.

"We really did," Arthur said, touching his lips.

When he had seen the map of the Whirling City, he'd imagined spiral-shaped streets, not a city of islands that actually *rotated like a galaxy*. Around the edge of the archipelago, torn right into the golden sky, were dozens of gated Rifts. Each one looked onto a different pocket-world—a sparkling forest, a desert of emerald, a frozen ocean . . . and on and on.

Arthur's head tingled as he imagined spending a lifetime adventuring through these pocket-worlds. Then it prickled with fear when he noticed the spindly, winged shapes coiling and tumbling in the clouds above. He wondered if the Duchess, Huamei's mother, was among them.

"*So*," Arthur said, anxious to get out of there before the dragons realized there were humans in their midst. "Which of those gates leads to the afterlife?"

Liza was scribbling something in her notebook. "That's for me to find out."

"What do you mean that's for you to—*ow ow ow!*"

Vines slithered out of the ground and around his ankles, jerking him upside down into the air. They whipped around his wrists, binding his arms and legs behind his back.

"Liza!" Arthur cried. "This island's booby-trapped! Quick! Write a knife and cut me free!"

Liza gave him a dull look and showed him her notebook. She had written the vines.

"Okay . . . ," Arthur said. "I'll admit this could be an effective way to float us from island to island, but wouldn't it be smart to still be able to use our hands? What if you wrote a floating lily pad instead?"

"You're staying here, Arthur," Liza said. "Now that we've reached the Whirling City, I don't need you anymore."

"Wha—?" Arthur flexed, trying to break his binds. "Why are you doing this?"

She flashed her eyes at him. "You know why."

Arthur stopped struggling. Liza knew. She had known this

whole time. That's why she hadn't asked him to bring her dad back from the dead. Only her mom. She knew the prospect of seeing the Rook might scare him away.

"It was an *accident*," he said. "I didn't know that spell would hurt your dad!"

Liza wasn't listening. She was writing something.

He continued, desperate. "The Rook unleashed *monsters* on Kingsport. I had to stop him."

Liza didn't look up from her notebook. "My father may have seemed like a harsh man from the outside, but you didn't know him like I did. He loved my mother, and he loved me. He wanted to reunite us."

She placed a period at the end of her newest sentence. Arthur braced himself for some grisly punishment—splinters under his fingernails, papercuts across his eyes . . . When nothing happened, he peeked up.

Liza turned in a circle, looking around the island, disappointed, as if she'd expected something to change. She turned toward the island's edge and started to write something new.

Arthur searched for an escape. A sharp rock to cut through his binds. An errant wind to whisk him to safety. But all he saw were chrysanthemums.

Liza made a huff of frustration. He strained to peer over her shoulder to see what she was writing. Her notebook held two sentences, struck through:

Pathway to the afterlife.
The Rift that leads to heaven.

For some reason, the spells hadn't worked. Arthur still had time to convince her.

"Your father killed a little girl," Arthur said.

Liza whirled to face him. "My father would *never*."

"He would," Arthur said. "Her name was Breeth. He created that Mirror Rook himself through all of his misdeeds in Kingsport. He destroyed *himself*."

Liza clenched her teeth and squeezed her fists . . . and then released them. She seemed to realize she was letting her anger get to her and started writing again.

"Liza," Arthur said. "If those dragons see me, they're going to *kill* me."

Liza's face remained unmoved. "Maybe you'll just go to dragon prison."

"Liza, *please*," he said. "You don't want to become like your father."

She locked on his gaze, steel glinting in her eyes. She had never looked more like the Rook.

She turned away again and considered her notebook. The spells weren't working. Arthur couldn't help but wonder if it was because there was no afterlife to find. But then Liza closed her eyes, breathed deep, then opened them and wrote,

The way beyond once filled with dread,
A path that leads to Kingsport's dead.

With these poetic, artful words, a sparkling trail shot off the edge of the island toward one of the Rifts, awash in gray, on the horizon.

Liza smiled at her work. Arthur hung slack in his binds.

"I'm sorry it had to end this way, Arthur," she said. "Just remember—you did this to yourself."

She wrote something, and a firework rocketed from her notebook and exploded in the sky directly above them, spelling out the words *I KILLED THE DUCHESS'S SON*. It caught the attention of two dragons, who coiled their bodies toward the island.

A stone turned over in Arthur's heart. "Liza, please!"

Liza hurried toward the sparkling line, writing as she went, and then leapt off the edge of the island. Arthur's breath caught, believing for a brief moment that Liza had sacrificed herself to the ocean below . . . But then a giant black bird soared up into the clouds, beating its massive black wings toward the swirling gray rift.

Arthur could do nothing but hang there like a pig about to be roasted as the dragons landed on the island like two lightning bolts. They shed their scales, revealing human forms dressed in black, decorative armor and wing-adorned helmets. Strangely, their hands and feet remained scaled and reptilian, while barbed tails extended from their lower backs. One dragon had eyes of green. The other of gold.

"Who are you?" the one with green eyes asked.

"And how did you come to be in the Whirling City?" asked the one with eyes of gold.

"My name is . . ." Arthur's voice failed him.

He glanced to the feathered shadow on the horizon, just now reaching the Rift. If he turned Liza in, they would catch her, and she would never see her mom and dad again. As much as her betrayal hurt, he tried to act like the Gentleman Thief.

"My name is Arthur Benton," he told the dragons. "I don't know how I came to be here."

"Arthur *Benton*," the golden-eyed dragon said, as if hocking up the name.

The green-eyed dragon scowled.

Arthur trembled. Did they already know about him?

The green-eyed dragon slashed his weapon through the air, severing Arthur's vines and making him fall to the ground.

"Pray the high court is in good humor today, boy," the green-eyed dragon said.

"The high court?" Arthur asked.

The golden-eyed dragon peeled their scaled lips. "*The floor is low, the dome is high, the walls are leaves, the judgement nigh. Bury the sword to its hilt, draw it out to bleed your guilt.*"

As the dragon spoke, the island's chrysanthemums began to grow and grow. Their leaves wilted and filled the sky, creating a rustling dome around the island. An invisible gong reverberated through the ground, and orbs of light sparkled to life.

Arthur found himself in a dragon courtroom.

Three blossom thrones towered before him. Each held a different dragon in human form. The executioner scowled his grim mouth. The judge stroked the scaly whiskers that hung from his chin. The last dragon looked familiar . . .

Huamei's mom, Arthur realized.

The Duchess's scaled face remained as placid as a sunbathing crocodile. Her eyes were as wide and white as pearls, with piercing black pupils. Her face was covered in scales. She had a wide, grim mouth with glass-sharp fangs poking through. It might have been Arthur's imagination, but her lips looked ready to peel open to unsettling proportions before she flapped down with her silken robes and devoured him.

"Rise, Arthur Benton of the Real," the judge said.

Arthur stood on shaky legs as the court stenographer began painting symbols with scented ink, filling the space with the aroma of spices.

"*I didn't kill Huamei!*" Arthur cried to the dragons on their thrones. "It was Alfred Moore! But he's *dead* now. I helped defeat him. The Duchess's son was avenged!"

As Arthur spoke, the leaves of the leaf dome rippled,

unveiling patterns of bright clouds and re-creating his words in images of light and shadow. An Arthur-shaped silhouette scaled the stairs of the bat-winged asylum to bring the mad author down . . .

The judge snapped his clawed fingers, and the dome of leaves fluttered shut.

"You are not on trial for Huamei's death," he said.

"I . . . I'm not?" Arthur said.

"The Duchess's shame was relieved the day her bastard son was sent to serve the Wardens of Weirdwood," the judge said. "The moment Huamei was banished from this kingdom, he was no longer royalty. His was the death of a mere Novitiate."

Arthur glanced at the Duchess and found her face was as calm as the sea at morning. He thought he could see the telltale shine of tears, but it was difficult to tell with her ivory-white eyes. Was she trying to hide her true feelings in front of the dragon court? Or did she really feel nothing at all for her son?

The judge's throat rattled, wrenching Arthur's eyes back to him.

"Arthur Benton," the judge said, "you stand before the court of the Whirling City, charged with stealing a dragon-bone quill and using it to break through the Veil into our realm."

Arthur was about to protest. To tell them he hadn't stolen the dragon-bone Quill. But then he'd be admitting that he knew what it was.

"A dragon-bone *whatsit*?" he said, feigning a puzzled look. "Never seen the like. As to how I came here, that's a funny story." He remembered each of the five elements needed to open a Rift to the Whirling City. "I was at a funeral for a truly terrible person when the love of my life strolled through the—"

The judge snarled, stealing the breath from Arthur's lungs.

"I should warn you," the judge said, pointing a claw toward the dome, which hadn't rustled so much as a single leaf. "Our dome shows only truths. If you attempt to use *Wordcraft* on us, you will continue this trial without a *tongue*."

Arthur's tongue retreated to the back of his mouth. He couldn't lose that. It was his best feature.

He glanced up at the leafy dome. If he revealed the truth, that Wally had taken the dragon claw from Huamei's body, then the dragons would swoop down on the Manor, seize Cooper, and put him on trial too. Arthur couldn't doom his best friend like that. Even if it did mean losing his tongue.

"Huamei's spirit gave permission to use his claw," Arthur said truthfully but leaving out the detail about his friend.

The leaf dome remained still.

Arthur looked straight into the Duchess's white eyes. "Your son and I were partners in the end. I tried to help him track down the dragon bone that the Fallen Warden stole from your ancestor's grave. He thought if he could return it to you, he would be redeemed in your eyes. That you would let him return to this kingdom."

The tragic memory played out across the dome.

The Duchess refused to look up.

The judge sneered. "Call in the witnesses."

A line of Fae-born filed into the courtroom. Arthur

recognized them all: a pirate from the *Treasure Bolt*, a bone-white nurse from the endless hospital, even the Ogre Oaker, the sewer gator, and the cloak-peddling pangolin from Mirror Kingsport were there. The only witness missing was a critter from the Dapplewood.

One by one, the Fae-born took the stand and testified about how Rifts had cut through their homes and disrupted their lives. The leaf dome fluttered with their stories. The pirate had lost his beloved pet rat in the chaos. The bone-white nurse had to calm her young patients after the hospital split in two. And the pangolin had to close up shop ever since the Mirror citizens had discovered he'd accidentally sold a cloak to a person from the Real.

Arthur listened and understood what the Wardens' patrolling of the Veil did for the *other* side of things.

The last witness took the stand. It was Gus from the Merry Rogues.

"Arthur Benton is nothing if not a gentleman and a *hero*," Gus said, striking his fist against the stand like a gavel.

Images flickered across the dome of Arthur and his band of Merry Skeletons saving Kingsport from the Corvidians. Arthur felt a stirring of hope.

"Of course," the Merry Rogue continued, kicking up his heels and crossing them on the stand, "he did use that quillity thing to retire my boss in a *permanent* sort of way. I'm not saying Arthur *killed* Garnett Lacroix necessarily. But the adventures sure have been tough without the Gentleman Thief around. That is until that young lady helped us out on our pirate adventure. What's her name? Liza? Now *she's* somethin'!" He blinked and seemed to remember where he was. "But Arthur's pretty all right too."

The judge dismissed Gus from the stand. As the Merry Rogue exited, he clapped Arthur on the shoulder, "Hope that helps some, Arthur. We'll see ya back in the adventure!"

Arthur's head hung heavy. It was no wonder the Wardens had made Wally a Novitiate and not him.

The judge smiled down from his high throne. "After hearing the testimonies of these witnesses, which further illuminates your past misuse of the Quill, I ask you again, Arthur Benton. How do you plead?"

"I'm . . . ," Arthur said, and felt his stomach cave. "I'm guilty."

The gavel crashed down. "Then you are sentenced to die three days from today. That will give us time to prepare the unmaker."

"Wait, *what*?"

The ground-trembling gong sounded once again, and the leaf dome tumbled like autumn, leaving behind the field of chrysanthemums. The Duchess flapped her robes and took off from her throne, fleeing the island.

Arthur swayed. The island grew blurry. He couldn't feel his face. He'd been perfectly willing to say he was guilty when he thought he'd only spend a few months in dragon prison. If he'd known they'd meant to kill him, let alone *unmake* him . . .

"Look into my eyes, Mr. Benton," the executioner said above.

Arthur looked up and tumbled into the black, ocean depths of the dragon's gaze.

"*Stripes of shadow, flash of gold. The dripping maw, thrashing bold. In the belly, close the fangs, where you wait, until you hang.*"

Arthur blinked and found the chrysanthemums had vanished. Replaced by what looked for a moment like tiger stripes . . . but were actually bars.

And that was how he found himself in an island cell, spiraling on the outer edge of the Whirling City. No one knew he was there. Not Harry. Not Wally. Not the Wardens.

Only Liza, who put him in this mess in the first place.

Arthur's fate was sealed.

15
ROSE

Breeth was too smart for Lady Weirdwood.

The old architect kept moving the impostor to quiet parts of the Manor, hoping that she, Sekhmet, and Rose could have a private conversation. But Breeth found them every time, giving that Rose ghost multiple scares she would never forget.

Finally, Lady Weirdwood led Breeth's body to the smithy where Rose had once forged weapons for the Wardens. "So she might remember the loyalty she once had toward us." But Breeth didn't want Rose in her comfort zone. She wanted her in a *discomfort* zone, hoping to pop the unwelcome spirit out of her body as easy as an avocado pit.

She creaked right after them.

It was hot in the smithy. The air wavered like a desert. Sweat gleamed on Lady Weirdwood's and Sekhmet's foreheads. The scales of the old woman's limp snake shone dully.

Breeth possessed the crackling wood of the forge and ignited it in an explosive blaze of flames, raising the temperature in the smithy by several degrees. Rose tumbled back, fearful of catching fire. But Breeth had been careful not to singe her own hair.

"Hello, Breeth," Lady Weirdwood said pleasantly.

She said it so casually that Breeth let the fire die down a bit.

"I need you to please stop assaulting my prisoner for a few minutes."

Breeth politely refused by smoldering black smoke into the room.

"I understand your frustration," Lady Weirdwood said calmly. "But I'm not going to get any answers out of my old Warden with you constantly attacking her. You draw more flies with honey than vinegar."

Breeth, who had once spent a short lifetime as a housefly, resented the comment.

"Don't you want to know what happened, Breeth?" Sekhmet asked. "Don't you want to know why Rose did this?"

"No!" Breeth shouted in an explosion of flames. But then her rage softened to embers. "Maybe."

Lady Weirdwood sat on an anvil and looked at Rose, who sat near the bellows. "Now that we have discovered who you are, Rose, there's no reason not to talk to us."

"She warn't s'posed to stay dead," Rose said, her face as hard as steel. "That little girl. It were Colson's idea from the start."

Colson. That must have been the Rook's real name.

"He said if we could see a person die, we could follow its spirit into the next life," Rose continued. "He could see his wife. I could see my Max. So he set out and borrowed a child from the city and brought her back to the Manor where we hid

— 167 —

her in the Thorny Passage." She gazed into the fiery reflection of a sword and saw the face of the girl she'd murdered staring back. She quickly looked away, her expression softening a bit. "I did the thing meself. Done it gentle-like and stitched up her hurts afterward."

Breeth wanted to scream fire at this. To remind this impostor they'd done a lot more than *borrow* her. She wanted to erupt in a great conflagration and declare that it was impossible to kill someone *gentle-like*. But there was something strangely comforting about hearing the story of her murder from her own lips. It was like she was breaking the horrifying details to herself.

"After it was over," Rose continued, "the Rook put on them necroglasses so's he could follow the kid's spirit to the afterlife. The *plan* was to snatch up her soul like a butterfly and stuff it back in its body before we crossed over to find our loved ones. It all went to plan until the girl's spirit rejected the afterlife and fled into the walls of the Manor."

Breeth's embers nearly extinguished. The plan was to *return* her to her body? She could have gone home . . . She could have lived some sort of life. But Breeth had been so frightened of the strangers in the masks that she had fled into Weirdwood Manor where she had quickly grown lost.

She had stayed lost for years. Until she found Wally.

Tears streamed down Breeth's cheeks. Both her body's and her ghost's.

"Like I said," Rose said, wiping her cheeks with the back of Breeth's hand, "she warn't s'posed to stay dead. We was gonna put her back."

"Leaving an innocent girl traumatized forever," Sekhmet said.

Rose's mouth set like cooling steel. "And giving my boy another chance at livin'."

"How did you come to possess your murder victim?" Lady Weirdwood asked.

"After you kicked Colson out the Manor, me and the other Wardens was summoned to the Neon Pastures where that bloody *demon lamb* gutted me." Rose looked at her old Novitiate. "I didn't blame you any, Sekhmet."

Sekhmet looked away, but her jaw was trembling.

"Ended up possessin' the grass beneath my body," Rose continued. "I tried soaking my spirit back inside myself, but . . ." She looked down at Breeth's stomach. "But my guts was too slashed to ribbons."

The smithy door opened, and Wally peeked his head in. "Sekhmet, can I talk to you for a second?"

Sekhmet kept her eyes on Rose. "Not a good time."

"It'll only take a second," Wally said.

Lady Weirdwood touched Sekhmet's shoulder. Sekhmet huffed and then followed Wally out, shutting the door and leaving Lady Weirdwood and Rose alone in the low firelight.

"Why didn't you go to your son then?" Lady Weirdwood asked. "Join him on the other side?"

Rose's lips locked up. "My Max was nothin' but five when he died. Had all his years ahead of him." She stared into Breeth's firelight. "I don't know what's waitin' for us in the hereafter. But I know the good here on earth. In the Fae. I wanted Max to see the beauty of it." She looked into Lady

Weirdwood's eyes. "Ain't it a mother's greatest joy to watch her kids grow?"

"Not if the cost is stopping a little girl from experiencing them," Lady Weirdwood said.

Rose frowned at the floor. "She warn't s'posed to stay dead."

"After your body was destroyed," Lady Weirdwood said, "your spirit returned to the Manor."

Rose's gaze arced up and around the ceiling. "I moved through the walls to where Colson'd hid the girl's body on ice. Figgered the little girl warn't usin' it no more." Rose held up Breeth's hand and wiggled her fingers. "Colson and me'd spent years tryin' to prove death warn't everlasting. That people can come back. So, I slipped into this body and left the Manor. I went and found the people I knew as would be willing to bend the rules of the Balance and help me find my son."

Flames danced in Lady Weirdwood's eyes. "And has your time with the Order of Eldar helped you realize that seeking the afterlife is a fool's errand?"

Rose flashed Breeth's green eyes at her, her face as unmovable as metal. "*We hain't done lookin' yet.*"

Lady Weirdwood sighed heavily. "Since the beginning of human history, people have tried to access the land of the dead. Every attempt has failed."

Rose almost smiled. "They didn't have the *Eraser*. Capable of *miracles*, it is."

Lady Weirdwood didn't show emotion on her face, but Breeth could sense her heart pulsing in the bits of ash around her. "Rose, if you are sincere in your regret for taking Breeth's life, then now is the time to set things right. I need you to give up this body."

Breeth's embers glowed hopeful.

Every muscle in Rose tightened. "I cain't do that."

"You can," Lady Weirdwood said simply. "If you leave now, maybe you can go to the place where your son is."

Rose smirked at Lady Weirdwood. "Whatcha gonna do, old lady?" She held out Breeth's hands. "You gonna *torture* me?"

Lady Weirdwood frowned.

Rose sat back, comfortable and satisfied in Breeth's body. "Well, then."

RREEEEEAAAAKKKKKKKKK!!!

A horrible shriek sounded outside the door, more ear-piercing and spine-chilling than any Breeth had heard in life. Or death. It was like a lamb being taken to slaughter. But its voice was echoed a thousand times in discordant cacophony— as if screaming to be heard from the bowels of the earth.

"No!" Rose cried, standing and backing toward the wall. "Oh Glycon. *Help me!*"

The smithy door burst open, and some *thing* came tearing into the room, bucking its head and kicking its hoofs and knocking holes in the wall. Its skin was desiccated, shrunken to its skull. Its fur dripped from its skin, and scorch marks stained its eyes, teeth, and tail.

Rose threw up her hands to defend herself as the demon lamb lunged. Breeth gasped as the horrific creature opened its dripping jaws wide, inches from her body's throat. She was about to creak out of the fire log to stop it, but then two things happened simultaneously . . .

Rose's ghost seeped out of Breeth's body like steam off of a hot lake, her arms raised in perfect parallel to the ones she'd just exited. In that same moment, the demon lamb jerked to a stop, its neck tied with a leash that Breeth had been too startled to notice.

Without a spirit inside it anymore, Breeth's body's arms flopped to its sides and it collapsed like a rag doll. Before her head struck the ground, Lady Weirdwood caught the body and gently laid it down on the floor.

Rose's ghost, who hadn't noticed the leash, fled into the floorboards and vanished into the walls.

Wally peeked into the room. "Did it work?"

He was wearing his gauntlets, having used them to herd the lamb down the hallway. Sekhmet stepped into the doorway beside him, holding the end of the leash. The lamb rounded and charged back toward them, but with a wave of Lady Weirdwood's hand, a vine shot from the floor, binding the raging lamb between two tethers.

Breeth was so shocked, she had barely registered what happened. But then she noticed Wally smiling at her fire log. And it started to sink in. He and Sekhmet had ventured into the Fae, into the Neon Pastures. They had collected the creature that had killed Rose and brought it back to frighten her spirit out of Breeth's body.

And it had *worked*.

Lady Weirdwood chuckled. "That's *one* way of getting Rose to leave. I only wish you had *warned* me." She waved to Sekhmet and Wally. "Come, you two. Let's get Breeth's body somewhere a bit cooler."

"Wait!" Breeth said, staring wide-eyed at her lifeless body. "What if I start to rot between here and there?"

Wally stifled a chuckle. "Sounds like Breeth's ready now."

"Perhaps, Breeth," Lady Weirdwood said, "you should have more training before you repossess yourself. We can keep your body on ice while—"

"No, thanks!" Breeth yelled.

"—you learn a few tricks," Lady Weirdwood continued, unable to hear her. "You have a tendency to get trapped in bodies when you possess them. Your own body will probably feel so familiar and comfortable that you—"

"Don't care!" Breeth said.

"—might be stuck in there forever. You'll lose all of your ghostly privileges, and I'll lose my haunted librarian."

Breeth thought of her lonely days in the Manor. Of the times no one could talk to her. She took a deep, ember-glowing breath. "I'm ready to be myself again," she said. "Except . . . wait a sec."

She took off through the Manor like a firework. She zig-zagged across the roof and spiraled through the hallways and thundered above the Abyssment. She visited all of her favorite places, relishing that feeling of being creaky then groany, stiff as a board and then spinny as a weathervane.

Breeth would miss this. But not that much.

When she finished her final ghostly tour of the Manor, she found everyone in the Throne Room. Sekhmet and Wally were laying her body down in the middle of the floor.

Breeth creaked into the ceiling right above them. "Okay, *now* I'm ready!"

Wally gave her a thumbs-up. Breeth took one last creaky sigh, plugged her ghost nose, dove out of the ceiling through the room, and then splashed down right into her own chest.

Breeth's eyes shot open, and she gasped, like waking from a dream.

She lay in shock a moment and blinked at the ceiling, feeling sensation tingle to life in every inch of her. She gave her fingers a twitch. She gave her toes a wiggle. She gave her nose a scrunch. Then she sat up, slowly, stiffly, and nearly buckled forward before Sekhmet caught her and sat her upright.

"How ya feeling, Breeth?" Sekhmet asked.

"*Sssstrrrraaaaaaange*," Breeth said, trying out her lips, tongue, and teeth for the first time in years. "'Slike . . . bein' . . . stuffed in a bone and meat *sssssssandwich*."

Sekhmet laughed.

"Hey, Breeth."

Breeth turned her stiff neck and blinked her wet eyes. She saw Wally. Not from the ceiling or the wall. Not upside down or through blazing bull eyes. Just *Wally*.

Breeth grabbed him by the collar and kissed him right on the lips. Her eyes were still open, and she saw the darkness of his pupils. She even felt his eyebrows leap up his forehead against hers.

"*Mmmwa!*" She pulled away with a great smooching sound, then instantly felt her cheeks grow warm. "Oops! Ha ha. Sorry! Jeez. Still getting used to having a body. People aren't supposed to just do that, are they?"

Wally blushed. He raised the back of his sleeve toward his lips, but Breeth caught it. "Don't you *dare* wipe that off!"

She hopped to her feet and twirled around the Throne Room, feeling as wobbly as a bumped vase, and remembering what it was like to have bendy legs and floppy arms that worked like pendulums to keep her balanced. She quickly grew dizzy and barely managed to catch herself against the waxen throne before falling over.

"Whew! Not used to *that* sensation! It's kinda fun, except . . . *Hurp*—"

She gagged and thought she might throw up. She squished her eyes shut until her brain stopped spinning in her skull and the dizzy sensation passed. It was immediately replaced with another, deeper feeling. Her hands leapt to her belly.

"*Food!*" she said, as if making a huge discovery.

She sprinted out of the Throne Room, down the hallway and toward the feasting hall, cackling the whole way. She heard Wally run after her. But even with Breeth in human form, he couldn't keep up.

16
THE PRISON ISLAND

Arthur lay in his island cell and watched the dragon city whirl like clockwork. The sunset was dying beautifully, shimmering the ocean with a million blood-red sparkles. Once it rose again, his death would come swooping in on scaled wings.

A fresh wave of fear brought him to his feet. He swiped a bit of slimy mold from the cell's corner and tried writing another spell on the wall.

"Come on, *come on*," he whispered.

The wall was covered in failed magical attempts. One read *A key appeared in Arthur's hand.* Another had an arrow pointing toward the lock and read *Open Sesame.* (Not that getting the lock open would do him much good. As far as he could tell, the only way off of the island involved a thousand-foot plummet to the ocean below.) Arthur had even tried following in Graham's footsteps, drawing a poor imitation of Kingsport on the cell wall. He'd nearly broken his nose when he tried to walk through it.

He finished writing *Grow Wings* in green slime and then patted his shoulder blades, hoping to feel feathers sprouting through. Nothing.

Arthur slumped back to the floor. If he had once believed that danger would awaken his magical ability, he now knew he'd been sorely mistaken. He was finally starting to accept that he didn't have a single ounce of magic inside him. Not even when he needed it the most.

***

Arthur was still awake when the sun rose again, swallowing the starlight and glittering the waves. It was his last dawn on earth. Or the Fae, for that matter. He was grateful for the beautiful view, at least.

He wondered how the people in his life would take the news. Harry would have no way of finding out, of course. Arthur would just be one of dozens of street urchins who went missing in Kingsport in every year.

If Liza heard about Arthur's death, she'd barely flinch. She would simply continue on her quest to the afterlife, feeling justified in condemning the boy who'd killed her father.

And then there was Cooper. Would the dragons inform the Wardens that they had executed Arthur? Would Wally shed a tear? If so, he might be the only one.

Arthur rubbed the ache from his eyes, hoping to take in the beauty of the world one last time. When he blinked his eyes open again, he found two fuzzy ears poking up against the brightening sky. He sat up, alarmed, as the furry creature scrambled over the floor's jagged edge and slipped through the bars as slick as butter. It stood upright in the middle of his cell and stared at him with glowing eyes.

"Hello again," said a familiar voice. "Did you crash through someone's roof here too?"

Arthur blinked. It was the ferret from the Dapplewood.

"Wha—How—Wh—?"

"You're gonna have to be clearer, sugar," the ferret said. "I'm not in the habit of answering incomplete sentences."

Arthur stood warily, not quite ready to believe that the ferret wasn't a figment of his imagination. "H-h-how did you get here?"

"After *someone* locked me in my wardrobe, I hollered at the top of my lungs, hoping one of my neighbors would come rescue me. I screamed myself to exhaustion, but to no avail. Eventually, I fell asleep."

Arthur listened, wide-eyed. By shoving her into that armoire, had Liza saved the ferret from whatever horror had happened in the Dapplewood?

"When I woke up," the ferret continued, "I found myself in a place that'd make a honey badger's head swim." She gestured toward the horizon, which was growing awfully bright. "Not only that, I was surrounded by a group of odd characters the likes of which I've never seen in the Dapplewood. I figured it was all a dream, but then a kindly creature called a *pangolin* told me we'd all been summoned to some *Whirly City* or other to testify against one *Arthur Benton* for creating havoc throughout the *pocket-worlds*—whatever *that* is."

The ferret studied her sharp claws. "I thought to myself, *y'know*, I *would* like to give that boy a piece of my mind. But I didn't have time to appear in any *court of law*. I had a shop to rebuild and a reputation to uphold! Some folks approached us with spears and armor, but they smelled like *reptiles*, and I never did trust reptiles. So I slipped over the island's edge with my claws and have been trying to sniff my way out of this Whirly City ever since. It was only last night that I smelled a familiar scent on the breeze. A scent that *filthied* up my laundry. I followed it here, and that's how I found you."

For the first time in three days, Arthur almost smiled.

"*Listen*," he said. "Ally."

"Audrey," the ferret said.

"Right. *Audrey*. I'm sorry about what my lady friend and I did to your shop. But I'm sure a lovely rodent such as yourself—"

"What did you just call me?" Audrey's eyes narrowed.

Arthur's jaw clenched. "A . . . rodent?"

Audrey's lips curled into a sort of smile. "I'm a *ferret*, sweetie. You must be thinking of Mrs. Rat. She lives at the bottom of the hill."

"Right again," Arthur said, breathing relief. "Surely, a *ferret* such as yourself could see to forgiving an innocent kid who fell through the wrong roof at the wrong time"—he decided it was best not to mention the armoire—"and possibly help me out of this cell and off this island? I promise I'll get you back to the Dapplewood and give you the *best* roof you've ever seen. It'll protect against rain, hail, *plagues of frogs*, anything."

The ferret turned up her muzzle. "If you think I'm the sort of lady that would break a *convict* out of *prison*, then you're about to be sorely disappointed."

Arthur's hope withered inside him.

"Now, if you'll excuse me," Audrey said, turning her tail. "I'm sure *someone* around here can instruct me how I can get home and resume my quiet, *respectable* life."

She started to slip through the bars.

"It was meant to be a surprise!" Arthur shouted.

Audrey looked back at him with her beady, caramel eyes.

He'd been going about this all wrong, promising her a new roof. Arthur's mom had read every single Dapplewood story to him before bedtime. He had all the information he needed.

"Your neighbor," he continued, "Mrs. Hedgehog. She told me and Liza that you needed a new thatched roof. It, um, *leaks*, yeah?"

Arthur made up this last detail, hoping beyond hope something like it was true. But the moment he said it, he felt a glowing in his chest, while the ferret's scowl melted like an ice cube in boiling soup.

"How'd you know about my roof?" Audrey asked. "Was that a lucky guess?"

"No!" Arthur said. "Like I said, Mrs. Hedgehog told me."

He wasn't sure if it had been a lucky guess or if his mom had once read to him about Mrs. Ferret's leaky roof and he'd only just now remembered it. Truth be told, he didn't even remember a ferret named Audrey living in the Dapplewood.

"When Liza and I fell through your roof, we realized

we'd spoiled the surprise," he continued. "Liza panicked and pushed you into the wardrobe. She felt bad about that."

Audrey reached up, and Arthur flinched, worried she might claw his face. But then she gently pinched his cheek instead. The ferret's touch wasn't nearly as unpleasant as it had been before.

"If you aren't lyin', then you're sweet as sugar," Audrey said, and sighed. "All *right.* I'd hate to see an innocent soul locked up for trying to help a ferret in need. I'll help you if I can."

"Great!" Arthur said, then gazed through the bars and over the island's edge. "Wait. How did you make it all the way over here? Can ferrets fly?"

Audrey sighed. "Well, now you've got me confused with Mr. Flying Squirrel. *He* lives in Redwood Heights." She pointed a claw. "There's lines connecting the islands. It seems just because these reptiles can make an island float, doesn't mean they can keep it *corralled.*"

Arthur squinted toward the ocean, but only saw the sparkle of waves a thousand feet below. "I don't see a line."

"That's 'cause it's practically invisible," Audrey said. "except to a soul that's been working with thread her whole life." She stuck her paw through the bars and traced her claw through the air, pointing at an indistinct spot a few meters below the prison island. "It's thin as a ray of light but strong as cable. Moving from island to island was as easy as scrambling across laundry lines—something I happen to be quite practiced at."

Arthur's stomach churned. How was he supposed to get

down to that line? He didn't have claws to cling to the island's exterior. In fact, how was he supposed to get through these *bars*?

A shriek cut across the sky, flattening Audrey's ears. Two winged shadows swept toward the prison island. They were so close, Arthur could see light glinting off their scales.

"We have to get out of here." Arthur gave the locked bars a jostle. "Think you can pick this lock?"

Audrey held up a paw. "Sugar, I use these claws for *sewin'*. Not jailbreakin'."

The island continued to rotate until the dragons were no longer in sight. But the bar's shifting shadows told him they would soon swing around again, placing them back in the dragon's view. If they were going to escape, they had to move *now*.

Arthur pulled at his hair in panic. "If it were up to me, every critter in the Dapplewood would have learned the subtle art of lock picking in school!"

The words stirred another glowing in his chest, just like the one he'd felt when he'd guessed at Audrey's leaking roof.

Audrey rolled her eyes. "They *did* teach us at school. In case any of our elderly neighbors locked their keys inside." She slid her claw into the lock and hooked it upward. "I'm just a little rusty is all."

A moment later, the lock clicked and the door swung open.

"That's to thank you for the future fixin' of my roof," Audrey said.

Arthur touched his chest just as the glowing sensation started to fade. He knew something significant had just happened, but he couldn't even begin to imagine what. And he didn't have time to figure it out.

The dragons were still somewhere behind the island as Arthur stepped through the bars to the edge and stared at the ocean far below. He thought he saw a razor-thin shimmer of sunlight.

"We're gonna jump," he said, "and you're going to hook the line with your claw. We'll hide under this island, wait until the dragons leave, then shimmy across the line to the outer islands. We'll find the Rift that leads to Weirdwood Manor, and Lady Weirdwood will get you back to the Dapplewood and me back to Kingsport. Deal? Say deal."

"*No deal!*" Audrey hissed. "I can't support both our weights. We'll be *fish food!*"

Arthur bit his lip, feeling suddenly uncertain. "Maybe you're stronger than you think."

Audrey placed her hands on her hips and gave him a flat stare.

They both stumbled as something heavy landed on top of the island cell. It was followed by another heavy something. Claws scraped the stone. Reptilian breath rattled the air.

Arthur removed his pants.

"Well now," Audrey said, covering her eyes. "I don't see how *this* helps."

As crumbling dust spilled over the top of the island, Arthur grabbed the ferret, slung her around his back, and jumped off the ledge. They plummeted through the air several yards before Arthur threw one pant leg over the shimmering line. He went to grab the other pant leg . . . and missed.

Arthur's stomach lifted into his throat as he fell. The line whipped past his nose, making his whole life flash before his eyes. But then Audrey scrambled up his back and launched painfully off his shoulders. Her hind claws snagged the pant leg Arthur wasn't holding right before her foreclaws hooked on the line.

They jerked to a stop and then dangled in the middle of the air, panting with fear. Arthur clasped his pant leg and blinked down at the ocean, shocked he was still alive.

"*Don't look up*," Audrey whispered, straining. "I'm wearing a dress. But I thought you should know that I'm losing my grip."

Arthur's sweaty hands were slipping.

"Can you pull us up?" Arthur hissed at her.

"I *sew*," Audrey hissed back, "not *heft bricks* for a living!"

Above, a snarl echoed in the island cell. "Where is the prisoner?"

"The Wardens must have discovered he was here and freed him."

This voice was royal and feminine. *The Duchess.*

Audrey's claws slipped lower. Arthur dangled from his pant leg, spinning in the middle of the air. He was torn between wanting the dragons to leave and having them peek over the ledge so they could pull him and Audrey out of this predicament.

"Summon a carriage for Weirdwood Manor," the Duchess said.

"I will attend you and keep you protected, mistress."

"No," the Duchess said. "I don't want Lady Weirdwood believing we're intimidated by her silly little plant magic."

On the other side of the island, a carriage formed out of starlight, pulled by two constellation koi fish. It was facing away from Arthur and Audrey. The Duchess swooped from the island to the carriage's roof, folded herself into human form, and then slipped inside.

Arthur's sweaty palms slipped lower and lower down the pant leg. He watched as the koi fish swam through the air, swooping the carriage in a great arc. It was going to pass beneath them.

"Audrey!" he whispered. "Get ready to let go!"

"What?" she said.

"Trust me!"

"Trusting you is what got us in this mess!"

A moment before the carriage was directly below, Arthur whispered, "*Now!*"

Audrey released the line, and she and Arthur tumbled several yards. Arthur landed on top of the carriage, but Audrey struck the corner and went careening over the side. He scrambled to grab her paw . . . and missed. Arthur peered over the edge, hand covering his mouth in horror. The ferret had vanished, swallowed by the waves below.

The Duchess poked her head out of the window to investigate the thump. But Arthur was already scrambling down the carriage's opposite side and nestling himself on the board beside the wheel's axle.

He stared down at the ocean, shaking. "You deserved better than that, Audrey," he whispered. "In a perfect world, you would have had longer claws and snagged yourself on the carriage wheel." The thought made another swell of feeling rise in his chest. He excused it as sadness. "I'm so sorry, Audrey. I only hope you're happy in the Great—"

"You *should* be sorry!"

Arthur jerked and nearly fell from the axle. He blinked. Audrey was right behind him. He just hadn't seen her.

"You're . . . ," he said. He pointed at the ocean. "How did you—? Weren't you just—?"

Audrey slapped him. "You *never* pick up a lady without asking first!" she said. "And what did I say about *incomplete questions*?" She placed a paw to her chest and took a shuddering breath. "I was barely able to snag the wheel, no thanks to you." She held up her paw and admired it. "I guess these claws of mine are useful beyond sewin'."

Arthur rubbed the sting from his cheek while he stared at her claws in disbelief. He could've sworn they were slightly longer than before.

Three times. Three times he'd felt that overwhelming glowing in his chest right before something about the ferret had *changed*—her roof, her lock-picking skills, her claws. But the ferret seemed completely oblivious to it.

"Listen," he said. "Ally—I mean, *Audrey.*"

"Close one."

"I'm sorry I picked you up. But I'm even sorrier for lying to you. Mrs. Hedgehog never asked us to fix your roof. I made that up so you'd save my life. But I meant what I said about getting you back to the Dapplewood and giving you the best roof you've ever seen."

Audrey sighed. "Guess I don't have any choice but to agree.

I *am* already an accomplice." She flexed her long claws. "That roof of yours'd better hold up till Armageddon."

Arthur smiled. "And beyond."

Exhaustion overcame him as the koi carriage sailed out of the Whirling City.

17
THE ROOFTOP DUEL

Wally watched in awe as Breeth devoured three roasted game hens, four ears of corn, two servings of green beans, a roll, another game hen, and a small mountain of mashed potatoes. When Pyra served dessert, Breeth shoveled a massive spoonful of chocolate pudding into her mouth and her face lit up like a fireworks display.

"Yum!" she said in a muddy gargle, and then promptly spat it onto an empty plate.

Wally laughed. "What's that about?"

Breeth patted her bulging stomach. "If I swallow one more bite, I'll pop like a volcano and erupt all over you and this table. But I haven't eaten human food in *three years*, so . . ."

She took a bite of the raspberry tart and then spat it next to the blob of chocolate pudding.

Wally shook his head, smiling. "What a waste."

"Three *years*, Wally," Breeth said, wiping a sugary smear from her chin. "I ate *lint* as a mouse thing and *poop* as a fly. You don't even want to know what I ate as that tentacle monster."

She continued to sample-spit the desserts like fine wines while Wally took in her features. He still couldn't believe Breeth was sitting across from him. No longer contorted in wood grain or spiraled in rope strands. But in the *flesh*. She had a freckled nose and strawberry blond hair and eyes big enough to take in the whole world. Her goofy grin was much better suited on her human face than on a bull or a shelf.

Breeth no longer seemed like an annoying kid he had to babysit. She seemed like an actual . . . *girl*. Wally's cheeks still burned with embarrassment when he remembered how she'd kissed him. Of course, now her lips were caked with butter and grease and jam and chocolate, so the thought of kissing her again hadn't crossed his mind. Yet.

"*So*," he said. "What do you want to do now that you're . . . *you* again?"

"Hmm." Breeth took a bite of peach cobbler. "First, I want to scratch an itch that's really hard to reach. Then I want to *floss*. And then . . . um, *oh*! Sneeze! I want to sneeze! Which room is the dustiest?"

Wally laughed. "I meant what do you want to do with your *life*?"

Breeth tapped her lips with her spoon. "Well, I can't go home. 'Cause, *y'know*. No parents." Her eyes grew shiny, but then she quickly cleared her throat. "And I can't possess books 'cause I'm not dead anymore. But that's good because being a ghost librarian was the *worst* job in the history of *everything*." She swiped a dollop of whipped cream and ate it. "Guess I'm just a tumbleweed, rolling in the breeze."

The ceiling let out a deep groan, and they both looked up. It might have been the wind. Then again . . .

"Rose is still in the Manor somewhere," Wally said.

Lady Weirdwood had warned them to remain on high alert and keep away from the walls while the staff tried to track down the blacksmith's ghost.

Breeth scowled at the ceiling. "I swear, if I catch her face in the wood grain, I'm going to punch it. I don't even care if I break my hand."

Something heavy thumped the roof, and Wally and Breeth jumped to their feet.

Breeth swiped up a fork and pointed it at the ceiling. "*Rose?*"

"I don't think that was her," Wally said. "You were never that noisy as a ghost. But . . . what *was* that?"

"Only one way to find out!" Breeth said. She turned to run and then promptly fell over. "*Whoops!* I keep forgetting that walking isn't the same as creaking." She picked herself up and pointed at Wally's face. "Erase that from your memory."

She took off again, and Wally followed her to the zigzag stairs that led to the roof. Before Wally could suggest that they should be careful, Breeth threw open the double doors.

Weirdwood's roof was an expansive, ethereal place. Mist caressed the spires. The towers were purple with moonlight. In the roof's center was a phoenix-shaped weathervane. Beside it was an ornate carriage pulled by two constellation koi fish. A woman stepped out of the carriage. Her robes were a delicate cream. Her face was scaled.

Breeth marched straight up to the woman. "Welcome to Weirdwood Manor, whoever you are! My name is Breeth. Please forgive my haircut. The last person in this body had terrible taste."

"I would speak with Lady Weirdwood," the woman said.

"I shall fetch her *presently*," Breeth said. "But please be patient. I can't move as quickly as I—"

Something jostled the carriage and two figures dropped from the bottom. For a moment, Wally thought he was seeing things. It was *Arthur* . . . and a giant ferret wearing a dress.

They scrambled out from under the wheels and sprinted toward the door.

"Cooper!" Arthur shouted. "She's going to execute me!"

The woman's head snapped unnaturally around her neck

as her lips peeled wide. She started to transform—like Huamei once had, only with the speed and grace of a striking serpent. Her robes unfolded into wings as her lips extended into a scaled muzzle, fangs sprouting toward her chin.

The ferret scampered behind the weathervane.

"*Oh*," Breeth said, taking a step back. "Should I not have welcomed her?"

Arthur had nearly made it to Weirdwood's door when the dragon lashed out and caught him in her claws. She brought him to her toothy mouth. Her grin sharpened.

Wally froze. His gauntlets hung from his belt. But he didn't put them on. He couldn't possibly win a fight against a dragon.

"Greetings, Duchess," a voice said behind him. "If I'd known you were coming, I would have prepared a cow or two."

Lady Weirdwood stood in the roof's doorway, her dead snake drooping from her shoulders. The Duchess lowered Arthur from her lips. Wally thought he recognized a gleam of fear in her ivory eyes.

Lady Weirdwood nodded at Arthur. "I'm afraid that boy isn't on the menu."

The Duchess squeezed Arthur between her claws, making him turn purple as a corpse. "This *boy* has been found guilty of magical *desecration*," she said in a bone-rattling voice. "He stole a dragon bone and trafficked it into the Real."

Wally stepped forward to tell her that *he* was the one who had taken Huamei's claw, but Arthur caught his eye and subtly shook his head.

"I understand your son's spirit offered his claw freely," Lady Weirdwood said.

"The child Huamei was no longer royalty. He lost ownership over his bones the moment he became your Novitiate."

Wally winced. The Duchess spoke of her deceased son as if he were a stranger.

"Are these your words, Duchess?" Lady Weirdwood said. "Or the court's?"

The Duchess's scales briefly smoothed. Then crumpled again.

Lady Weirdwood continued. "Arthur used that Quill to save his city from monsters sprung from the imagination of a madman. His actions restored the Balance."

"Only to undo it shortly after," the Duchess responded. "We watched witness testimonies play out in our dome of leaves."

Lady Weirdwood clicked her tongue. "And here I banished Arthur from this Manor so he would cease his meddling." She sighed. "Still, I can't in good conscience let an innocent boy die. Even a foolish one."

Lady Weirdwood removed her snake from her shoulders. It lay lifeless as a leather belt in the doorway. She stepped out onto the roof and pulled up her sleeves as the Duchess rose up to her full height, stretching her wings as wide as the Manor. Wally backed away.

The Duchess flapped Arthur several yards into the air, her eyes flashing as bright as collapsing stars. Her voice took on a dark shimmer. "In a far-off country, in a land between hills, was a forest that caught a terrible disease. It chewed the roots and withered the leaves and wilted the branches so they hung like dead serpents . . ."

As the Duchess spoke, the Manor's roof began to boil and rot, like centuries were passing in seconds. The spires and towers melted and collapsed as the roof sucked up the phoenix weathervane like quicksand. The ferret scrambled toward its top. Only Lady Weirdwood and the starlit carriage floated, unharmed.

The wood melted beneath Wally's feet. The moment before he fell, Breeth just managed to grab his wrist and clasp the tip of a drooping spire. The roof parted beneath them, revealing the feasting hall, which crumbled and collapsed into the Abyssment below.

"I've got you, Wally!" Breeth said, straining her muscles, which she'd slipped back on hours before. *I think!*"

The roof slanted them toward the pit. Wally managed to climb up Breeth's arm and grab on to the drooping spire. Arthur tried to wriggle free of the dragon's claws as the ferret tried to balance her paws on the tip of the sinking weathervane.

In the center of all the chaos stood Lady Weirdwood, unfazed. She had her eyes closed and was mumbling something. Moments before the weathervane and the ferret collapsed into the Throne Room, little mushrooms popped out of the rotting wood like tiny umbrellas. They grew across the seam like stitching and then cinched together, closing the hole with a great squelch and saving the entire Manor from buckling in on itself.

Wally and Breeth climbed to solid mushroom ground.

The Duchess started to hiss another spell. "A young woman pricked her finger on a needle. Her blood began to *flow.* It created rivers and waterfalls and entire oceans, drowning everything in its—"

Before the Duchess could finish her spell, Lady Weirdwood raised her hand and squeezed it into a fist. There was a crackling sound. The Duchess looked and found that vines had grown around her starlit carriage, encasing it completely. The more Lady Weirdwood tightened her fist, the more the vines squeezed, splintering the carriage within.

"If you don't set that boy down this instant," she told the Duchess, "I will crush your only means back to the Whirling City like a peanut shell."

The Duchess flapped silently in the air a few moments. The stars of her eyes dulled and she swooped down and dropped Arthur beside Lady Weirdwood before folding herself back into human form. Lady Weirdwood unclenched her fingers, and the vines fell away from the starlit carriage.

"The Wardens' mission is to protect the Veil," the Duchess said, her voice no longer dark and shimmering. "You betrayed your oath the moment you decided to play *babysitter* to street urchins. Perhaps it's time the dragons replace you with someone else."

"This wasn't the Wardens' fault!" Arthur said. "It was m—"

He was silenced by a raise of Lady Weirdwood's hand.

"To remove the Wardens from the Veil now would not only be unwise," she said, "it would be catastrophic. There are rumors that a Void walks the Fae. It seems to have intelligence. It even gave itself a name. The Eraser."

The Duchess's scaled face did not so much as twitch. But she remained silent.

"You need me to take care of this problem," Lady Weirdwood said. "You need my Wardens."

The mist twisted around the Duchess and coiled up the spires. "I will leave you to handle this *Void* . . . but then I will return with two of my strongest dragons. That should be more than enough against your *plant* magic." She extended a claw-sharp fingernail at Arthur. "Should you continue to harbor this fugitive, we will be forced to destroy this Manor and everyone in it."

With that, the Duchess stepped back into her starlit carriage. The constellation koi fish swam down from the stars and carried it into sky.

"Welp, it's official," Breeth said, climbing down from the tower. "I hate dragons."

Wally followed after and helped Arthur to his feet while the ferret descended the weathervane and worried her paws together. "What *have* I gotten myself into?"

Wally noticed that Lady Weirdwood had slumped to the roof and ran to her side.

"Oh, stop making such a fuss," she said, waving him away.

Wally stepped back, speechless. The old architect looked . . . *different*. Not so old, in fact. The liver spots on her hands had faded. The wrinkles on her face had smoothed. Black hairs sprouted from her gray head. It was as if casting those spells had not spent her years but rejuvenated them. Made her . . . *younger*.

Arthur didn't seem to notice. "Thank you for saving me, Lady Weirdwood," he said, stepping forward. "As far as the Quill goes, I can explain. I—"

Lady Weirdwood shot him a chilling look. "You have brought chaos and madness down upon my Manor."

Arthur's mouth snapped shut. Even Lady Weirdwood's voice had changed. It was more youthful and had more fire in it.

She got to her feet, less hunched than before. "I must go tell the staff to fix the roof and fortify it against a possible dragon assault." She gave Arthur one last look. "And to make the decision between one boy's life and my Manor."

In the doorway, she retrieved her limp snake and wrapped it around her shoulders. As she descended the stairs, the old architect regained her hunch, leaving behind a trail of black hairs that shed from her gray head. Simultaneously, the snake seemed to *coil to life*, a healthy gleam returning to its scales. Wally shook his head in confusion.

"*Whew!*" Breeth said. "Glad we didn't die. Hi, Arthur! I'm Breeth. I saved your life like a *billion* times in the Abyssment. Nice to officially meet you. I'm not dead anymore. Great, right?"

Arthur shook her hand, too shocked to register what she was saying. The dragons were coming for him.

"Why didn't you *stay* in Kingsport, Arthur?" Wally said. "You just made things so much more complicated. Like you *always* do."

"I know," Arthur said, taking his hand back from Breeth. "It's just . . . Liza had the Quill, and she wanted me to help bring her mom back to life, and then the Order was chasing after me, and the dragons somehow knew I had used Huamei's claw, and I . . . I was trying to do something good. But I messed up. I *know* I messed up."

This was a lot of information. But Wally dwelled on one detail in particular. How would the dragons know that Arthur had the Quill? Unless they'd heard it from a *little birdy*.

"Anyway," Arthur said. "I won't be able to cause any more trouble after Lady Weirdwood hands me over to the dragons."

"Lady Weirdwood would never do that," Wally said, but his throat tightened. She had said she was going to choose between her Manor and one boy's life.

He saw the broken expression on Arthur's face, and the tension melted from his shoulders. He wasn't so much mad at Arthur as he was *afraid* for him.

Wally threw his arms around his friend, pulling him into a tight hug. "I'm glad you're okay."

Arthur hugged him back, and Wally realized just how much he'd missed the kid.

"Aww!" Breeth said. "Second reunion!"

"Well, if *Arthur* isn't gonna introduce me," the ferret said, smoothing her dress. "I'm Audrey. Arthur fell through my roof. Could anyone tell me how to get back to the Dapplewood?"

"There's a whole *town* of critters like you?" Breeth asked. "More like when can *I* go to the *Dapplewood*?"

Audrey the ferret. Where had Wally heard that before?

"Once Lady Weirdwood finishes her meeting," he told Audrey, "I'll ask her to open a door to your home."

Audrey nodded, and they all fell quiet.

"Welp!" Breeth said, slapping her hands together. "What should we do now?"

Wally's stomach squeezed. He couldn't stop thinking about Lady Weirdwood's final words.

"Now," he said, "we go to the Throne Room."

***

Wally, Arthur, Audrey, and Breeth crept like shadows to the Throne Room's entrance. While the others pressed their ears to the door, Wally peeked through the keyhole and spotted Lady Weirdwood's snake, coiled on the floor and seemingly *un*-shedding its skin.

He shifted his head and found Amelia standing before the waxen throne.

"And where does my eye currently reside, Lady?" Amelia asked as if quizzing a student.

"Oh, you worry too much," Lady Weirdwood said in her usual dusty voice. "Your eye is in the Abyssment atop that monstrous mushroom. My memories are just *fine*. I was only out there for ten minutes."

Amelia sighed. "Just know that I refuse to be the one to bottle feed you and change your nappies."

Lady Weirdwood gave her a look. "There are more pressing matters."

"I've put a bed in our guest's cell," Amelia said, "but I still can't get her to agree to sign—"

"I meant Arthur," Lady Weirdwood said.

Breeth pressed her cheek to Wally's, trying to peek through the keyhole herself. "*Wow*," she whispered. "Keyholes are *terrible* for spying. I'm not gonna say I wish I was still a ghost, but . . ."

"*Shh*," Wally said.

"Even after the disastrous events in the Mirror City," Amelia was saying, "Arthur still went *out of his way* to disrupt the Balance."

Lady Weirdwood didn't respond to this. Wally's heart started to pound in his chest.

"He even caused destruction on his *way* to the Whirling City," Amelia continued.

"And then *lied* about it," Audrey whispered.

"I came clean!" Arthur hissed back.

Wally hushed them, pressing his ear to the keyhole so he could hear better.

"One pocket-world saw the worst of it," Amelia said. "While sewing up the many Rifts Arthur left in his wake, I came to a place that looked like it had been . . . erased. It was nothing more than a mailbox, a half an oak tree, and some pipework against a paper-white background—like scraps cut from a storybook."

"What was this pocket-world called?" Lady Weirdwood asked.

"The Dapplewood."

At the mention of her hometown's name, Audrey pressed her ear closer to the door.

"The Order pursued Arthur through the pocket-worlds he broke into," Amelia continued. "When they reached the Dapplewood, they kidnapped its citizens. We believe the Order's plan was to use them in one of their Fae-born zoos."

Audrey lifted a paw to her muzzle. Her eyes grew wide with horror.

"There was only one witness," Amelia continued. "A

white-feathered duck was overlooked because she blended in with the empty background. Between sobs, she told me the other critters in the town ran from the Eraser but were funneled into a Rift where cages awaited them. Even if we manage to find the Dapplewood citizens, they won't have a home to return to."

Audrey slumped to the floor, too heavy to stand. Breeth stroked her ears to soothe her.

"Audrey . . . ," Arthur whispered. "I don't know what to say. I'm the one who led the Order there. I—"

"I don't understand what's happening," Audrey interrupted. She looked right at Arthur, whiskers sagging, eyes shiny with tears. "But it doesn't sound like it was your fault."

Arthur's hands fell to his sides. He clearly didn't know how to respond to that.

Wally continued to listen through the door.

"Do we have any idea where the Order took the Dapplewood citizens?" Lady Weirdwood asked.

"None," Amelia said. "Ahura found yet another Rift in *Kingsport*, believe it or not, but no zoo. We have reason to believe the Order may have discovered a pocket-world that's even *more* profitable."

"*Kingsport?* Again?" Lady Weirdwood asked, mirroring Wally's thoughts exactly. "That city draws Rifts like cheese draws holes." She stood and gathered her snake. "Summon a Trackdragon so the Wardens can head to the port city immediately."

Amelia nodded. "And Arthur?"

"We must focus our resources on stopping the Order, not fighting our allies," Lady Weirdwood said, draping her snake around her shoulders. "While I couldn't allow the Duchess to defy me in my own Manor, I can't sacrifice this place and everyone in it for one selfish child. As much as it injures me to say it, when the dragons return, we will give them Arthur Benton."

Wally's mouth fell open. Arthur turned even paler than before.

"What do we do, Wally?" Breeth whispered.

He was still piecing together what he'd just heard. How could the same woman who'd made him, a *penniless thief*, a Novitiate also condemn Arthur to such a terrible fate? Yes, Wally had been hurt by Arthur's recklessness in the past. But when it came down to it, Arthur Benton was *good*.

"Wally?" Breeth said.

"We're getting Arthur out of this Manor," Wally said, and turned to head down the hallway.

"Cooper, *no*," Arthur said, catching Wally's wrist and stopping him. "You could lose your Novitiateship."

"In case you forgot," Wally said, "*I'm* the one the dragons should be executing. Huamei gave his claw to *me*. But the dragons don't know that, do they, Arthur? They don't know because *you* refused to tell them. To keep me safe."

Arthur bit his lip.

"Besides," Wally continued, "Breeth made me realize that I've been following orders my whole life. It's time I took things into my own hands."

Arthur released Wally's wrist. "You know, I'm the one who usually makes the heroic speeches."

"How things change," Wally said.

They smiled at each other.

"Aww," Breeth said.

Wally hurried down the hallway. "*Come on!*"

Arthur and Breeth followed, but then a sniffling stopped them.

"What about me?"

It was the ferret in the dress.

"There's no use putting you in danger," Wally told her. "You should stay here."

"Aw, man," Breeth said. "But I *like* that ferret lady."

"Lady Weirdwood might not be able to get you back to your home," Wally told Audrey, "but she and the Wardens will rescue the other Dapplewood citizens and then get you all to a different, safer pocket-world."

The ferret nodded uncertainly.

"*Audrey*," Arthur said. "I owe you more than a roof now. I owe you an entire—"

Audrey held up a paw to silence him. "Don't promise what you can't provide."

Arthur let the rest of his breath escape. He gazed back at the ferret as they continued down the corridor.

"Hopefully one of the northern exits opens on the Real," Wally said, and then stopped when they hit a dead end that he could have sworn wasn't there before.

"Oh no," he said.

He tried to backtrack, but the hall began to crack like a dying branch. Passageways pinched shut. Doorways puckered and vanished. Soon they were trapped in a small space, encased in dried bark and dead leaves.

"Um?" Breeth said.

"Lady Weirdwood must know we're trying to escape," Wally said.

He slipped on his gauntlets.

18
ESCAPE FROM WEIRDWOOD MANOR

The little forest room was as quiet as the autumn woods, save the pleasant popping of firewood. Shortly after Arthur, Wally, and Breeth had become trapped in there, a fireplace had flowered in one of the walls, lending a bit of warmth to the cold mulch air. Breeth tried to not enjoy the smoky aroma. Everything was too sad.

Arthur sat in a mulchy corner, holding his head, waiting for his death to come. Wally, meanwhile, slammed his gauntlets over and over again into the barky wall. He didn't make so much as a dent.

"Give it up, Wally," Arthur said. "Before you break your knuckles."

Wally tried punching another wall, wincing when the tree bark wallpaper remained as strong as concrete.

"Even if we *do* find a way out of this room," Arthur said, "Lady Weirdwood will have sealed the Manor's outer doors. We couldn't get back to Kingsport if we tried."

Wally pulled his hand from his gauntlet and shook off

the pain. "We don't need a door. Lady Weirdwood said the Wardens are taking a Trackdragon to Kingsport in one hour. We just have to get on that train. The question is *how*?"

Breeth sat in the center of the room, tearing leaves to bits. "If I was still a ghost, I'd just possess the wall and peel it open."

"I'd *write* us an exit," Arthur said, "but it turns out my stories are about as useful as the paper they're written on."

Wally's eyes went wide. He dug into his pocket and pulled out a small strip of paper.

"What's that?" Breeth asked.

"It's a riddle. My brother gave it to me."

Arthur got to his feet. "So you *have* been talking to your brother?"

"It's complicated," Wally said, and then read the poem. *"When lost in the woods full of surprises, keep in mind what a forest despises. What once was extinguished now you stoke, what once was exterminated now is woke."*

Arthur stroked his chin. "What do forests *despise*? Loggers?"

"There's something they hate more than that," Wally said, and walked to the fireplace. He took a deep breath and, using his gauntlet, rolled one of the flaming logs onto the floor. Breeth leapt to her feet as the rug started to smolder.

"Um, *Wally*?" Arthur said, panicked. "Maybe warn us the next time you decide to *kill us all*?"

"Yeah!" Breeth said, covering her nose and mouth. "I *just* got my body back!"

"I'm trusting my brother," Wally said. "His last riddle gave me clues for how to extinguish a fire, and it would have done a lot of good."

"There's a big difference between that and *setting a fire in a small space!*" Arthur said.

Billowing black smoke filled the room, stinging Breeth's eyes and throat. Her lungs started to panic. What if Wally had answered the riddle incorrectly?

But then the fire crept up the wall, which started to blossom like a pinecone seed. The gap ventilated the smoke, leaving an opening behind. The kids squeezed through and found themselves in a smokeless corridor.

"Okay, all right," Arthur said. "Maybe your brother was onto something."

Wally put a finger to his lips, and then they quickly and quietly snuck down the strangely empty Manor. The floor seemed to groan louder beneath their footsteps, and every little creak in the walls made them jumpy.

"This is *terrifying*," Arthur whispered.

Breeth giggled. "Yeah it is!" The hairs on her arms went electric with the promise of adventure.

"The good news is we're in the east wing of the Manor," Wally said. "The Trackdragon Station is directly north of here."

They came to three doors, carved with a tower, a scythe, and a wheel.

"Okay, Breeth," Wally said. "Which one gets us there?"

Breeth pointed to the scythe door. "That one's fastest, but I once watched it turn a rat inside out before putting it back together again. So . . . *that* one."

Wally opened the door with the wheel. This hallway was tall and wide and every inch of it was covered with doors. The doors were upside down and sideways, circular and triangular, tiny as mouse holes and big as vaults. There were even doors on the floor and ceiling. Not one of them was marked.

Breeth slapped her forehead. "The *Everywhere* Room. Each of these doors will transport you to a different part of the Manor. Usually, I could just stick my ghost face through each of them and see which one leads north, but . . ."

"That doesn't really help us right now," Wally said.

Breeth squeezed her fists in frustration. No longer being able to creak through the walls made her feel constipated in her whole body. Still, she'd been in this hallway before. Boredom and immortality had caused her to try every single exit. If only she could remember which one led where . . .

She placed her hand against several doors, feeling for vibrations, just like she had when she was a ghost. She touched a white porcelain doorknob and thought she sensed the rumble of a train behind it.

Breeth patted it. "It's this one."

"Are you sure?" Wally asked.

"Positive."

She turned the handle, threw open the door, and then screamed when the black vacuum behind it slurped her, Wally, and Arthur inside. They tumbled through the root-filled darkness between the Manor's walls before being spat out into a blue swirl room where they landed on grassy carpet. The ceiling coiled with storm clouds. The air smelled of rain.

"Breeth!" Wally said, getting to his feet. "You brought us to the wrong side of the Manor!"

"*Thorry!*" Breeth lisped. "Being on the wrong *thide* of the

Manor wa*th* never a problem a*th* a gho*th*t. Having a body again i*th thre*thful!"

She had bitten her tongue in the fall—a sensation she had been happy to forget. But it didn't hurt as much as disappointing Wally and putting them in even more danger.

"No use crying over spilled milk," Arthur said as he stood and brushed himself off. He examined the room's three exits, marked with a lantern, an anvil, and a cloak. "Where now?"

Breeth pointed to the cloak. "I want to say it's that one, so"—she swept her finger toward the door with the lantern— "I'll say that one instead?"

Wally bit his lip, clearly questioning Breeth's advice, and then headed toward the door. Before he could reach it, lightning struck across the wallpaper, making him retreat. The room shook with thunder like it was going to come apart. Breeth, Wally, and Arthur fled to the room's center as the clouds on the wallpaper coalesced into a stormy face that stretched across the entire ceiling.

"Turn back, children," Lady Weirdwood boomed. "Don't make my Manor make mulch of you."

Wally stood his ground. "Promise me you'll protect Arthur."

"I can't do that, Wally," the face said. "Arthur chose his fate the moment he used that dragon-bone Quill."

Wally linked his arms through Arthur's and Breeth's. "Then I've chosen mine."

The cloud face flashed in anger and then broke apart, swirling toward the cloak door and covering it so completely, it looked like it had never existed.

"This way!" Wally said, running to the door with the lantern—Breeth's first choice.

Breeth sprinted after him and Arthur, feeling frustratingly slow on her two feet. The clouds raced overhead, trying to beat them to the lantern door. All around them, lightning bolts struck the grassy carpet, making it explode in ashen plumes.

Wally jumped over a crater in the floor, then lunged forward and just managed to get the door open and Breeth and Arthur through before a mass of thundering clouds filled the frame.

The three breathed heavily, like escaping prey. Arthur smoothed his staticky hair straight.

They were in a new space, as dark and expansive as a moonless night save the electric green swoops of fireflies. The air was cool and smelled sweetly of swamp water. They couldn't see any walls. The carpet was damp and squishy underfoot and decorated with occasional bouquets of cattails. Feathery branches whispered pleasantly against the top of Breeth's head.

"Lady Weirdwood knows exactly where we are now," Wally whispered. "She'll have blocked all of the exits."

Crickets played a silvery song while everyone fell to thought.

Arthur snapped his fingers. "Everyone walk in a different direction!"

"Seems like a bad idea," Wally said, blinking into the swampy gloom.

"Trust me," Arthur said. "I have a theory."

They put their backs to one another and then set off in three directions through the darkness.

The way was tangled. Breeth kept tripping over serpentine roots and stepping in invisible water holes. Her socks grew soaked—another miserable sensation she'd forgotten. If she was still a ghost, she would have been able to squish through every inch of this expansive room in five seconds flat, and then safely lead Wally and Arthur to an exit.

Breeth wondered if having her body back meant she would never save the day again.

Finally, her fingertips found the soggy wall. She felt along it until she ran into some hanging moss curtains, which she parted. Behind the moss, she found a stone door lit by fireflies. She tried the handle. It wouldn't budge.

"Let. *Go! Lady!*" Breeth said, straining to turn the handle like she was arm wrestling the old architect.

A liquid coiling made her freeze. Something was swimming through the missing parts of the carpet. Breeth's skin prickled. Her heart started to panic. She'd almost forgotten she could die now.

"*Found one!*" Wally's voice rang out in the darkness.

Breeth hustled toward him and found a rectangle of light.

Wally held open a door that led to a new hallway. "I don't get it," he told Arthur. "If she knows we're in here, why didn't she seal this door with moss or something?"

"*Because*," Arthur said, sloshing in from the other direction. "Lady Weirdwood can only control one part of the Manor at a time! The clouds in the Room of Fathers proved it. Her clouds uncovered one of the doors so she could sweep toward the one we were running toward. Why wouldn't she just block them all?"

Wally clapped him on the shoulder. "Smart."

Breeth wished Wally would clap *her* on the shoulder now that she had one.

The door led to a short corridor of bedrooms where the Wardens slept. Breeth had steered clear of this area as a ghost to avoid accidentally catching Ludwig getting dressed.

Wally slipped into one of the rooms and came out holding several paper slips. They read *Shadowrail Company* with a steam *S* for the logo. "Trackdragon tickets," he said, smiling at Breeth. "It's good we came to the opposite side of the Manor after all."

"Well, *obviously*," Breeth said, grinning like an idiot. "That's what I had planned the *whole time*."

They continued east to the end of the hall and stepped into the wide-open center of the Manor.

"Ugh," Breeth said. "*This* place."

The Bookcropolis looked less like a library and more like a labyrinthine city whose walls were replaced with countless shelves of books. The roadway aisles were made of squeaky marble, and the ceiling was forever twilit, orbited by two moons.

"How do we find our way through, Breeth?" Wally asked.

Breeth held out her arms like a weathervane. "We're in the Reach right now. If we cut through the Wilds of Wee and the Mytherlands, we can enter the north wing. Unfortunately, we'll need to work our way around Monster's Hollow. *There Be Jerkwads*."

The three wound their way through the twining stacks. Wally kept his gauntlets raised, eyes darting left and right.

"I hate books as much as the next person, Wally," Breeth said. "But they can't *hurt* you."

Wally kept his gauntlets up. "Lady Weirdwood might use them to attack us."

Breeth snorted. "You don't know Lady Weirdwood very well. She wouldn't harm a book if it crushed her pet sn—"

A book flew off the shelf and cracked Arthur in the side of the head. "*Ow!*"

"Wow, Arthur," Breeth said. "She must really be mad at you."

Wally punched the next book out of the air, but then dozens more flapped off the shelves, and came wheeling toward them like floppy bats. The kids ran through the stacks as a tornado of ruffling pages and manic tomes tried to consume them.

Breeth swatted a book away and felt a sliver of pain on her finger. "Gah! Papercut!" She hadn't missed *that* feeling either. "You know!" she said, sticking her finger in her mouth, "if I was still a ghost, then—"

"Again!" Wally screamed. "*Not helpful!*"

They reached a crossroads and came to a stop.

Wally turned in a circle. "I can't tell which way is north! Breeth?"

"I don't know! I'm sorry!" She couldn't see anything through the whirlwind of pages.

A giant tome tried to clamp onto Arthur's face, but he caught it, forced it shut, and read the title. "*Thirteen Ways to Bring Your Cat Back to Life.* Breeth, where's the Necromancy section?"

"West!"

"Brilliant, Arthur! The titles will tell us where we are!" Wally squinted through the storm of pages, then pointed. "*How to Cure Unicorn Kidney Stones!*"

"Potions!" Breeth said, and then pointed left. "That way's north!" They ran through the chaotic pages. "I never thought all that boring reading would actually amount to anything!"

They reached the northern door, but it was blocked by a gigantic flower made of shed pages. A book blossom. It unfurled its paged petals and snapped its serrated teeth.

Breeth gulped. They wouldn't survive that many papercuts.

"This way!" she yelled, leading them west.

The Bookcropolis was so torrential with pages, they couldn't see what was carved into the next door they came across. The moment they passed through it, the way behind them sealed with paper.

They stared down the plain hallway—stately lit and stuffy as a courtroom.

"Looks safe," Arthur said.

"That's what you said the last time we were in here," Wally said. He held a finger to his lips. "No one say a word."

They had only made it halfway down the corridor when the door at the far end creaked open and Sekhmet stepped out, her sword unsheathed.

She sighed. "Why am I guessing you aren't on your way to get a midnight snack?"

Wally stepped in front of the others. "I have to save Arthur, Sekhmet."

Sekhmet flipped her sword over her hand, igniting it in flames. "Then I hope you remember your training."

Wally raised his gauntlets.

Arthur placed a hand on Wally's shoulder. "I know you can't take her alone. We're here to back you up."

Breeth wanted to possess the door and smack Sekhmet in the back of the head, but she settled with, "I'll grab her legs!" Goose bumps rippled up her arms. Everything was scarier when you weren't a ghost.

Sekhmet strode down the hallway, sword flaming. It was enough to make Breeth, Arthur, and Wally back away. Wally's eyes darted to the paper-blocked door behind them, looking for some sort of escape. He looked left, then right, then up, then down.

Wally lowered his gauntlets and hooked his arms through Arthur's and Breeth's.

"I apologize in advance," he told them.

"For what?" Breeth asked.

Wally stared Sekhmet dead in the eye. "I love fighting."

With that lie, the floorboards of the Judgment Passage parted, and they all fell through.

19
SCARABS

Wally, Breeth, and Arthur landed with a wet *smack*.

They were on a muddy incline that sloped into a black pit. Overhead, giant roots snaked out of the darkness, gleaming with carapaces, which clung to the roots with their dead metal legs.

The Abyssment.

"Sorry about that," Wally said, picking himself up. "I didn't know how else to get us out of there."

Breeth, who had somehow managed to belly flop in the mud, turned herself over with a grunt. Her eyes went wide. "Oh no." She sat bolt upright and hugged herself. "Being down here was bad enough when I was a *ghost*."

Wally's gaze traveled around the chasm. "At least Lady Weirdwood can't find us down here."

"She can't save our souls from being eaten by a *maniac mushroom* either!" Arthur said, his voice muffled. For some reason, he had both hands clamped over his nose and mouth.

"Oooo*kay*," Wally said. "Breeth, where are the exits?"

Breeth pointed while trying to rub the goose bumps from

her arms. "Up three levels. But trust me when I say, that way lies a million deaths. *Gross* ones."

Wally headed toward the steps that led up from the mud pit. "We'd better get moving or else we're gonna miss the train."

"Uh-uh," Arthur said, backing away. "No way am I going up there."

"But . . ." Breeth gazed into the mud pit that descended into infinite blackness. Flapping jackal heads grinned back at her. "The monsters only get worse the deeper we go."

Arthur looked up the stairs, then down the pit; then he sat in the mud, firmly planting himself.

Sshhhhhhhhink!

A sharp sound in the distance brought him right back to his feet.

"What was that?" Wally asked, eyes wide.

"The monkey mummies must have heard us," Breeth said staring wide-eyed into the darkness. "Why didn't the Mycopath get them?"

"Because Amelia whipped off its tendrils to save *me*," Arthur said. "That's why."

Shink . . . shink . . . shink . . .

The sounds were getting closer.

"Um," Wally said, backing away. "What's a *monkey mummy?*"

"Imagine a mummified monkey," Breeth said. "Only it's the size of a barn and has scissors for fingers. And it has children."

Shinkshinkshink. Shinkshinkshink.

The sounds were multiplying.

"Oh, except the kids *ate* their mom," Breeth continued, "and now it sounds like they're all grown up."

Wally's gauntlets hung heavy on his fists. He didn't think he could take on a single Fae-born, let alone a *swarm*.

He searched the Abyssment. One way led to the slicing monkey mummies. The other to a jackal-filled mud pit. They were trapped.

"Don't worry, guys," Breeth said. "Dying's not so bad." She gulped. "Once you get used to it."

Wally was about to resign himself to a sharp, painful death when he remembered that he still hadn't solved the end of Graham's riddle.

When lost in the woods full of surprises,
Remember what a forest despises.
What once was extinguished now you stoke.
What once was exterminated now is woke.

Wally gazed up at the dead Scarabs clinging to the roots. *What once was exterminated . . .* What if Graham had never been trying to destroy the Manor? What if he'd been giving them a chance to escape?

"Climb the roots!" Wally shouted as he leapt and grabbed the tip of the nearest one.

Breeth and Arthur followed, and the three scrambled up the massive roots toward the Abyssment's cavernous ceiling. They dug their fingernails into the bark while using their legs to winch their way up. High above, Wally spotted a Scarab that had broken down the moment its pincers met the underside of the Manor's floorboards.

"Breeth! How did you and the staff stop the Scarabs?"

"I possessed Ludwig and crushed 'em to pieces!" Breeth shouted. "But before that, Amelia whipped open their wings so Ludwig could fly his paper butterflies inside!"

Shink shink shink shink shink shink.

Sounds flooded the darkness below. The creatures were so close, Wally could hear their breaths, wheezing from dozens of dusty throats.

He reached the Scarab and stuck his hand through its open carapace.

"Um, Wally?" Breeth said. "I don't want to stress you out, but they're here!"

There came a juicy sound below as the monkey mummies plunged their sharp fingernails into the roots, climbing higher and higher with terrifying agility.

Wally's fingertips sought the oily gears inside the Scarab and felt along their edges until he found the obstruction. He wrenched the scrunched paper butterfly free.

Nothing happened. Wally waited a moment. Then another. Below, the monkey mummies climbed higher and higher—*SHINK SHINK SHINK*. Panic set in.

The Scarab shrieked as its internal gears started to rotate, and the mechanical insect bucked forward, its metal jaws munching a hole straight through the floorboards.

"*Thank you, Graham,*" Wally whispered. "Breeth! Arthur! Climb up!"

They scaled up and around him just as the creatures came into view below, nails slashing, dry tongues whirling. Wally managed to climb up the Scarab's back to the floorboards, where he pulled on his gauntlets and raised his fists, ready to punch any skeletal face that showed itself.

But the Scarab seemed to smell the creatures' desiccated bones. It rotated its pincers downward and chewed one of the mummified creatures into sawdust. The other creatures saw what happened to its sibling and then, hissing, descended the roots and vanished below.

"Well, *that* was lucky," Breeth said.

"Yeah," Wally said, tossing the paper with his brother's riddle into the hole. "Lucky."

The Scarab crawled up and out of the Abyssment and then continued to chew holes through the Manor's walls, straight toward the northern passage. After it had passed through its second wall, a pair of fuzzy ears peeked around the corner.

Audrey stared at them with wide caramel eyes. "Y'all see that cockroach? *Whew!* They don't grow 'em that big where I come from."

"*Yesssssss,*" Breeth whispered to herself. "Ferret lady."

Arthur was smiling even bigger than she was.

Audrey climbed through the wreckage to join them. "Honestly, I'm glad I ran into you. After that hallway shifted, I couldn't find my way back to that old woman in the wedding dress."

"Station's this way," Wally said.

He led them through two of the Scarab's holes and then down a long passageway. It ended in an eerie platform with a single lamppost that struggled to glow behind writhing coal steam. Blazing through the darkness was a dragon-headed engine.

"*Come on*," Wally said, starting to jog as he pulled out his Trackdragon ticket. "Before Lady Weirdwood realizes we're ba—"

The hallway began stretching like taffy, making the station grow farther and farther away. They ran faster, but to no avail. They couldn't get any closer.

Breeth shoved Wally and Arthur toward the station.

"*Run!*" she said. "Audrey and I will keep Lady Weirdwood distracted!"

Wally opened his mouth to argue.

"Just *save Arthur*!" Breeth said. "You can thank me later!"

Breeth grabbed Audrey's paw and ran away from the station, screaming, "Hey! Lady Weirdwood! Look at us! We're escaping!"

A few steps later, the hallway's carpet rolled over them like a giant tongue. Breeth and Audrey screamed.

Wally's heart sank. He wanted to go back and save them, but instead he grabbed Arthur's arm and ran toward the station, balancing on the stretching hallway like a tightrope, racing to make it to the station before the passageway became thin as a thread.

They leapt onto the station platform. Wally nearly collapsed to the ground, but Arthur spotted the conductor and immediately turned on the charm.

"Evening!" he said, breathing heavy, as if they were running just to catch the train. "The Wardens are sending us Novitiates on a special mission. We can't tell if we're more nervous or excited."

The conductor took the tickets, clearly uninterested in their reason for boarding.

Wally had planned to hide in the luggage compartment so the Wardens wouldn't see them. But Willa, Cadence, Sekhmet, and her parents were nowhere to be seen.

As they boarded the Trackdragon, Wally stared past the platform and down the hallway, trying to assure himself that Lady Weirdwood would never hurt Breeth . . . and wishing he believed it.

20
THE HOUSE OF SPIRITS

Arthur and Wally stepped out of an alley and into a hazy Kingsport day. The city was as gray as winter even though it was June. The sky was ash-streaked and infested with seagulls, and the rooftops were greasy with rain. Arthur tried breathing in the fresh ocean air, but all he smelled was drainage from the fish factory.

A steamy snarl turned them around, and they watched as the Trackdragon's tail caboose whipped under the dock and vanished into the waves.

"I guess that's it, then," Wally said. "No more Weirdwood."

Arthur's heart clenched. It was his fault that his best friend had lost his place as a Novitiate and would have to return to a life of thieving. Kingsport would no longer be something to save but to plunder. He wanted to tell Wally that they would return to the Manor someday. That they'd both become Novitiates and then Wardens together. That Wally would finally tap into his magic.

But if Arthur had learned anything, it was that delivering heroic proclamations did not make them come true.

He put his arm around his friend's shoulder. "Thanks for saving my life, Wally."

Wally patted his hand. "Don't mention it."

"Let's get lunch, eh? On me. Harry owes me money."

They left the docks and took a back-alley route to the Wretch and the slumped tenements they had once called home. Compared to the wonders they'd seen in the Fae, the collapsing building looked almost quaint now, the scowling cutthroats that haunted the front stairs as harmless as buzzing flies. Wally slipped on his gauntlets so no one would mess with them as they scaled the collapsing steps and entered the splintered doorway.

The inside of the tenements smelled of ale and dust, old mattresses and sickness. The boys climbed to the fourth floor and took the second hallway to the last door on the right, the one with peeling yellow paint.

Arthur gave a special knock. "Get decent, Harry! We've got company!" When no answer came, Arthur opened the door into a waft of clean-smelling steam. Harry stood shirtless in front of the mirror, humming a pleasant tune and trimming his nose hairs.

"Harry!" Arthur said. "Put a shirt on! And if you don't have one, sweep up that nose hair and start knitting."

Harry jerked around, his face clean-shaven, spots of shaving cream and blood dotting his face. "*Arthur*," he said with heartwarming relief. "You're *alive!*" But the moment he saw that his son was in perfect health and well-dressed, he scowled and pointed his tweezers at him. "Where in unholy *blazes* have you been?"

"Long story," Arthur answered. "Cooper and I would love to tell you over the stew and rolls you owe me."

Harry set the razor on the sink, rubbed his face clean, then grabbed his fanciest shirt. "No time for food now, son. We're headed downtown."

He struggled to button his buttons, and Arthur noticed his father's fingers were shaking.

"Is the landlord taking us to court again?" Arthur said, stepping up and buttoning his dad's shirt for him. "Because we paid three months in *advance*. Granted that was six months ago, but—"

"*Son.*"

Harry gathered Arthur's hands in his, making Arthur slightly uncomfortable.

"How do I say this . . ." Harry searched Arthur's eyes. "Your mother. She's come back."

Arthur pulled his hands away from Harry's. "What?" He smelled the air for telltale signs of alcohol. But all he smelled was tooth powder.

"It's true," Harry said. "I didn't believe it myself at first, but then Hank saw his mother down there, and Mickey saw her husband. He was in the mine when it collapsed. That's why I'm getting myself all fancy." He looked in the mirror and swiped a bit of shaving cream from his ear. "I'm a little rusty."

"Dad . . ." Arthur's head moved slowly back and forth. "Mom's dead. She's been gone for *four* years. She can't just *be back*."

"But she *is*, son," Harry said. "She is." He pointed at Wally.

"And your parents will be there too. Everybody who ever died in this cursed city is waiting for us downtown!"

Wally looked too shocked to respond.

Harry stepped to the dirty window and peered out. "They say it's on Fortune-Teller's Alley. The miracle. In a place called the House of Spirits. I heard there's a line that'd make a *monk* weep." He stared down at the holes in his socks. "But I'd stand in line for a year to see your mother again."

Arthur backed away toward the door. If Harry raised his hopes any higher, he feared his heart might shatter.

"Come on, Cooper," Arthur said. "Let's get out of here."

Harry waved a towel after them. "I'll finish getting ready, then meet you boys on Fortune-Teller's Alley! There's nothing to be afraid of! You'll see!" He chuckled gleefully as Arthur shut the door. "You'll see!"

The boys hustled down the hallway toward the splintered stairs and out into the gray morning.

"Well, it's official," Arthur said. "Harry's lost it."

"Arthur," Wally said. "Lady Weirdwood said a Rift opened in Kingsport. That's why the Trackdragon came here."

"Rifts don't bring back the dead, Wally," Arthur said, heading west on Center Street. "The Rook proved that when he tried to bring back Liza's mom."

"Then where are you going?"

Arthur threw an arm around Wally's shoulder. "What sort of ex-magician gentlemen thieves would we be if we didn't at least investigate?"

What he didn't tell Wally was that the expression on Harry's face had been so content—so *convinced* that his mother was still alive—that Arthur had to see what was happening for himself.

***

Fortune-Teller's Alley was packed with crowds, which overflowed onto Center Street. Thousands of people were lined up before an unassuming three-story building, beneath a sign hastily painted *THE HOWSE OF SPIRUTS*. Arthur and Wally slipped through the crowd, trying to get a better look.

"It's all poppycock!" a woman shouted from the fringes. "I stood in that line till my toes bled, and I didn't see *nothin'* behind that old curtain but cobwebs and an old ballet slipper!"

"Smoke and mirrors, you gullible sods!" a man shouted.

The crowd turned their backs on the disbelievers. They rumbled and shifted like ocean waves, desperate to break through the House of Spirits' front door. And they might have tried were it not for the rusty-toothed man guarding it.

"*Rustmouth*," Arthur and Wally said at the same time.

"We gots sights for sour eyes!" Rustmouth said. "For less than a month's wages no less!" He plucked a bill from a well-dressed gentleman at the front of the line. "You won't be regrettive, sir."

He opened the door for the gentleman, and the crowd tried to steal a peek inside. The door shut again, and they groaned in disappointment.

"This is just like the Fae-Born zoo," Wally said. "Only they're selling tickets to . . . the *dead*."

"That's what they're saying, anyway," Arthur said. "At least I know Harry's still playing with a full deck."

As the boys tried to squeeze their way closer through the ever-tightening crowd, a hush fell over the alley. A well-dressed woman stepped out of the House of the Spirits. She held her hat in her hands and looked as if she'd seen a ghost.

She blinked at the expectant crowd. *"She was real,"* she said quietly. A smile spread across her face as she threw her hat into the air and screamed. "My sister was real!"

The crowd erupted in cheers while the nonbelievers booed. The well-dressed woman quickly worked her way back through the line and rejoined the end.

"We gotta get in there," Arthur said.

"Right behind ya," Wally said.

They pushed through the line, ignoring the shouts of "Hey!" and "No cutting!"

Arthur recognized someone toward the front and waved his hand in the air. "Mrs. Blythe! Remember me? I wrote the eulogy for your son!"

The woman smiled at him. "And a right memorable one it was," she said, then jabbed her umbrella at his chest. "Now get to the back of the line before I *stick* ya."

More people started hissing and heckling, some even threw food, until Wally and Arthur retreated to the back of the crowd.

"Great," Wally said. "We'll be waiting in line till next week."

Arthur snorted. "Cooper, you've been following rules in that Manor too long." He tilted Wally's head back and pointed to an open window on the third floor of the building. "It's time we returned to our thieving days."

***

They made their move at nightfall. It was simply a matter of scaling the building on the other side of the alley, shimmying across a plank that extended high over the crowd, jumping a gap, picking open a caged gate, and finally slipping over the lip of the roof through the window of the House of the Spirits.

They found themselves in a small room filled with cob-webbed sewing machines and dusty mannequins fancily dressed. There was a wardrobe in one corner and in another a rack that held hats for gentlemen. They crept out of the room and heard distinct sounds emanating from behind the door across the hallway—clucking snores, whistling breaths.

Wally gazed through the keyhole. "Well, Arthur. Looks like you might have a chance to make amends."

Arthur peeked through the keyhole, and his heart nearly broke at the sight. Inside were the Dapplewood citizens: a duck, a mouse, a badger with a badge, a chickadee, an aproned hedgehog, a shabbily dressed fox, and a small bunny with a vest. Those who weren't sleeping sat miserable, muzzles and beaks hanging heavy. Claws, paws, wings, and webbed feet were all locked in chains.

"I don't get it," Wally said. "Why didn't the Order stick them in a zoo?"

Arthur remembered the strange storm cloud city. "It's like Lady Weirdwood said. They must have found something better that caught their attention."

Wally took out his lock pick, but Arthur stayed his hand.

"We should investigate the lower floors first. I don't want any of these critters getting hurt."

They continued down to the second floor and found a different set of stairs at the other end of the hallway. Before they reached them, they heard noises behind another door—a girl's voice . . . and what sounded like *static*.

Arthur pressed his ear to the door.

"If you or any of those freaks downstairs come within five feet of me, I'll add a *k* to the *Roo* in my notebook. I'll fly away, and you'll never see this Quill again."

Arthur's eyes went wide. He looked at Wally and mouthed, *Liza*.

The static sound returned. It hissed and popped and squealed, like someone was trying to find a clear signal on the radio. The boys gave each other uncertain looks.

Arthur peeked through the keyhole, but all he could see was the blur of his eyelashes and Liza, who held a strange listening device to her ear.

"If that really is the afterlife behind that curtain," Liza said, "then why isn't my mother there? I've seen dozens of Kingsport's dead. But not her. Why?"

Strange, Arthur thought, remembering the disbelievers. Why would some of Kingsport's citizens believe they'd seen their dearly departed but others didn't?

The radio started to tune again—*crackle*, *spit*, *shriek*—and Arthur's nerves went cold. That wasn't a radio. It was someone's *voice*. He shifted his eye and realized that the blur wasn't from his eyelashes. It had a human shape.

"Well, figure it out," Liza said. "Otherwise, I'll find someone else who can help me find my mom. I'm sure plenty of people would love to get their hands on this Quill."

So, Liza was making a deal with the Order. Her mother in exchange for the claw Quill. Arthur wanted to kick down the door and tell Liza not to hand it over under any circumstances. But he was afraid of the blurred shape.

Wally tapped him on the shoulder and gestured that they should get going before they were caught. Arthur followed him to the top of the stairs.

"That's the answer," Wally said. "The Order is creating fake spirits with the Quill."

Arthur shook his head. "I told you. The Rook *tried* that. It doesn't work. All he could make was a creepy wax imitation. Can you imagine what horrific monstrosity Rustmouth would make? A *revoltergeist* or something."

"Good point," Wally said.

"Besides," Arthur said, "Liza just told that staticky radio thing, whatever it was—"

"The Eraser," Wally said with fear in his eyes.

"The Eraser?" Arthur shuddered at the nothingness he'd just seen. "What is it?"

"A Void," Wally said. "A hole where a storybook character once existed. But not even Lady Weirdwood knows how it's moving around."

Arthur's thoughts spiraled down a dark drain of possibilities, but he gave his head a shake. "Liza told the *Eraser* that she wouldn't turn the Quill over unless they could produce her mom's spirit. I don't know how the Order found Liza, and I don't know what's downstairs, but they must have promised her something big in exchange for that Quill."

The boys stared down the shadowy staircase. What answers awaited at the bottom?

"I'm right beside ya, Arthur," Wally said.

They descended the stairs to the first floor, which had an L-shaped hallway. Candles flickered against the blue flower wallpaper. At the short end of the hall was the front entrance. Rustmouth's silhouette stood crooked in the door's fogged window.

"Settle down, the lot o' ya! Otherwhiles, my friend the Astonishment'll come out here, and you'll be disposaled of propermanently!"

Arthur and Wally crept to the hallway's corner and peered around it down the longer corridor. The Astonishment stood guard before a door, stony arms crossed over her chest.

"How do we get past her?" Wally said. "We don't have any tickets. And the moment one customer leaves, the next comes in right after."

Arthur smiled. He hurried back around the corner, up two flights of steps, and then returned with two top hats and jackets from the third-floor room they'd first entered. "Hope I found one in your size."

Wally put them on without asking questions. Arthur had never felt so flattered.

They hid in the shadow at the top of the staircase until the previous customer rounded the corner, mumbling to himself. "*Three* years since I buried Mother, and all she wants to know is if I've watered her bloody *gardenias*. Well, I'm going straight home and throwing those gardenias in the *trash*. That's what *I'm* gonna do."

The front door creaked open again. "You'll find my intimidazing partner 'round that corner, misseses," Rustmouth said to a pair of newcomers. "Don't be cockled by her appearage. Just give her your tickets."

When the door clicked shut, the two women found two boys in top hats and tails waiting for them.

"Good *evening*, ladies," Arthur said bowing deeply and sweeping off his hat.

Wally quickly did the same.

Arthur gave a low whistle as he looked the women up and down. "Are you visiting a *queen's* spirit this evening? You're dressed to the *nineties*!"

The older woman smiled. "We were hoping you have *pets* behind that curtain." She placed a hand on the younger woman's shoulder. "See, my daughter and I have lost quite a few over the years. Fluffy. Taffy. Snarky."

"*Quicky*," the daughter added.

"We'd just like to give each of them a little *scritch* under the collar," the mother said.

"Of *course*," Arthur said. "There's a whole *kennel-full* of fuzzy relatives waiting just for you. They've been panting about it all day." He gestured up the stairs. "If you'll just provide us with your tickets, you can head on up."

The daughter's smile quickly vanished. "The man outside told us to go down the hallway and around the corner!"

"*Shh, shh, shh*," Arthur said, checking the silhouette in the fogged window to make sure Rustmouth hadn't heard. "We don't want to disturb the spirits."

The mother quickly covered her mouth. The daughter folded her arms.

Arthur leaned in close to the women and whispered conspiratorially, "The instructions we give outside are merely a security measure to keep any loonies from trying to sneak in. Why, not one hour ago we had two thieves sneak through a third-floor window. Had to throw them out on their behinds."

The mother looked convinced, but the daughter remained skeptical. She noticed Wally's gauntlets clacking at his hip, but Wally quickly swept them behind his jacket.

Again, Arthur gestured upstairs. The mother headed up and the daughter, sighing, followed.

"Third floor," Arthur said. "Last door on your right. Enter, and then sit perfectly still in the darkness until Buffy and Flarky and all the others come bounding into the room. Be patient. It can take a while."

"I do hope Taffy hasn't been peeing all over the fancy upholstery in the hereafter," the mother said as the two women faded into the shadows of the second floor.

Arthur and Wally headed down the hallway, two tickets in hand.

"I feel kinda bad," Wally said, smiling. "But it's always a pleasure to watch you work, Arthur."

"Couldn't have done it without your convincing performance, my friend," Arthur said.

They rounded the corner and approached the Astonishment, who stood as still as a scowling statue. Wally turned his nose toward the floor, keeping his face covered by his hat.

"Here you go, ma'am," Arthur said, handing over the tickets while covering his face with one sleeve. "Apologies. All this dust."

A stone hand reached out and took them, and then Arthur and Wally were inside.

21
BEHIND THE CURTAIN

On the other side of the door was a chair and a desk and a frail woman with a sickly smile. Wally kept his nose turned down. Just the sight of Silver Tongue made his fists tingle. Like any moment they would betray him and start punching him in the face.

"Whaddaya call your dead, darlins'?" Silver Tongue asked in her sugar-cracked voice.

Arthur swallowed. "Margery Benton."

Wally kept his head down and lowered his voice. "Beatrice and Omar Cooper."

Silver Tongue spun around in her chair. "I can't promise they'll show, spirits bein' unpredictable and all, but we'll give it a shot!"

Wally peeked up as the woman stuck her head through the dingy orange curtains that covered the back wall.

"*Hey!*" she shouted. "Is there a Margery, an Omar, and a Beatrix back there?"

It all felt so cheap and ridiculous that Wally nearly laughed.

He quickly lowered his face again as Silver Tongue dropped the curtains.

"They're comin'," she said, as if Wally and Arthur had just ordered sandwiches. "Your tickets are good for *ten minutes*, and not a millisecond more. And your loved ones *must remain in this room*. No trying to break 'em out or else my stone friend'll come in here and cave your little heads in." She rolled her chair toward the corner of the room. "I'll give you some privacy." She turned to the corner and started filing her nails.

Wally and Arthur looked at each other and then stared at the orange curtains, waiting to see what would or wouldn't happen next. The curtains were still for a moment, but then billowed forward, revealing a swirling gray light.

"I . . . I've seen that place," Arthur whispered. "On my journey through the Fae."

Wally only stared.

Three figures formed in the hazy cloud light. At first, they were as formless as falling rain, but as they grew closer, they developed depth and definition. As the figures stepped through the curtain, they looked . . . human.

Wally took a step forward as Arthur took a step back.

"*Mom?*" Wally whispered. "*Dad?*"

The woman covered her mouth, then wiped the tears from her eyes. She stepped up to him and ran a finger down his cheek. "Hello, my sweet baby Wally."

Wally tried to speak, but words failed him. He threw his arms around his parents and buried his face between their shoulders. Only once he was completely convinced that they

were solid and breathing and wouldn't evaporate into cloud stuff did he pull back.

Wally took in his mom's features. Her smile. Her hair. The crow's feet in the corners of her eyes. He never had to worry about memories of her wilting away again. She could make him pancakes again.

"I barely recognized you!" Wally's father said, giving his chin a pinch. "You're near as big as your old man!"

His dad's features blurred in Wally's tears. His wrinkled eyes. His tilted smile. The bad haircut he'd insisted on giving himself.

Wally looked in the middle of the room to see if Arthur was witnessing the same miracle he was. Arthur stared at his mom, arms folded tight across his chest. He didn't look happy to see her. His mother looked like him but with longer hair. She had his smile, but the witty sarcasm in his eyes was replaced with a soft kindness in hers. She held her hands out to Arthur for a hug, but Arthur didn't budge.

"Where's your brother?" Wally's mom asked, her eyes searching the door.

His dad chuckled. "I'm not sure I want to see him! He's probably bigger than me!"

"Graham is . . ." Wally's voice stopped, unsure how to explain it. "He has powers. He can see into the future. In fact, he knew that you two were going to . . . That when the Pox came it would—"

"*Shh shh shh*," his mom said. "You don't have to say it now. We'll find your brother, and then we'll all be together again."

Wally smiled so big it hurt. He didn't have to worry about making a living as a sneak thief. He didn't need to master any magic. Wally could finally be a kid again.

"*Five minutes*," Silver Tongue blurted out in the corner, still filing her nails.

Wally swallowed. He didn't want this moment to end. He gazed through the curtain into the infinite swirl of gray.

"Do you have to go back?" Wally asked his parents.

His parents looked at each other, then back toward the curtain. Wally felt a hand on his shoulder.

"Cooper?" Arthur said. He was pale as a sheet. "May I speak to you a moment?"

Wally pulled away from him. "We only have five minutes."

"It's an *emergency*," Arthur said.

"*Go*," Wally's mom said, giving his hand a squeeze. "We'll be right here."

Wally let himself be dragged to the corner opposite Silver Tongue.

"Those aren't our parents," Arthur whispered.

Wally crossed his arms. "I think I'd know my own mom and dad, Arthur."

But a pressure was building in his head. Something wasn't right. Wally tried to push the feeling away.

"I may not know magic," Arthur said, "but I know enough about fiction to spot a lie from a mile away." He nodded to the woman behind the desk. "That woman is not my mom. She's smiling too much. As much as I would *want* her to smile. See? She might as well be made of *wax*."

Wally glanced at Arthur's mom, whose grin looked plastered on her face. Almost like a mannequin. But then he looked at his own parents, whose smiles melted Wally's heart.

"Yeah, well," Wally said, "my parents look exactly the way they did when I last saw them, so—"

He tried to take a step toward his parents but stopped when Arthur touched his arm.

"Wally. *Listen.* I don't know what's going on. Those people might look like your parents. They might talk like them—"

They even smell *like them*, Wally thought. Her like wool and the minty oil of the tooth powder factory. Him like sawdust and lye soap.

"*—but that's not them*," Arthur said.

Wally's fists clenched. He stared at the cheap orange curtain and the swirling gray light behind it. Everything he'd learned back in the Manor told him that he was looking at a Rift. That the figures in this room were nothing but Fae-born, sprung from someone's imagination. But who would have created them? Not Graham. He couldn't draw that much detail. And certainly not Wally. He didn't have a creative bone in his body. No one else knew their parents this well.

"You said yourself that the Rook tried and failed to make a convincing copy of his wife," Wally said, trying to keep his voice from trembling. "So how are my parents standing right there?"

"I don't think they are," Arthur said.

Wally's jaw clenched. *"You don't understand."*

"What it's like to lose a *parent*?" Arthur hissed. *"Of course I do! I want to see my mom again more than anything in the world. My real mom. Not some trick the Order conjured."*

Wally grabbed Arthur by the shirt and pressed him against the wall. *"No,"* he hissed. "You don't understand what it's like to lose *both* parents. You still have Harry. I'm an *orphan*, Arthur. I don't have any family left. Even my own *brother* ran off into the Fae somewhere. I almost had a new family in the Manor. Breeth and Sekhmet and Lady Weirdwood. But I lost them the moment I decided to save *you*."

In the corner, Silver Tongue gave an exaggerated yawn. "Two minutes!"

Wally realized his hands were shaking with rage. And Arthur wasn't putting up a fight. He released Arthur's shirt and looked at his parents, smiling, waiting for him to come back.

"You know what I think? I think it doesn't matter if those

are my mom and dad or not. Because they have all of their traits, and they love me. So, I'm going to spend every last moment with them that I can. And if I can't bring them home with me, then I'll go outside and get back in line and keep coming back until I find a way to sneak them out of here."

Wally took a step toward his parents.

"*Wally*," Arthur said.

Wally stopped.

"What if this is the kind of thing the Manor is trying to protect us against?"

Wally turned to look at him. "What if it's what the Manor is keeping us from?"

There was a commotion outside. "We want to see our puppers!"

"We gave our tickets to two boys in ill-fitting suits, and they sent us *upstairs*. There's nothing up there but cobwebs and lace! I want to see my Sparky, *now*!"

"Astonishment?" Rustmouth said right outside the door. "You wouldn't happen to have accepted two filthified urchins in place of these gentlerwomen, would ya?"

A stone grumbled in response.

The door handle started to turn, but Arthur lunged and quickly locked it.

Wham!

He and Wally backed away as a heavy fist struck the door, knocking free a few splinters. In the corner, Silver Tongue spun her chair around to see what was happening.

"Hey!" she said, squinting at Wally with her colorless eyes. "I know *you*."

She pulled the flask from her belt as the door started to splinter in earnest.

"Mom! Dad!" Wally shouted. "Get behind the curtain! I'll come find you!"

They and Arthur's mom hustled into the gray cloud swirl. Wally yanked his gauntlets from his belt loop and sprinted toward the window to throw them outside before Silver Tongue could speak.

But just as he was about to wrench the window open—

"Stop!"

—the silvery word shrieked in his ears, freezing his limbs.

"Turn around."

Wally's feet followed the command.

"Gooooood." Silver Tongue smiled her blue lips. "Now," she said, and nodded toward Arthur. *"Kill your friend."*

22
LETTING GO

After being rolled in a rug as tight as twins in a womb, Breeth and Audrey were squeezed through the rooty in-between of the Manor's walls before being spat out into the Throne Room, right in front of Lady Weirdwood.

"Quick, Audrey!" Breeth said, leaping to her feet. "Claw the old lady's eyes out! I'll kick open the door!"

Lady Weirdwood chuckled. "There's no need to *claw my eyes out*. I'm not going to hurt you, and you're not in trouble."

"Don't believe a word she says!" Breeth told Audrey. "Why aren't your claws out?"

Audrey looked at the old woman sitting on her waxen throne. "I don't scratch old ladies on principle."

"I never intended to hurt any of you," Lady Weirdwood said. "*Least* of all Arthur."

"You *sure* about that?" Breeth said, showing her papercut.

Lady Weirdwood nodded toward the Throne Room door. "I knew you all were listening when I told Amelia I'd be turning Arthur over to the dragons. But I can assure you that every word I said was nothing but theatrics. The dragons have a leaf dome that's able to draw memories from a person's mind. If they ask me why Arthur isn't here, I can honestly show them that I tried to hand over their prize."

"*Wait a minute*," Breeth said. "We were never in any danger at all? You just scared the ever-loving shivers out of us as a part of a *performance*?"

"Yes," Lady Weirdwood said.

Breeth let her arms flop to her sides. "That's hilarious."

"Wait," Audrey said. "What if the dragons see *this* memory?"

"They would have to know to ask about it," Lady Weirdwood said. "It's not likely."

Breeth sat on the floor crisscross applesauce. "Well, that was a fun, pointless adventure."

"Don't get too comfortable, Breeth," Lady Weirdwood said. "There's a Rift in Kingsport, and it's spreading like gangrene. The Order is selling tickets to commune with what look like *spirits*, telling people they've discovered an opening to the *afterlife*."

Breeth felt a stirring within and her face lit up.

"It's not real, Breeth," Lady Weirdwood said kindly. "I don't know what pocket-world the Order has found—full of stormclouds and rainy spirits. But as I told Rose in the smithy, there's only one way to reach the afterlife: and that's through death."

The stirring in Breeth died away. *Sometimes not even then*, she thought.

"But that's the least of our concerns right now," Lady Weirdwood continued. "Kingsport is dangerously close to falling into Daymare."

Breeth leapt to her feet. "Well, what are we waiting for? We gotta go save Wally and Arthur!"

"*You*, young lady," Lady Weirdwood said, "are human now and just as vulnerable as the rest of us. *More* so, since you've never studied magic. You're staying here."

"*Waaaiiiit*," Breeth said. "Is this one of those times where you're telling me *not* to go and save Arthur and Wally's lives because the dragons might be watching this in the future, but really you actually want me to? Wink if yes."

***

Two minutes later, Breeth and Audrey were locked in Wally's Moon Tower room.

Breeth sat on the bed, eyes shut, teeth clenched, fists squeezed. "*Rrrrrrrrrrrrrrrrrrrr.*"

"Well, if that isn't the most unladylike sound I've ever heard . . . ," Audrey said. "What on earth are you doing?"

Breeth scrunched up her face tighter. "Trying . . . to . . . *die*."

"You're *what*?"

Breeth released her tension with an exasperated sigh. "I'll be *fine*. If Lady Weirdwood won't let me help, I'm just gonna leave my body, go save Wally and Arthur real quick, then return here and slip it back on."

"*Oh*," Audrey said sarcastically. "Well, when you put it *that* way."

Breeth scrunched up her face as if she were trying to break a brick with her bare hands. Meanwhile, outside the window, the color of the horizon shifted. A pink sunset was replaced with an ashen sky and the hazy outline of a bustling port city.

"*Rrg!*" Frustrated, Breeth stood and paced the room. "Amelia told me that in order to release from my body, I needed to just . . . *let go*."

"Let go of *what*?" Audrey asked. "Bones? Muscles? The will to live?"

"*Anger*. See, I got murdered once." She lifted the side of her shirt and showed Audrey the scar.

Audrey's eyes went wide. "Who killed you?"

"A blacksmith named Rose." Breeth wrinkled her nose at the ceiling. "Her ghost is traveling through these walls somewhere."

Audrey looked up and hugged herself. "That's . . . off-putting."

"I have to find a way to forgive Rose for murdering me," Breeth said, and flopped on Wally's bed. "Which, y'know, is *impossible*."

Audrey sat next to her. "Ain't no harm in trying, sugar."

Breeth squished her eyes shut again, trying to focus.

"Hey," Audrey said, poking Breeth's nose with her claw and releasing the tension. "Forgiveness isn't like lifting a piano. It's more a relaxing. Hating someone is a lot more strenuous than forgiving them."

The thought made Breeth's muscles relax a little. "How did you forgive Arthur so easily after what he did to the Dapplewood?"

The ferret stared at her paws. "It wasn't his fault that

some *vermin* followed him to my little village. You can't go blaming everyone with good intentions, otherwise we're all doomed."

Breeth sat upright. "But Rose *did* mean to kill me."

Audrey took Breeth's hands in her paws. Breeth tried not to enjoy the way they tickled in this somber moment.

"Sometimes we have to learn to forgive," Audrey said. "Even when that person is undeserving of forgiveness. If not for their sake, then for our own well-being."

A lonely wind sailed in from the sea, making the Manor creak. Audrey's words sounded nice, but Breeth still didn't know how to start forgiving.

"Why did Rose do it?" Audrey asked.

Breeth's muscles tensed again. "Because she's a heartless, no-good, spirit-thieving, child-hating, evil piece of—"

Audrey laid a paw on Breeth's arm. "There had to have been a *reason*. Most people don't just go killin' for fun."

Breeth tried to clear the snarling thoughts from her mind. She remembered the conversation in the smithy where she'd wanted to punch Rose so badly, she'd barely listened to what she was saying.

"Rose killed me because . . ."

Breeth started to tremble, and Audrey combed her hair with her claws to soothe her.

Breeth remembered the blacksmith's rough voice, speaking with Breeth's own lips.

"Because . . . because . . . she wanted to see her little boy again." The tension melted from her shoulders. "*Max*. That was his name. She wanted him to have a chance to see the wonders of the world. And if she was going to bring him back to life, then . . ."

"Then what?" Audrey asked.

Breeth looked at the whorls in the ceiling. "Then she was willing to do anything for the person she loved most in the world."

And with that, Breeth dropped dead to the floor.

Audrey, clearly not used to seeing people die, fell to her knees and shook Breeth's shoulders. "Breeth? *Breeth?*"

Breeth was in the floorboards. She watched with knotted eyes as Audrey frantically pressed her paw to Breeth's lifeless wrist, feeling for a pulse.

"Breeth, how do I know if you're okay?" Audrey asked. "Can't you give me some kind of sign?"

"*BOO!*" Breeth seeped back into her body and sprang to life, scaring Audrey so badly she screamed and fell back on her tail.

Audrey growled. "You nearly made me wet the floor!"

"You did it, Audrey!" Breeth cried. She leapt up, seized the ferret's paws, and spun her in circles. "Amelia was all stuffy about it! But you found the perfect words to kill me!"

Audrey tried to smile. "I'm very happy you died, Breeth. But could we stop spinning? I'm gonna be sick."

Breeth released Audrey, who nearly crashed into the wall.

"I thought dying again would be scary!" Breeth said. "But I can just slip my body back on anytime I want, like a glove!" She lay on the floor and then seeped in and out of herself. "Alive! *Dead.* Alive! *Dead.*"

Audrey laughed uncertainly.

Breeth became alive again and sat up. "I'm going to go save my friends!"

She stared at her hands. While she was gone, her body would be vulnerable—open for Rose to come take up residence again.

Breeth took Audrey's paws. "I need you to stay here and keep an eye on me for me, just in case Rose tries to get into my body."

Audrey pulled her paws away. "Wait, *what*?"

"I forgive her for killing me," Breeth said. "But she still wants to see her kid, so she might try and steal this body back." She shot the ceiling a searing look. "She's *sneaky* like that."

"I'm not worried about the reasons *why*, darlin'. I'm worried about *how* I'm supposed to keep your empty body safe from a *ghost*."

"Just keep it away from *organic materials*," Breeth said.

Audrey glanced around the wooden room, at the cotton sheets on the bed. "How on earth am I supposed to—"

"You're smart! I'm sure you'll figure it out." Breeth flopped down on the bed and hugged herself. "Well, body. If this is the last time, it's been good." She shook the numb feeling out of her fingers. "*Whew!* Okay. Gonna save my friends. Here we go." She closed her eyes, relaxed her face, and promptly died again.

23
THE ERASER

Wally circled Arthur, gauntlets dripping with his friend's blood.

Silver Tongue stood on the desk, hissing silvery commands. *"Again!"*

Wally strained against his own muscles, but his fist swept forward, striking Arthur in the mouth. Silver Tongue cackled. The door splintered again as the Astonishment tried to break in.

"I'm sorry, Arthur," Wally told his friend. "I'm so, so sorry."

Arthur spat blood onto the floor and smiled. "I'm just glad you're not stronger, Cooper." His voice was beaten, exhausted. "Otherwise I'd *really* be in trouble."

Wally couldn't laugh. Arthur was doing his best to deflect the blows with his arms, but the gauntlets were made of metal.

"Hit him harder!" Silver Tongue squealed.

Wally's fist obeyed, knocking Arthur to the ground. Wally's fists throbbed with fury while his heart broke.

Silver Tongue coughed wetly into her hand, looked at the spray of blood on her palm, and sighed. "This stuff'll be the death of me," she said in a non-silvery voice. She jutted out her bottom lip, giving Wally a pouty face. "Time to say good-bye to your friend."

As she tipped the flask to her lips, Wally tried to shake off his gauntlets, but his fists remained poised, casting a shadow over Arthur's beaten face. This was it. She was going to make Wally kill his friend. And there was nothing he could do about it.

Strangely, Arthur didn't seem too bothered by the idea. In fact, a smile crept across his lips into a full bloody-toothed *grin*.

"Hey, lady," he said to Silver Tongue. "Before you make my friend kill me . . ." He nodded to the flask in her hand. "Is that a belt flask or just a regular one?"

Silver Tongue swallowed the liquid, then gave him a questioning look. "*Belt flask.*"

Wally found his fists obeying the command, pulling him across the room where he belted the flask right out of her hand. The flask exploded in a hundred pieces. The silver liquid splashed onto the floor. Silver Tongue cried out and fell to her knees, desperately trying to scoop up what was left. But the mercurial fluid seeped away between the board slats.

"That was a nasty, *filthy* trick!" she said, backing toward the splintering door. "You think you're *so clever*. But there's more silver stuff where that came from."

She opened the door, and the Astonishment came at Arthur and Wally like a rockslide. Wally raised his gauntlets while the stone woman raised her boulder-sized fists, ready to cave in the boys' heads. But before she could bring them crushing down, a single board popped loose from the ceiling and broke itself over the Astonishment's face.

The blow was enough to knock any human unconscious. But the Astonishment rubbed her cheek and frowned up, annoyed. Arthur gave the ceiling a confused look.

"*Breeth!*" Wally said, smiling at the familiar face above them. "Where's your body?"

"Being guarded by a trustworthy ferret!" she yelled back. She scowled down at the Astonishment. "How do you hurt a *rock*?"

Another board came loose from the ceiling, swinging like a baseball bat and cracking the Astonishment right in the ear. It, too, buckled as harmless as a toothpick. The Astonishment searched the ceiling for the culprit. And that's when the floorboards beneath her feet broke in half, snapping shut like a bear trap and locking the stone woman in place.

"Nice, Breeth!" Arthur said to a random floorboard.

Silver Tongue was nowhere to be seen, having slipped down the hall, which echoed with drums and Rustmouth's screams. "Bring it on, *Snoredens!*"

Wally felt a lifting in his chest. "The Wardens are here!"

Arthur took a step back. "To take me to the dragons."

"Oh!" Breeth said. "About that."

She told Wally about the dragons' leafy memory dome and why Lady Weirdwood had no choice but to scare the dickens out of Arthur.

Wally smiled. No wonder Lady Weirdwood had sounded so heartless. No wonder Sekhmet hadn't immediately slapped magma manacles on them when she'd caught them in the hallway. And no wonder there were no Wardens on the Trackdragon.

Wally hadn't even noticed how strange it was that Lady Weirdwood had summoned a Trackdragon instead of simply opening one of the Manor's doors onto Kingsport. She had been giving him and Arthur an *escape*.

A wave of relief washed over Wally so complete it almost brought tears to his eyes. He didn't have to be a thief. He could return to the Manor with a clean conscience.

"What's wrong?" Arthur said.

"Nothing at all," Wally said. He explained what had happened.

"You mean . . . she *didn't* want to kill me?" Arthur laughed in relief. "That old woman's talents are wasted as an architect. She should be in the theater!"

The boys ran down the hall and peered around the corner just as the Wardens broke through the front door. Linus's sword sparkled with green fireworks. Cadence's drums rattled the walls. Willa's kites whirled like knives.

Rustmouth blocked the hallway with his body. He breathed his putrid, rusted breath into the air, shriveling Willa's kites before catching one of Linus's swords in his teeth and crunching through it like bone meal. Cadence lifted his drumsticks, but then froze when a silvery voice called out from the stairs.

"Don't play on your drum, silly! Play on your head!"

Cadence started to beat himself with his own drumsticks while Willa unfolded more kites from beneath her moth wings. The kites dive-bombed toward a shrieking Silver

Tongue, lashing at her with their sharp edges, while Linus unsheathed a copper dagger from his belt and swung it at Rustmouth, making him retreat. The Wardens pursued him down the hall.

"*Astonishment?*" Rustmouth screamed over his shoulder. "We could use some assisterance!"

Back in the spirit room, the Astonishment strained against Breeth's wooden trap, making it splinter.

"Breeth?" Wally whispered to the ceiling. "Can you help the Wardens take care of Silver Tongue and Rustmouth? We'll keep an eye on the Astonishment."

"Uh, *yeah I can*!" Breeth said. "Man, does it feel good to be a ghost again!"

She rippled the ceiling like piano keys and headed down the hall—but then froze halfway to the entrance.

"What?" Wally whispered. "What is it?"

Breeth didn't answer. Her knotted eyes gazed toward the front door.

Silver Tongue was cackling. "Get 'em, Mr. 'Raser!"

A shape was coming down the stairs. Wally's eyes saw it, but it wouldn't quite fit in his mind. It didn't look like a man but the *space* where a man should be. Like a negative silhouette.

The Eraser.

Linus raised his dagger to slash at the thing . . . but the blade melted the moment it touched the impossible shape. Willa's kites swarmed toward it, but they disintegrated like crumbling leaves. The Eraser came at the Wardens, who quickly backed into a side room, calling out Wards to no avail. Once they were all inside, the Eraser blurred a hand over the door, leaving behind a purple nothingness, as if there had never been a door—or a room—at all. The Wardens screamed and pounded at the walls, unable to escape the impossible trap.

The boys retreated to the spirit room as the Eraser continued down the hall. The thing turned the corner and then raised its static fingers, pointing them at Wally and Arthur, who backed away toward the curtain.

Before the Eraser could reach them, the door slammed in its face, showing Breeth's expression.

"What the crap was that thi—*Augh!*"

The Eraser passed through the door as if it were made of dust. It carried Breeth's ghostly form with it, squeezing her throat in its nonexistent hands. Breeth's legs kicked. Her head whipped back and forth. Her entire form flickered like a dying candle flame.

"What's happening?" Arthur asked, wide-eyed.

"It has *Breeth*," Wally said, breathlessly.

"*How?*" Arthur said. "She's a ghost!"

Wally could only shake his head in horror.

Breeth caught his eye and screamed. "*Run, Wally!*" Her voice was garbled . . . like she was *drowning*. "I'll beat this thing and then go tell Lady Weirdwood to come get you!"

But how could she possibly beat the Eraser? Nothing had ever been able to *touch* Breeth, let alone strangle her. Her ghost was starting to fade.

"*Go!*" Breeth cried.

"What's happening?" Arthur asked.

"Breeth's telling us to run," Wally said.

"*Great idea*," Arthur said, grabbing his arm and trying to pull him through the curtain.

Wally resisted. He couldn't stop staring at his struggling friend. Even though Wally knew he'd be helpless against the Eraser, he couldn't just leave her.

"She's a *ghost*, Cooper," Arthur said, pulling harder. "She'll be *fine*."

Breeth wrenched her head to the side and caught Wally's eye. "If the Eraser kills you and you become a ghost, I *will* slap you."

Wally tore his eyes from hers and allowed Arthur to pull him through the Rift.

They were standing on the edge of a city made of storm clouds. The ground was as damp and buoyant as vapor, as if one wrong step would send them hurtling through. The longer they stood in place, the lower their shoes sank. Wally lifted one foot, then the other, trying to keep his legs from sinking through the quicksand-like clouds. Arthur's mom and Wally's parents stood in the distance, looking concerned.

On the other side of the curtain, Silver Tongue was giggling. "Whatcha got there, Mr. 'Raser? It looks like you's stranglin' nothin' at all!"

With the Wardens sealed away, the Order members had gathered in the spirit room.

"There, there, Astonishment," Rustmouth said. "Allow me to help you out of this predicamess."

Wood crunched behind the curtain as Rustmouth chewed through Breeth's trap like a termite.

"Quick, Wally!" Arthur said. "Use a Ward and close this Rift before the Order comes through!"

Wally hesitated. "If I close it, it may never open on Kingsport again." He looked at his parents, waiting for him on the distant cloud bank. "My mom and dad might never come home."

"*Wally*," Arthur said, "for the last time, those are not your—"

"For the last time, I don't *care*!" Wally said. "I've dreamed of this moment for *four years*, and *nothing* is going to stop me from reuniting my family." He nodded toward the storm cloud city. "Breeth said she would get Lady Weirdwood to open a door to this pocket-world." He shoved Arthur's shoulder. "*Go*. Get our parents to safety and then find the entrance to the Manor. Lady Weirdwood is the only one who can help us. I'll keep the Order distracted."

Arthur gazed back through the curtain where, to his eyes, the Eraser was crushing something between its nonexistent hands. "But Breeth is . . ."

"The most resilient person I know," Wally said. "You're right. If anyone can handle that thing, it's her." He nodded toward the storm cloud city. "The faster you find the Manor, the safer I'll be! Now *go*!"

Arthur backed away, hesitant, then turned and vanished in the storm clouds.

Just then, the curtain parted, and Rustmouth, the Astonishment, and Silver Tongue stepped through.

"*Well, well, well*," Rustmouth said, cracking his fingers. "Quite the setting for a scuffle, eh?"

"Blech!" Silver Tongue said, touching a toe to the cloud stuff. "It's wet!"

The Astonishment was having trouble not sinking through.

Wally raised his fists as the Order approached.

Where were his brother's riddles when he needed them most?

24
A CITY MADE OF STORM CLOUDS

Breeth couldn't breathe. Or whatever it was that spirits did to remain conscious.

The Eraser burned as purple as a sunspot in her vision. It clasped her ghostly throat so tight, she could barely move. She wiggled and writhed, kicked and thrashed, helpless against its hands of nothingness. She felt an impending sense of death deeper than any she'd felt before. Not only would she never return to her body, she would cease to *exist*.

She needed to get away from this thing. She needed to get back to the Manor and tell Lady Weirdwood that Wally and Arthur were in trouble in the storm cloud city. She needed to get her body back and *never leave it behind again*.

But how could she do any of that if she couldn't even reach the walls?

Breeth remembered her time in the Mercury Mines when she'd stretched her entire being through the rope. She quickly unraveled her legs and slipped them into two floorboards, which she bent up like the claws of a hammer. She wrapped them around the Eraser's shoulders to try and pry him off her. But the boards merely blurred through his form.

The Eraser squeezed her throat tighter. Shocks of nothingness pulsed through her.

Next, Breeth unraveled her arm into the wall, breaking the lit candelabra free and angling it at the Eraser's head, hoping to light its nonexistent hair on fire. But the flames extinguished the moment it came into contact.

The Eraser's hands started to twist. The world flickered and dimmed in Breeth's vision. Her spirit was about to snuff out completely.

As a last-ditch effort, Breeth stretched her fingers through the bones of the house, feeling from room to room—the walls, the floor, the furniture—grasping for help. She sensed a young girl. The girl held an object in her hands. On a whim, Breeth touched the thing, and her senses *exploded* with volcanic energy.

She had felt something like this object before. It was a dragon-bone quill. The energy channeled through her like a conduit right into the Eraser's hands. The Eraser flinched. Its hands loosened around her throat. The hallway regained its shape.

"Don't like that, huh?" Breeth said.

She clasped her fingers around the Quill again, and the sensation shot back through her, like touching a live wire. The Eraser jittered and winced like sputtering electricity and released her completely.

Breeth fled toward the house's exit, through the door and down the steps. As she ruffled through the grass, she felt a slight tingling, like the Eraser had seized hold of her toes. But it was barely a tickle compared to when he'd had her by the throat.

She continued to unravel herself like fishing line down Fortune-Teller's Alley, then passed through the door of an out-of-business china shop and into the Manor, all the while reeling her toes back in.

She shot through the foyer and the forest room and then up to the Moon Tower to make sure her body was still safe. Audrey had been busy. The ferret had removed the glass panes from the windows and created a box around Breeth's body.

Breeth tried spiriting back into herself but found she couldn't penetrate the box.

"Audrey, you *genius!*" Breeth said from the ceiling.

Glass was nonorganic.

It was a little disconcerting, not being able to access herself. But once this was all over and everyone was safe, she could have Wally tell the ferret to unbox her.

"Thank you, Audrey!" Breeth called out soundlessly. "I love your ferret guts!"

She whipped back down the tower and toward the nearest corridor that would take her to the Throne Room . . . but instead of a corridor, Breeth found a howling void.

"Uh," she said. She could've sworn there had been a hallway there. "That can't be good."

She creaked down to the Manor's foundation, constantly checking over her shoulder as she wound her way through the roots then up into the Throne Room, where Lady Weirdwood was conversing with Sekhmet.

"Lady Weirdwood!" Breeth shouted, rattling the walls. "I accidentally let something bad into the Manor! It clung onto my toes like an evil piece of gum, and now it's inside, and it's erasing the hallways! We have to get out of here!"

Lady Weirdwood stared at the rattling walls. "Rose? Is that you?"

"*What?* No! It's *Breeth!* The *nice* ghost!"

She was searching the Throne Room for a way to communicate when Ludwig burst in. The arm that had been gnawed off by Scarabs had been slowly growing back. But now it was gone. *Erased.*

"Somesing is eating ze Manor!" he said. "Ze front entrance . . . it is *vanished!*"

With that, the giant carpenter passed out.

There came a great staticky groan far down the hallway, and Lady Weirdwood stood from her throne. "The Eraser is in the Manor."

"*That's what I've been trying to tell you!*" Breeth screamed from the wall.

Sekhmet stared down the hallway. "What does it want?"

"I wish I knew," Lady Weirdwood said.

Ludwig suddenly sat up from the ground, making Sekhmet jump.

"Lady Weirdwood!" Breeth shouted with the giant's voice. "It's Breeth! Arthur and Wally are trapped in a storm cloud place with the Order!"

Lady Weirdwood made a frustrated sound as she stood from her waxen throne. "The whole point of sending those boys back to Kingsport was to keep them *safe*. Sekhmet, tell

Amelia to gather the staff. They'll need to fight. Without a front entrance to the Manor, our Wardens can't get back in."

Sekhmet left through the Throne Room's south door while Lady Weirdwood swept through the north, wrapping her snake around her shoulders. Breeth seeped out of Ludwig, leaving him to nap on the floor, and followed the old architect, rippling the carpet beneath her feet.

"Breeth, I need you to help me get the Eraser *out* of my Manor. Can you guide him toward the northern exit?"

"I think so?" Breeth said, creaking the floorboards.

"Do whatever's necessary. The Manor can heal broken corridors, but it will not recover from being erased." She swept toward the heart of Weirdwood. "I'll transport us to this *storm cloud* place and then meet you at the northern exit."

"Done!" Breeth said.

She zoomed through the west and eastern wings, trying to figure out how to get the Eraser to head north. She considered pinching certain doorways shut, but the Eraser could simply erase the walls and stroll through . . .

But what if she could manipulate the corridors so all ways led from the Eraser's location to the northern exit?

She used her full ghostly strength to tie a grass hallway into a knot, snapped a wooden corridor in half by splintering the ceiling, walls, and floorboards, and finally, delicately bent a hallway made of reeds so it no longer connected to the Manor but led straight outside.

As Breeth made her way north, the light in the windows grew dark with rain. She reached Lady Weirdwood, who stood in front of the open exit that led to the storm cloud city.

"I did it!" Breeth said. "I dunno how quickly some of those hallways are gonna heal, but—*oh*."

Lady Weirdwood's eyes were fixed on the corridor before her. The Eraser approached like spreading blindness.

"I asked you who you are," Lady Weirdwood said.

The Eraser tilted his staticky head.

Lady Weirdwood pointed her fingers beyond the figure, summoning vines and mushrooms, expanding moss and explosive flowers, trying to push the Eraser toward her and the exit. But the plants wilted to nothingness the moment they touched the Eraser's pulsing form.

"I see," Lady Weirdwood said.

The Eraser swept his left hand and made a door vanish. He swept his right hand and evaporated a corridor. Normally, Breeth would hurl herself at danger, confident nothing could harm her as a ghost. But just the sight of the Eraser shook her to her ectoplasm.

"Breeth?" Lady Weirdwood said. "Are you here?"

Breeth wriggled the rug beneath the old woman's feet.

"I'm going to draw the Eraser outside. But once we're out there, you might not recognize me. And if you try to communicate with me, I might not remember you."

"*What?*" Breeth said, somehow even more afraid. "What do you mean?"

"If that happens, I need you to get me *back inside* the Manor, okay?"

"But—but I still need to save Wally!"

The old architect didn't hear her. She raised her hands, and the entire Manor started to tremble. Then it shifted, sliding along its foundation. A window shattered. A corridor broke. Breeth briefly worried about her body upstairs but could not tear her eyes away from the Eraser. As the Manor shifted, the negative silhouette floated in place, sliding closer and closer to Lady Weirdwood. The old architect stepped backward through the exit and onto the cloud bank. The Eraser slid through the door.

Breeth flipped her senses to the Manor's outside wall just as Lady Weirdwood waved her hand. The Manor flashed with a bubble sheen, presumably barring the Eraser from reentering.

"Be brave, Breeth," Lady Weirdwood said, and took off into the storm clouds.

The Eraser blurred after her.

Once the pair was out of sight, Breeth gazed across the storm clouds, searching for Wally. The Order thought *this* was the afterlife? It looked nothing like the place she'd briefly seen after she died. It lacked that impossible light and the feeling that her parents were waiting for her with open arms.

Breeth saw buildings made of clouds. But no Wally. The land seemed to be made of vapor. There was no organic material to possess. How was she supposed to search for him?

Something slithered into the hall behind her. Breeth gazed back into the Manor and found Lady Weirdwood's boa constrictor flicking its tongue at the wall, as if it could sense her presence.

"You'll have to do," Breeth said.

She slipped into the snake and winced at the panicked hissing that filled her brain.

"Snake!" she said. "Sorry, I don't know your name! But it's me. Breeth. Lady Weirdwood's friend."

The snake's long muscles relaxed at the name. Breeth didn't have to think about juicy rats or tree branch naps to comfort it. It seemed to understand.

"I need you to do me a favor," she said.

Moments later, she was slithering across the clouds. The surface felt as tenuous as water. She sensed in her scales that if she didn't keep moving, she and the snake would sink and tumble through the clouds beneath. That wasn't the only difficulty. The snake was blind. She couldn't see where she was going.

Fortunately, the snake's other senses were sharp. Breeth licked the air with a forked tongue and tasted familiar blood in the distance.

She slithered as quick as she could and sensed a Wally-shaped heat signature, badly beaten and slowly sinking through the cloud bank. She wound down to him.

"I'm here, Wally," Breeth said. It came out as tongue flicks against his cheek.

She coiled her golden tail around his ankle and then slithered him back to the cloud's surface and toward the Manor. After several hundred winding movements, she made it back to the Manor.

Breeth quickly wriggled Wally through the open door, then slipped out of the snake's body and ruffled into the rug, which she folded over Wally like a blanket.

Just then, Weirdwood's staff came running down the hall,

armed with their artistic weapons. They stopped in the doorway, and Amelia assessed the storm cloud city with her one eye.

"Pyra?" Amelia said.

Pyra poured ingredients into her cauldron, creating a wintery blue concoction, the ghosts of snowflakes pinging out the top. She poured the liquid into one of her bomb vials and then hurled it outside where it exploded across the clouds, freezing the water vapor to a solid if bumpy surface. Now they could walk across it without sinking through.

Ludwig rubbed the space where his arm had been. "Vhere is Sekhmet?"

"She's grabbing weapons that don't *rust*," Amelia said. "We don't have time to wait for her." She saw Wally folded in the rug. "Or him," she said sadly.

Amelia, Ludwig, Weston, and Pyra ran outside, easily passing through the bubble sheen shield, and leaving the door open for Wally and Sekhmet to catch up.

Breeth stroked Wally's cheek with the rug's fringe. "*Be safe*," she told him, wishing she could kiss him one more time.

She spirited to the Manor's roof and gazed out through the storm. Weirdwood's staff approached the center of a great field of frozen clouds.

The Order was waiting for them.

"No place like the hereafterward to die, eh, Snoredens?" Rustmouth cried.

"Ve are not *Snoredens*!" Ludwig shouted back. "Ve are not even regular Varden-types!"

"*That so?*" Rustmouth said, delighted. He turned to Silver

Tongue and the Astonishment. "Hear that, ladies? Sounds like we packified the last of the Wardens away like sardines in a tin can!" He licked his teeth and nodded to the staff. "Once we handle these pestilences, the Manor'll stop metaling in our affairs once and for always. Let's get 'em!"

Rustmouth, the Astonishment, and Silver Tongue ran across the cloud bank as Ludwig, Weston, Pyra, and Amelia prepared their spells.

Just then, four shadows swept across the battlefield. Three dragons perched on a cloud bank on one end while a giant black bird perched on the other.

They didn't attack. Only watched, like royalty in some otherworldly chess match.

Breeth had always hated chess.

25
PUPPETS

ally awoke folded in a soft rug. He tried to sit up, but his muscles screamed in pain.

He was back in Weirdwood Manor. But how had he gotten there? And what had happened to this place? The door to his right was gone, replaced with a solid wall, and the passage to his left looked like it had a *bite* taken out of it. Or like it had been . . . *erased*.

Wally pushed himself upright as everything came rushing back: the staticky figure, the storm cloud city, his parents. He remembered his brief fight with the Order and taking a knockout hit from one of the Astonishment's rock fists. As Wally sank through the clouds, consciousness starting to slip away, Rustmouth had screamed, *Let the kid capsize! We's got bigger fish to fry.*

"Wally!" a voice called out behind him. "Don't just sit there! Help me get this thing open!"

He looked behind him and found Sekhmet trying to force open the Manor's northern exit. A pile of aluminum weapons leaned against the wall beside her. He hesitated a moment. The last time he'd seen his mentor, she'd threatened him with a sword.

"Am I . . . am I still a Novitiate?" he asked her.

"Not if you don't help me get outside!" she yelled back.

He got to his feet and peered through one of the windows. Rainy ghosts—the ones the Order had ushered into the House of Spirits—had drifted from their homes and gathered around a field of frozen storm clouds to watch what looked like a battle. Wally squinted. Amelia, Ludwig, Weston, and Pyra were doing their best to fight off Rustmouth, Silver Tongue, and the Astonishment. They were losing.

Wally peered past the fight to the rainy cloud city. Wally's parents were still out there somewhere. So was Arthur. They needed his help.

He tried opening the window, but it wouldn't budge. He ran down the hall, testing another and another while Sekhmet failed to break open the northern exit. He punched a window, but his gauntlet bounced off the glass like it was made of rubber.

"Don't bother," Sekhmet said. "It's Fae material." She slashed her flaming sword against the door one last time, then grunted with frustration. "I don't get it. The Manor's doors don't just *seal* themselves. They open when Lady Weirdwood decides they'll open."

"Was it the Eraser?" Wally said.

"He doesn't *lock* doors. He *erases* them. It's in his name."

Wally crouched and peered through the door's keyhole to

see if he could try and pick it open. And that's when he noticed the texture around the doorframe. It looked as if thorny vines had been carved there . . . They hadn't been there before.

"Are you seeing what I'm seeing?" Wally asked, tracing the wooden thorns with his finger.

Sekhmet blinked. "A doorframe?"

Of course. He was the only one who could see ghosts.

"It's Rose," Wally said. "She spread through the walls and is holding the exits shut."

Sekhmet slammed the butt of her sword into the frame. "Let *go*, Rose!"

Wally's heart dropped. "She must have locked us up to give the Order a better chance at winning the fight."

"How do we make her let go?"

Wally shook his head. "I could never make Breeth do anything."

"*Find Rose*," Sekhmet told him, heading west down the hallway. "I'll check the doors and windows on the upper floors. She might have missed one."

Wally headed east, searching the walls for telltale signs of a ghostly face.

"Keep those gauntlets ready!" Sekhmet called after to him. "The moment we get back outside, we fight!"

Wally traced Rose's thorns along the baseboards and crown molding, past missing doors and truncated hallways. The Manor felt like a half-demolished forest. The hallways that weren't splintered or missing were *bent* like young tree branches. One led to an exit it had not before.

The thorns led Wally to the Bookcropolis at the center of

the Manor. He was about to follow them through the labyrinthine bookstacks when he froze mid-step.

A devil puppet sat on a bookshelf, staring at him.

A dozen thoughts swirled through Wally's head. How had Graham gotten into the Manor? And *when*?

Wally turned to follow the thorns. He didn't have time for riddles right then. He needed to get outside and fight alongside the staff. He needed to find Arthur and his parents . . . But what if his brother's newest riddle helped Wally find Rose and unseal the Manor?

He jogged to the shelf and plucked up the puppet. He almost screamed when he found a hand underneath.

"*Surprise!*" the hand yelled.

"*Graham*," Wally said, gripping his chest to slow his pounding heart. "What are you *doing* here?"

"I'm here to see *you!*" the hand said pleasantly.

"Okay," Wally said. "How did you get in here?"

The hand bowed. "I couldn't have done it without you, dear brother."

Wally's skin went cold. "What do you mean?"

"Every time you solved one of my riddles," Graham's hand said, "you brought me one step closer to the heart of the Manor."

He gestured toward a hole in the wall of the Bookcropolis. Beside it was the mechanical Scarab that Wally had resurrected in the Abyssment. Its pincers were filled with splinters, and it had finally broken down.

"When you set that fire," Graham continued, "one of the Manor's entrances bloomed open to let out the smoke, allowing *me* to sneak in. And when you revived that Scarab, it chewed through the more precarious hallways, allowing me to sidestep Lady Weirdwood's many traps."

Wally was having trouble seeing straight. Graham had told him he would help bring down the Veil. But he never thought he'd do it out of ignorance.

"The first riddle turned out *differently* than I expected," Graham's hand said. "You were meant to collapse the water tower at the Fae-born zoo. That would have extinguished Rustmouth's magma manacles so he could steal the Mimic Map back from Sekhmet. I was going to use that map to track Lady

Weirdwood's movements and enter the Manor the moment she came to rescue her stranded Wardens."

Wally was only half listening. How had he been so easily manipulated? He had tried to think for himself, refusing to be a puppet for the Wardens or the Black Feathers. But in the end, he'd become his *brother's* puppet.

"Still," Graham said pleasantly, "your distraction allowed Rustmouth to escape and extinguish his manacles elsewhere. I knew I couldn't enter the Manor without a diversion, so I told Rustmouth that a certain boy in Kingsport was in possession of a coveted dragon-bone Quill. Arthur didn't have it yet, of course, but he would soon enough."

Wally had almost forgotten. Graham, the *little birdy*, had given the Order *and* the dragons information about Arthur. That put Wally over the edge. He rounded the bookshelf, seized Graham's hand, and pulled him toward the exit. It wasn't too late to make this right. Sekhmet was still in the Manor. She'd know what to do with his brother.

Graham didn't put up a fight. "You're not even going to ask why I went to such great lengths to get here?"

Wally could feel his brother's talking hand moving between his fingers.

"No," Wally said. "You told the Order, a *murderous organization*, where to find my friend. You lied to the dragons and told them that he stole one of their bones."

Graham's hand smacked its lips. "Guilty."

"Arthur could have *died*, Graham."

"But he *didn't*. Do you think I'd ever send a child into a

dangerous situation I knew he couldn't get out of? Let alone your best friend? I'm not a *monster*. My actions may seem terrible in the moment, but that's only because you aren't able to gaze across the pool of time and see the ripples my movements create."

Wally stopped walking. He looked down at his brother's hand, which had twisted its wrist to look up at him. How could he blame his brother for his recklessness when Graham could gaze into the future and see how it all turned out?

Wally released him.

"Besides," Graham's hand said, stretching its wrist like a throat, "if Arthur knew what I did for him, he would *thank* me! His time in the dragon prison awakened his *art*. Just like tying you up when you were younger made *you* a better thief."

"Arthur doesn't *have* an art."

"Oh, but he *does*," Graham whispered excitedly. Then he snorted. "But you know how I hate to spoil the ending."

"Graham . . ." Wally was almost too afraid to ask the next question. "What is *my* art?"

"*Your* art, dear brother, does not exist."

Wally expected the words to sting. But he didn't feel anything. Perhaps because his brother had confirmed what Wally had suspected all along: He wasn't magical.

Outside, raging storm clouds trembled the Manor.

Wally stared up at the Bookcropolis's double moons. "I saw Mom and Dad."

"I know you did."

"Were they . . ." Wally steeled himself. "Were they *real*?"

Graham sighed. He lowered his hand and placed it behind his back, dropping the puppet façade. "Does it matter?"

This *did* sting. But not as badly as Wally had expected it to. He'd told Arthur that he didn't care whether those were his parents or not. They looked like them. They talked like them and *smelled* like them. His memories couldn't do that.

"If the Veil comes down, brother," Graham said, "you could see those versions of our parents every day."

Wally squeezed his eyes shut, fighting off tears. His mom could still make him pancakes.

Graham took Wally's shoulders in his hands. "Having our parents back is just the *beginning* of the possibilities. Lady Weirdwood and her Wardens patrol and maintain the border between the Real and the Fae. I ask you, brother: When have border walls done anything other than separate people? When have they developed interactions between worlds? The Wardens are a *wall*, Wally. They are the theater curtain that refuses to rise."

Wally couldn't quite accept that. He saw the Wardens as a group of good people trying to protect the innocents of the Real.

"After witnessing the miracle of Mom and Dad's revival," Graham said, "can you really go back to the Wardens, whose very role is *preventing* miracles?"

Wally stared at the floor. He loved being a Novitiate almost more than anything in the world. But not as much as he loved his parents.

Graham smiled. "Are you ready to see the next part?"

Wally's stomach clenched. "There's a next part?"

Graham gestured to the empty Bookcropolis. "We're locked in this Manor for the foreseeable future, so we might as well make the most of it."

"This isn't another riddle, is it?"

"No, Wally. We're beyond riddles now. When was the last time you checked the Abyssment's prison cell?"

"*Ahem.*" A voice cleared behind him. "Stop to read a book?"

Wally turned and found Sekhmet giving him a strange look.

He looked back and found Graham had vanished.

"What's that in your hand, Wally?" Sekhmet asked.

Wally looked down and found he was still holding the devil puppet. He dropped it and walked straight past Sekhmet toward the exit.

Sekhmet came after him. "Is this where Rose went?" She searched along the floor, looking for signs of thorns.

He continued to ignore her as he approached the entrance to the Abyssment. The armored guard had been erased. Well, half of it, anyway. Wally stepped over the empty metal legs and headed down the stairs.

"Whoa, Wally," Sekhmet called after him. "*Wait up!*"

Wally increased his pace. He beat her to the first floor and found someone locked in the cell. A young woman. Wally recognized her. In fact, the last time he'd seen her, she'd been locked in another cage at the Mad Zoo.

"*Jamie*," Wally said. "What are you doing down here?"

Jamie's head jerked up. She saw the worried expression on Wally's face and her fear melted away. "I . . . I don't know." Her voice was hoarse with exhaustion. "I asked that woman with the eye patch why my drawings were coming to life, and she brought me here. She said I could return to my home once I agreed to stop painting. But—but my art is my *livelihood*."

Wally saw what his brother had wanted him to see. Jamie's paintings had sparked the public's imaginations so completely that her creatures had come to life in the Fae. The Order had tracked the Fae-born down and exploited them to open a Rift. Now the Wardens were ensuring Jamie could never do anything like that again.

Not only was the Manor keeping magic from the people . . . they were taking it away.

"Come back upstairs, Wally," Sekhmet said behind him.

Wally didn't turn around. "Why did the Wardens lock up this woman?" He knew the answer, but he wanted to hear Sekhmet say it.

"We've kept her comfortable," Sekhmet said.

Wally turned around, barely able to contain his anger. "By holding her hostage?"

"It isn't that simple. We can't just release her back into the Real. She could be working for the *Order*. And if she's innocent, then we're protecting her from being kidnapped again and being used as a weapon." Sekhmet nodded up the stairs. "We can talk about this later. Let's go find Rose."

Wally didn't budge. "Why didn't you tell me the Wardens did stuff like this?"

"You're barely at the beginning of your studies, Wally," Sekhmet said. "The more you interact with the Veil, the more you understand the necessity for extreme measures."

Wally felt stuck. He couldn't just leave Jamie locked in this cell. But he didn't think he could abandon his promising life as a Novitiate.

"We don't have time to argue about this," Sekhmet said. "We need to be outside fighting with the staff and saving *your* friend."

Wally remembered his brother's words: *Do you think I'd ever send a child into a dangerous situation I knew he couldn't get out of?*

"I think Arthur's going to be just fine," Wally said.

He took out his lock picks and moved to free Jamie.

Sekhmet drew her sword. "I can't let you do that." She locked eyes with Wally, and something seemed to dawn on her. "That puppet . . . Did Graham give it to you?"

Wally didn't answer.

"He's trying to bring down the *Veil*, Wally. I don't care if he's your brother. If you're helping him, then you are an enemy of the Wardens."

Wally eyed Sekhmet's sword warily. He hadn't been able to beat her in the courtyard. And even though she only had one weapon now, he knew he was still no match for her. But he couldn't just stand by while an innocent woman rotted away in a cell.

He slid his pick into the lock. Sekhmet's sword ignited.

She took a step toward Wally, but then Graham's hand

snaked out of a crack in the wall and grabbed hold of her arm, wrenching the sword from her grasp.

"Run, Wally!" Graham's hand said, mouth full. "We'll save Jamie later. Just *run*!"

Wally dropped the pick, dodged past Sekhmet, and fled upstairs.

26
THE HAUNTED BATTLE

The fight raged across the storm clouds—swinging stone fists, chattering rusted teeth, a screeching silver voice—while all around them, the rain people howled like a hurricane.

Breeth wanted to be everywhere at once: in Ludwig's branchy bones, in Pyra's bubbling cauldron, in Amelia's cracking whip . . . But then she heard a pot shatter and sought Weston in the chaos.

The Astonishment had punched the gardener's potted plant, destroying his only weapon. The second punch came with a spray of blood and teeth and his command whistle, which flew out of his mouth and clinked across the frozen clouds.

The Astonishment hefted a stone foot and was about to stomp the broken plant to pieces when it suddenly scooted out of the way. The stone woman quirked her head in confusion, then swiped up the plant in her massive hand to inspect it.

Breeth stretched the branches like fingers, poking the Astonishment in both eyes.

The Astonishment reeled back, grinding her teeth and clutching at her face. The stone woman distracted, Breeth quickly checked on Weston. The gardener was knocked unconscious.

"Come on, Weston!" she screamed soundlessly at him. "Grab your whistle! I can't make this plant grow by myself!"

The Astonishment blinked the pain from her eyes, shook her head, raised her fist and brought it down like a falling boulder, crushing Breeth's plant to pieces, spraying bits of leaf and soil across the clouds. Breeth was disoriented. One moment she was flying through the air, the next she was in what looked like a massive cave with two arching rows of rocks, one above, one below, and a bumpy tongue-shaped rug.

"*Ew*," she said.

Her tiny leaf fragment had soared straight into the Astonishment's mouth. She tumbled and whirled around the stone tongue, fearing she would be swallowed. But then a whistle echoed outside the cave, and Breeth's little bit of leaf started to expand.

She grew tendrils, which she slithered out of the Astonishment's mouth, wrapping them down and around her stony arms. The Astonishment flexed, splitting her leafy binds, but then Weston regained his feet, whistled again, and bound the vines tighter.

"You're welcome!" Breeth screamed, as she swung from the vines and spirited to the next fight.

Ludwig and Rustmouth circled each other across the clouds. The giant's face hung slack with fear while Rustmouth grinned like an old bear trap. Ludwig used his remaining hand to fold a paper bat and sent it flapping at Rustmouth, who merely breathed his orange breath, making it disintegrate.

Rustmouth sniffed. "You ain't made of humany stuff, is ya?"

Ludwig gulped and faintly nodded. "Ja. I am made of ze human stuff."

"Nah," Rustmouth said. "You's made of vegetables. That's *good*. I got my iron when I anibblated that fightin' girl's sword, but I ain't had me *greens*." He looked the giant up and down, chomping his rusted teeth. "I'll start with your toes. Pop 'em like big ol' corn kernels."

Ludwig whimpered and took a step back, right into Breeth's ghost.

"Hi again!" she bubbled into his sloshy brain.

Ludwig screamed.

"*Well now*," Rustmouth said, licking his brown lips. "Been a while since my food's screeched in fearment."

"Ludwig, it's me!" Breeth said. "Your favorite brain guest! Mind if I drive for a minute?"

Ludwig trembled. "Just don't let him eat my toes!"

Rustmouth stopped in his tracks. "Him whom? Me him?"

"I'll treat them like they were my very own!" Breeth said.

She stretched her being straight to Ludwig's precious toes. Then she stood tall and scowled at Rustmouth.

"That's better," Rustmouth said, smiling afresh. "Food tastes better when it puts up a fright."

Breeth bellowed with Ludwig's booming voice and ran at Rustmouth, who suddenly looked uncertain about challenging a vegetable to a fight. She tackled him to the clouds and used her one fist to punch Rustmouth in the nose. The man tried to catch her hands between his teeth, but Breeth simply uppercut his jaws shut. Then she punched him again and again and again and again and—

It was only when Rustmouth rolled away, crying "*Uncle!*" and wiping blood and rust from his chin, that she decided it was time to help elsewhere.

"I weakened him for ya, Ludwig!" Breeth said, releasing the controls of his brain. "Like a jar of pickles. You take care of the rest!"

She skipped out of the giant, who quickly sat up and started folding paper bats.

The next fight was strange to behold.

Silver Tongue stood on a high mound of cloud, mouth dripping silver and howling at two figures below. "*Bleed her!*"

Below, Amelia cracked her whip, sending waves of energy at a snarling Pyra, opening gashes across her arms, which Pyra quickly healed with her med vials. Amelia's face looked pained, like she was trying to stop her arm from attacking. But then her whip cracked forward again, striking Pyra's cheek.

"*Now,*" Silver Tongue said, taking another sip from her flask and turning her colorless eyes on Pyra. "*You hurt* her *a while.*"

Pyra pulled poison vials from her bullet belt and hurled them toward Amelia while Silver Tongue clapped her hands and giggled.

This was a tricky one. If Breeth uncorked all of Pyra's vials, Silver Tongue would make Amelia whip Pyra to pieces. But if Breeth tried to bind Amelia's hands with her whip, Pyra would blind Amelia with a potion . . .

But then Breeth saw it. Something she had never possessed before.

She was not looking forward to it.

Breeth slipped into Silver Tongue's hair. It was greasy and limp and in dire need of a comb. But Breeth separated two strands from the sides and lifted them straight outward, giving them a sharp yank.

The moment Silver Tongue gasped in pain, Breeth swung each strand across the woman's cheeks and between her teeth like a horse bridle. The woman's blue fingers tore at her hair to pull it free, but Breeth continued to sweep the strands around the back of the woman's head where she tied them into a perfect, if greasy, knot.

"Isn't that better?" Breeth asked, stroking the woman's cheek with a strand of her own hair. "Now you can't say such nasty stuff."

Below, Amelia stopped attacking Pyra. Breeth decided to see how the others were faring.

"Oh crap."

The Astonishment had broken through Weston's vine binds and was crushing him between her stony arms. Rustmouth had regained his confidence and was chomping after the terrified Ludwig. And while Breeth wasn't looking, Silver Tongue's blue fingers had managed to undo the grease-slippery knot in her hair.

Breeth took a breezy breath. "Okay. It's okay. This is fine. I can help them all again."

The moment Silver Tongue got her mouth freed, she spotted a strong rain ghost in the audience and took a quick sip from her flask. "*Heya, ghostie!*" she said, and raised a blue-veined hand, pointing toward the Weirdwood staff. "*Murder them, pretty please.*"

Rustmouth stopped chasing Ludwig and smiled. "Now that's a swelluva idea! S'matter of fact . . ." He placed his hands to his brown-stained lips and called out to the other rainy figures. "To any disembody who fancies seeing their sweet famililies behind that curtain again, it's time for an *onslaughter!*"

Dozens of rainy dead swept across the battlefield like a gray tsunami, overwhelming the staff. Amelia's whip was torn from her hand. Ludwig's bats disintegrated in the dampness. Pyra's cauldron tipped over, spilling its contents across the clouds.

"*Hey!*" Breeth screamed. "From one ghost to another! Stop being jerks!"

They didn't hear her.

"You guys aren't ghosts at all," she whispered to herself. "But . . . what *are* you?"

Better yet, where were Wally and Arthur when she needed them?

27
BUTTERSCOTCH

A rthur wandered the storm cloud city—its rainy towers, its billowing shopfronts, its squat cloud homes. At
one point in his journey, an icy layer had swept across
the clouds beneath his feet, and he'd stopped sinking through
the ground. He didn't know who or what had done it. But he
was grateful.

Something still seemed so familiar about this place, but
he couldn't quite put his finger on it. Had he read about it?
Dreamt about it? How long had this pocket-world existed
before he and Liza had stumbled on it and the Order started
exploiting its inhabitants?

He supposed it didn't matter right then. He had to find
the Manor and save Wally.

Arthur had told Wally's parents, or whoever they were, to
go to their cloud home and lock the door until the battle was
over. That he would save their son's life. When they'd left, they
looked as worried as any real parents would. Arthur hadn't
been able to look his mom—or whatever she was—in the eye.

The expression on her face when she'd turned away nearly broke his heart.

A sound roared in the distance as gray shapes flooded across the battlefield. It seemed the ghosts, or whatever they were, had joined the Order and were attacking Weirdwood's staff. The staff didn't stand a chance now.

A part of Arthur wanted to jump into the fray and do everything he could to save Ludwig and Pyra and Weston and Amelia. To finally prove that he was worthy of being a Novitiate. But it was like Amelia had said. There was no Garnett Lacroix in this fight. Arthur would be useless.

Arthur turned his gaze to the winged giants, perching on either side of the battlefield. The dragons waited patiently, like predators poised for the kill, while on the other end, Rook Liza watched with the dragon-bone Quill in her bill to see if the Order would survive to help find her mother's spirit.

Arthur considered trying to convince Liza to join the Manor's side. The claw Quill would vanquish the Order in a matter of moments. But he had the terrible feeling that if he stepped within her black bird sight, his life would end in a quick snip of her giant bill.

Arthur walked deeper into the storm cloud city.

***

The clouds shifted into houses, streets, and lampposts. The sun refracted through the droplets in a rainbow of colors, making the neighborhood shine bright and pleasant. Arthur hustled across the water-vapor lawns, checking every door, hoping to find the Manor waiting on the other side. But the handles simply evaporated in his hand.

"Stranger!" a young voice cried out in alarm. "*Stranger!*"

"Hey! Stop trying to break into those houses!"

Two small, rainy figures stood at the end of the sidewalk. It seemed not all of the ghosts were fighting in the battlefield. The children of the storm cloud city were as gray and translucent as their parents. Their eyes glittered like lightning.

Arthur held up his hands in surrender. "I'm looking for a door that leads somewhere other than these houses. Have you seen anything like that?"

The kids gave him questioning looks.

Arthur dropped his hands. "What are you doing outside?" He nodded back toward the battle. "It's dangerous."

One of the kids pointed a ghostly finger. "A mean wind got our house."

Sure enough, several water-vapor homes had been destroyed by one of Amelia's errant wind attacks.

"Come on," Arthur said, guiding the kids farther away from the battle. "I'll keep you safe."

As they continued down the sidewalk, the boy grabbed Arthur's pinky. His hand felt like damp laundry static. He was trembling.

"Don't worry," Arthur said. "If any trouble comes our way, I'll cast a thousand spells and banish those bad guys back to whatever hole they crawled out from!"

The little boy nodded.

"Do a spell now!" the little girl thundered.

"Oh, well," Arthur said. "It wouldn't be appropriate right now."

"*Pleeeeaaaaaaase?*" the little girl said, and she reached into her pocket. "I'll pay you!"

She uncurled her fingers and offered him an oval cloud candy that shined like translucent caramel.

Arthur snorted. "You pay in candy?"

The girl smiled. "Butterscotch!"

Arthur's heart skipped a beat. He stared at the candy, trying to work out why it was so familiar. *Butterscotch.* And then it hit him. The first tale of comfort he had given back in Kingsport. That old lady's cobbler husband had adored butterscotch before he died. Arthur had told her that children in the afterlife gave him this very candy in exchange for his shoes.

Arthur picked up the bit-of-cloud butterscotch, which almost felt like nothing between his fingers. "What do you call this place?"

The boy snorted. "You don't know?"

"*Duh.*" The girl giggled. "It's the Great—"

"*Elsewhere*," Arthur finished.

He turned in a circle, taking in the houses, the trees, the street. This was *his* pocket-world. *He* had invented it. The dead were *Fae-born* that *he* had created by spinning stories for the grieving back in Kingsport. Arthur may not have been able to write a spell to save his life. But if he spoke it like it was a story . . . it came to life here.

He remembered the tingly sensation that had coursed through his veins every time he'd talked about the Great Elsewhere. He'd thought it was the satisfaction of doing good in the world—soothing the people of Kingsport with his eulogies or assuring Wally in the hospital that his parents were in a better place . . .

Arthur felt a wave of sadness when he realized that Wally's parents and his own mother were just as fake as Arthur had feared. He hadn't wanted to be right. Not really.

"What's happening to your face?" one of the cloud kids asked.

"Yeah, it got *sad*."

Arthur tried to smile at them. Why focus on the sad things? He could do magic!

"Now you're *giggling* to yourself," one of the rainy kids said.

"Is he—?" the other whispered, spinning a rainy finger around his temple.

Arthur popped the cloudy butterscotch in his mouth. It tasted *heavenly*.

"Good news!" he said, heading back toward the wreckage of the kids' home. "Your home wasn't destroyed by that wind. It was just lifted into the heavens and then placed gently, perfectly unharmed, at the other end of the street."

The kids skipped after him, excited to have their home back. But when they reached the site, they found nothing but cloud rubble.

"That doesn't *look* gentle," one of the kids said.

Arthur's confidence deflated. "That should have worked . . ."

Just then a meteor shot out of the sky and landed in the middle of the street. Arthur blinked the spots from his eyes.

It wasn't a meteor at all but a girl on a bike. A bike made of *starlight*.

One of the kids waved. "Hey, Maddie."

Maddie. Arthur had comforted this little girl's grieving father by telling him that she was riding her bicycle across the heavens.

Things started to click. Arthur may have invented the Great Elsewhere, but once it had formed in the Fae, he had to follow the rules he'd made up for the place. Not only that, he had to follow the rules the grieving back in Kingsport had contributed through their own tales.

Arthur was a character in his own story.

Arthur turned to the kids. "You guys want to help me beat up those bad guys?"

"Yeah!" the boy shouted

The girls nodded fervently.

"*Great.* Do you know where Joe's shoe shop is?"

"Of course!" the girl said, lifting a cloud-soled shoe.

Arthur smiled. "How much butterscotch do you have on you?"

He told the kids his plan, giving special instructions to Maddie with her starlight bike. Then he ruffled their cloudy hairdos and sent them on their way. "Remember to tell Joe that his wife misses him terribly and regrets the last thing she said to him! Tell him she wants him to eat all the butterscotch he can shake a stick at!"

***

Arthur Benton approached the battle in cloud-soled shoes.

On one end loomed the Duchess with her dragon guards. On the other, Rook Liza. He would handle them when the time came.

The rainy ghosts howled across the field, overwhelming the Weirdwood staff and giving the Order cheap shots. Ghosts pinned down Weston, whose chest was being crushed by the boulder foot of the Astonishment. Ludwig was being smothered by even more ghosts, while Rustmouth cruelly chomped his teeth closer and closer toward the giant's toes. Only Amelia and Pyra were spirit-free, attacking each other at Silver Tongue's command.

The sight infuriated Arthur. The memories of the dead were not meant to be wielded as weapons. They were not supposed to haunt or to cause guilt. They were there to be remembered. To uplift. To teach the living to not repeat their mistakes.

Before he could lose his nerve, he placed his hands to his mouth and called out the names of the men who had died in the mine collapse. "Andy Rickshaw! Dale Calloway! Harris Means!"

Several rainy ghosts flashed their lightning eyes at Arthur, surprised to hear their names in this place.

"The mining company still hasn't paid your life insurance!" Arthur told them. "Your wives have been struggling to keep your kids fed!" He pointed to Astonishment. "But that lady is trying to bleed your families dry, just for one last look at your ugly mugs."

The miners looked at one another and then scowled at the

woman of stone. They released Weston and walked toward the Astonishment, rainy pickaxes manifesting in their hands. The stone woman turned and ran, and the miners chased after her.

Meanwhile, a streak of starlight cruised up to Weston, leaving him with a pair of cloud-soled shoes.

"Sandra!" Arthur called out.

Another pair of lightning eyes fixed on him. This woman's husband had come to Arthur for comfort after she had died of a tooth infection.

"I told your husband that all rotten teeth were removed the moment the sufferer stepped into the Great Elsewhere. Was yours?"

The woman smiled, showing a gap in her cloud-white teeth.

Arthur looked at Rustmouth and clicked his tongue. "Looks like one of the new arrivals is *desperate* for some dental work." He squinted toward the horizon. "The dentist must be a little behind schedule is all."

Not two seconds later, a pair of pliers came snipping through the air like a silver bird.

Rustmouth saw the thing, and his lips clamped shut in fear. "What accidentistry is this?"

He too ran across the clouds as the pliers chased him.

The streak of starlight left a pair of cloudy shoes in Ludwig's hands.

One more. Arthur took a deep breath. "Aubrey D—"

"Stop! Stop talking! Shut your mouth!"

Arthur's lips pinched together like a sealed can.

During his first two skirmishes, Silver Tongue had been

too busy making Pyra and Amelia torture each other to notice what was happening. But now her colorless eyes were fixed on Arthur.

"*Pinch your nose!*" she screamed.

Arthur's fingers obeyed, plugging up his breath.

"*Hold it,*" Silver Tongue said.

His lungs started to strain.

"*Hold it . . .*" She giggled and clicked her tongue. "Tick tock tick tock tick tock."

Arthur's body began to spasm. His eyes sought the streak of pedaling starlight, which made its final stops at Amelia and then Pyra. The cook snarled until Maddie whispered something in her ear and handed her a pair of cloud-soled shoes.

Arthur's chest convulsed. His throat pounded. He smiled.

"What?" Silver Tongue said, wearing the same expression she had when Wally belted the flask out of her hand. "What is it? *Stop smiling.*"

Arthur lips obeyed. But he couldn't help but enjoy watching Rustmouth and the Astonishment sprinting across his version heaven, trying to escape their own personal nightmares.

They're going to be so embarrassed when they realize they aren't wearing the proper shoes for this fine establishment.

Having slipped on her cloud-soled shoes, Pyra pulled a steamy red vial from her bullet belt and hurled it downward. It exploded across the clouds, shattering the icy layer. Without Joe's specialty shoes, Rustmouth, the Astonishment, and Silver Tongue started to sink.

Silver Tongue took a quick sip from her flask, and Arthur

briefly feared that she was going to command Maddie to bring her a pair of cloud-soled shoes. But then Ludwig brought his giant fist down, pounding the woman on the head, driving her like a nail through the clouds. He gleefully did the same to Rustmouth and the Astonishment, like a life-size game of Wack-a-Mole, then lifted his arm above his head and, without his usual accent, bellowed, "I am Ludwig! Pounder of jerkwads!"

Arthur's fingers finally released his nose. His lips unsealed. His lungs sucked in the sweet stormy air. Amelia hugged Pyra, while Ludwig gathered Weston up in his one arm.

Arthur caught his breath and called out to them. "We need to go get Wally!" he said, pointing toward the Rift that led to Kingsport.

"He's back at the Manor!" Ludwig called back. "I dragged him back there when I was a snake!"

This didn't make any sense to Arthur, but he still felt the tension uncoiling from his muscles. His friend was okay.

The relief didn't last long. Rook Liza and the dragons had taken flight from the shattered cloud bank and were now circling the sky. He expected them to start dive-bombing the staff. But they simply circled and watched.

A low pulsing turned Arthur around. The Eraser had not fallen through the clouds like the others. Its massless form still hovered against the sky. It cut toward the battlefield, leaving a trail of nothingness in its wake.

The staff braced themselves.

"Where's Lady Weirdwood?" Weston asked.

"I don't know," Amelia said, her voice trembling.

The Eraser came closer. It waved its fingers, vanishing a storm cloud building. Closer. It collapsed a clouded spire. *Closer.* With a flick of its fingers, three rainy ghosts evaporated in a breath of steam.

Amelia cracked her whip, but it was sucked into the Eraser's black hole form. Pyra threw her bomb vials, but they melted like snowflakes.

Weston stepped in front of the others and, sputtering with fear, blew his whistle. His pot-less plant expanded, interlocking its leaves into a kind of topiary shield. The Eraser walked straight through it, rendering the leaves to bare veins, then nothing at all. In one smooth motion, it clasped its hands around the gardener's head. Weston's face fell slack as the Eraser's fingers passed through him like putty, melting away his layers, showing skin, muscle, bone . . .

"No!" Ludwig screamed, lunging forward to catch what was left of his twin. "*Nein!*"

But it was too late. Weston's bones fell away to nothingness.

Ludwig attacked, but the Eraser caught his fist. His skin started to peel away like shedding bark.

Arthur had to act before the entire staff was erased. This was *his* pocket-world. But what could he do?

Before he had an answer, Arthur stepped forward. "You're not welcome here!"

The Eraser turned its nonexistent eyes on Arthur.

"This is the Great Elsewhere!" he cried, trying to sound braver than he felt. "It belongs to the grieving people of Kingsport. Not ugly ink spills like you."

The Eraser released Ludwig, who fell back into Amelia's

arms. It swept toward Arthur like a black tide. Arthur started to panic. His body was numb with fear.

The Eraser grew bigger and bigger in his vision, like flames spreading across a photograph. Arthur's brain scrambled for answers in the eulogies he'd given back in Kingsport. But the impending nothingness seemed to erase all thoughts.

How could he banish something that didn't exist?

The Eraser filled the world, closing its hands around Arthur's head. Arthur felt everything in that moment. Every nerve. Every ache. Every memory, painful and good. Images of his loved ones flashed through his head: his mom, Harry, Wally. Arthur experienced everything he'd ever felt for all of them—love, frustration, fear—for one last time as it all tumbled down a bottomless well.

In Arthur Benton's final moments of consciousness, he only had one thought.

I hope I was more gentleman than thief.

Something changed.

Deep in the depths of the Eraser's nothingness, a swirl of light appeared. A wrinkle of movement. It looked like a coalescing galaxy. Like a photograph trying to develop . . .

The darkness in Arthur's vision receded ever so slightly as the Eraser took a step back. Its head jittered and contorted. Its limbs wavered like bolts of electricity.

Arthur blinked at the cloud light, relieved to be alive, and tried to piece together what he'd just seen. There was *something* in all that nothingness.

"You existed once," Arthur whispered. "You're trying to exist again."

The Eraser's form continued to tremble as if it was going to come apart at the seams. Its body and arms made odd unpredictable shapes. But then . . . for the briefest of moments . . . the shape of the Eraser's head swept into a wide-brimmed hat.

Arthur gasped. "*Garnett?*"

Bright, golden eyes flashed through the nothingness. They gave Arthur a pleading look. Then the Eraser fell through the clouds, leaving behind a steaming black hole.

Arthur sat in shock, feeling tingling back into his body. Had he just seen what he thought he'd seen? Was the Eraser *Garnett Lacroix*? Or rather . . . the absence where the Gentleman Thief had once been?

A shriek jolted his heart. Again, there was no time to piece together what had happened. Now that the Eraser was gone, the Duchess and her guards were descending on the staff.

Arthur struggled to his feet and limped as fast as he could toward the far end of the battlefield. Every fiber of his being told him that approaching Liza was a bad idea. But he felt confident. If he could beat the Eraser . . . what couldn't he do?

Arthur reached the field's edge and gazed up at the Rook, circling above. The dying sunlight shined on Liza's black wings. Huamei's claw Quill hung from her beak.

"Liza!" Arthur called to her. "I need you to give me the Quill! It belonged to the Duchess's son, and I think it's the only thing that will satisfy her. Otherwise, the Manor is going to be destroyed, and there will be nothing standing between the Real and the dangers of the Fae. Lots of people will die. I *know* you don't want that."

Liza only flapped and stared. Arthur's reflection was tiny and helpless in her giant, dark eyes.

Behind him came the beating of scaled wings as the dragons swept close.

He pointed to the Quill in Liza's beak. "That won't bring back your mom and dad. I'm certain of that now."

The giant bird continued to stare. In the distance, Pyra snarled while Ludwig screamed.

"Liza, will you just please turn back into yourself so we can talk?"

The Rook circled.

Arthur sighed in frustration. "I know the Order promised to help you find your mom in exchange for the dragon-bone

Quill. But they *tricked* you. This"—Arthur swept a hand across the clouds—"isn't the afterlife. I know because I made it up. It's called the Great Elsewhere. I created it when I was sad about my mom and needed to imagine her somewhere nice. It came to life in the Fae and then continued to grow whenever I told stories about other people's lost loved ones. *That's* why your mom and dad aren't here. I never tried to comfort you for losing them. But I should have. I felt too guilty for accidentally making you an orphan."

Arthur stared into the Rook's eyes, but he couldn't *read* them. Was Liza still in there?

There was only one way to find out.

"Your mom loved you very much," he said. "She still saw you as her baby girl, even after you were all grown up. That's why she held your hugs a little too long and rocked you back and forth."

As he spoke, a silhouette formed in a nearby cloud bank and then stepped out of it.

Liza's cloud mother clasped her hands in front of her and looked around, searching for something familiar. Arthur watched Liza as she circled through the air, feathered head tilted, watching her mother. And he caught the moment Liza saw the truth. A dark shine of grief in her big bird eyes.

All Liza had to do was turn back into herself and she could hug her mother again. Or a version of her. But she'd already done that when she hugged the waxen woman her father created. Wax. Clouds. She didn't want a hug unless it was the real thing. Arthur knew how she felt now.

He gently took Liza's cloud mother by the shoulders and

pointed her toward the storm cloud city. She headed toward it, confused.

Back on the battlefield, Amelia was screaming.

"I'm sorry," Arthur told Liza. "Someday we'll be reunited with our mothers in the true afterlife. But for now . . . I need that Quill."

Liza squeezed her bill, and the Quill made a cracking sound.

"No, Liza!" Arthur said. "*Please!*"

Liza was angry. He had shattered her dreams of reuniting with her parents. And now she would shatter his hopes of saving the Manor.

She narrowed her beak, splintering the Quill again. And again. Arthur clutched his hair, waiting for his last hope to splinter to pieces.

But then Liza opened her giant black bill and dropped the cracked but still intact Quill into his hands.

Arthur sighed relief. "Thank you, Liza!" He patted his pockets. "Let me find a notebook, and I'll write you back to normal . . ."

But without warning, the great black bird angled her wings upward. She flapped once, launching straight into the sky before rounding her neck and diving straight downward, her bill piercing through the clouds.

And just like that, Liza was gone.

Arthur stared at the hole in the clouds, trying to understand. But before he could come up with anything, Weirdwood's staff cried out behind him. Arthur sprinted back toward the fight.

"Duchess!" Arthur screamed, waving the Quill in the air.

He would offer Huamei's claw as an olive branch to the Duchess and then write her son the best eulogy ever heard on either side of the Veil. He would show the Duchess how much her son had loved and respected her. How he had tried to restore honor to his name and return to his kingdom. He would show her why Huamei had given Arthur and Wally the claw Quill. How the dragon boy had been trying to restore the Balance. To reunite his family. To save the Manor as well as Kingsport.

"Duchess! I have Huamei's claw! I need to tell you about his last—"

He had barely set foot in the dragon's shadow before she swooped down . . . and swallowed him whole.

28
THE FALLEN NOVITIATE

Wally sprinted through the Manor, making tight turns and entering random rooms while purposefully avoiding the dead-end corridors he'd noticed earlier. Shortly after he'd exited the Abyssment, Sekhmet had managed to escape Graham's grip, and now she was chasing him through the Manor like a machine. Her lungs seemed to be made of iron.

Wally sprinted into the Bookcropolis, scaled a tower of shelves, and lay flat across the top. He tried to quiet his heaving lungs. Sure enough, moments after Wally had flattened himself across the top of the shelf, footsteps entered the Bookcropolis.

Wally held his breath.

"I know you're up there, Wally," Sekhmet said. "The moonlight's gleaming off your gauntlets."

Wally winced. He should have left the gauntlets behind. They wouldn't do him any good anyway.

"Come down," she said below. "Don't make me cut this shelf in half."

He removed his gauntlets and wiped sweat from his forehead. "I don't want to fight you, Sekhmet."

"Turn yourself in, then," she said.

Wally didn't move.

A fiery blast of air struck the bookshelf, which started to tilt. He barely managed to jump up and step onto the next bookshelf before the first tipped over. He skipped along the tops of the other shelves, then dropped to the ground and ran out of the Bookcropolis.

How was he supposed to get away from her? Sekhmet knew the rest of these halls like the hilt of her sword. There wasn't a single passage she didn't know about. Unless . . .

He passed a window and glanced at the frame. The thorns were gone. Wally had a terrible feeling about what that meant . . . but he could use it to his advantage.

He headed north, then far enough east so that the shortest route back to the Abyssment would be different than the one he'd taken to the Bookcropolis. Only then did he stop running.

He turned just as Sekhmet rounded the corner.

"You win," he said, raising his hands. "I'll turn myself in."

She kept her flaming sword raised. "What changed your mind?"

Wally stood tall like a loyal Novitiate. "I let my emotions take over when I saw my brother. I've been protecting him for so long that it's hard to stop now. But you're right, Sekhmet. People can't be trusted in the Fae." He held out his palm, still burned from the flaming bull's cage. "The things they bring back create chaos."

Sekhmet lowered her sword but kept it alight. "I gotta lock you up until Lady Weirdwood gets back and decides what to do with you."

Wally's eye twitched. "Makes sense."

She escorted him back toward the Abyssment.

"We'll have a long discussion after this fight is over, Wally," Sekhmet said. "The Manor's actions really are for the greater good."

"I'll look forward to it," Wally said.

Sekhmet opened the door, expecting to find a corridor back to the Abyssment, but instead it led outside to a field of clouds. "Wait, wh—"

Wally gave her a push, slammed the door behind her, and locked it.

Sekhmet hammered at the door, hitting it with blast after fiery blast. Wally rested his head against the frame and let his heart settle itself while he quietly thanked whatever force had twisted the Manor's hallways so that they led to new places.

He gazed into the empty Manor. "No turning back now."

Wally went to find his brother.

29
SPORES

Breeth had seen it all happen.

As the Eraser approached Weirdwood's staff, she had fled to Amelia's eye patch, too frightened to face the negative silhouette again. From there, she had watched Weston, her friend, the man who had spared her when she was a helpless mouse thing, peel away at the Eraser's touch, layer by layer, until nothing was left of the gardener general.

It was more painful than any death Breeth had experienced herself.

She splashed back into Ludwig's frazzled brain to comfort the giant over his twin brother's death. But when Ludwig uncharacteristically attacked the Eraser and his crackled bark skin screamed out in pain, Breeth had retreated to Pyra's vial bullet belt.

Breeth felt ashamed. She was a ghost again. She was supposed to be able to save the day. But she didn't know how to beat the Eraser.

Lucky for her and the staff, Arthur did.

Unfortunately for Arthur, he was dumb enough to then

stroll straight up to a dragon like a fish flopping toward the open mouth of a crocodile.

When the Duchess devoured him, even Amelia cried out in terror.

But it was finally Breeth's time to shine.

A dozen solutions twined through her head. She would possess Arthur's clothes and haul him up the dragon's throat. No . . . That hadn't worked in the Abyssment. Instead, she would possess the bacteria in the Duchess's belly and give her a tummy ache, making her puke Arthur up! But Breeth had never possessed anything microscopic before . . . It seemed hard.

She gritted her ghostly teeth. The longer she brainstormed, the more Arthur was being digested.

That settled it. Breeth would just have to possess the Duchess herself. Hopefully she'd be able to find her way out again.

She reached her ghostly senses toward the dragon's, but then bounced off of the scales like they were made of solid concrete.

"*Ow!*"

Breeth wiggled the shock from her being, then felt the first chill of fear that Arthur was not going to survive this. She might already be too late.

She scanned the field of clouds for something that could defeat a dragon in battle. But there was nothing save rainy ghosts. She needed a blimp-sized puffer fish or a monkey mummy or . . .

Breeth gasped.

She whipped toward the Manor as fast as the clouds would carry her. She creaked through the northern entrance and down the main passage, then nosedived into the hole of its erased center, straight to the Abyssment. She passed the ghostly ocean and the mummy-infested desert, and arrived at the fungus-filled third floor, which, compared to the Eraser, wasn't that scary anymore.

The Mycopath sensed her presence and howled with the voice of a million Fae-born souls trapped in eternal misery.

"Quiet, grouchy!" Breeth cried over the sound. "I need a favor."

A dark wind blew from the Abyssment, and a cloud of greenish spores wafted toward Breeth, whispering sick nothings in her ear. She waited to see her parents' images form in the falling spores, raised from the leaf mulch of the dead. But the spores wafted right through her.

"Doesn't work on ghosts," she said a little sadly. She watched the spores drift downward and smiled. "Never mind about the favor!"

She possessed one spore and then another and another, linking them together like she had Ludwig's paper birds the last time she'd been down here. She quickly grew her collection of spores from a dozen to a hundred, then a thousand and then ten thousand, until she had a nice little Breeth-shaped cloud.

She floated up and out of the Abyssment through the vents. Meanwhile, the spores hissed at her with their tiny, dusty voices. *Infect! Destroy! Take over the world!*

"Oh, *shush*," Breeth told them. "Get those slimy thoughts out of my face. We're not thinking like that anymore."

As Breeth breezed through a keyhole and back outside, she pulsed a new kind of energy through her spores. Amelia had said the Mycopath recycled *dead* matter. That *sounded* dark and depressing, but it was the opposite. It made dead things *alive* again. Gave them a second chance to speak. That was good. Breeth focused on the goodness.

The spores were so simple, they started to change their minds. One moment they were hissing death and destruction, the next they hummed a different tune.

Breeth soared her spores into the sky where the dragon duchess flapped her wings and whispered poetic destruction upon the staff. The clouds below churned and washed over Ludwig, Amelia, and Pyra like waves, trying to drown them. Somewhere, a child was sobbing.

It wasn't easy keeping a cloud of spores together. Especially while being buffeted by the swooping gusts of dragon wings. But Breeth managed to hold tight to her many separate parts, like clinging to thousands upon thousands of balloons, as she whirled and whooshed toward the dragon's mouth. The Duchess took a deep breath to whisper another spell, and Breeth's spores were slurped right into the dragon's throat.

She disappeared down the long tunnel of a sea-salt gullet and went whirling into cavernous lungs where she lost track of most of her spores. Another deep breath sucked her into a dark-blue bloodstream, as frosty as churning waves.

Breeth rode through the dragon's arteries up and up toward the dragon's head until . . .

***

She was staring at a baby. A boy. He was cute and chubby and wrapped in purple silk. Every time Breeth pressed her gem-encrusted fingernail into the baby's tummy, he made raspberries with his lips.

"*My beautiful*," Breeth told him in a language that was not her own. "My Huamei."

She watched him grow up. He was her little secret. Not her husband's child, but another's. And no less perfect for it.

Huamei was a happy boy, reveling in the delights of the Whirling City. The waterfall islands. The maze islands. The ones populated by Fae-born whose pocket-worlds had been demolished. Huamei was also very studious. He mastered calligraphy at a young age and proceeded to correct the aristocracy's techniques. And then he started to label things.

When not attended, young Huamei would paint the symbol for *pot* on the pots and the symbol for *dress* on his mother's favorite gown. The ink refused to come out of the gown, no matter how many times her servants scrubbed it, but Breeth—the Duchess—wore it into the city proudly. It started a fashion trend that lasted for three seasons.

It was this very event that started the tragedy. How was she to know that Huamei's artistic flare would make her husband suspect that the boy was not his son?

The Duchess wore a face of scales the day she was brought

before the dragon court. She watched emotionless as the memories of Huamei's true father—a mere merchant—flickered across the leaf dome. The scales remained on her face as her husband, the Duke, told her that if she didn't repent and disown Huamei, he would see them both executed. She wore the scales the day Huamei was banished from the Whirling City. She had worn them ever since.

The painful memories began to waver and then disintegrate into what looked like *spores*. The Duchess did not know what had happened to her son after he'd departed to join the Wardens.

The spores briefly formed a young human girl's face before coming back together to show scenes the Duchess had never seen. *Huamei walking the halls of Weirdwood with royal pride. Tracking his ancestor's stolen bone so he could bring it home, regain his honor, and rejoin his mother in the Whirling City.*

The Duchess's scales started to smooth as she watched her son leave his hospital bed, skin still softening after having turned to porcelain. Her heart trembled in fear as she watched him attack a monster asylum in this fragile state.

She did not look away. Huamei deserved to have his mother beside him when he passed over to the imperial light above the clouds. She watched the asylum come hurtling down. She watched his scales split open and then shatter.

And she watched her son, her Huamei, die.

. . .

But the memories weren't finished.

With a shattered heart and a smooth face, the Duchess

watched as Arthur, the human, the *thief*, grieved for her son and blamed himself for Huamei's death. She watched as he tried to sacrifice himself to set things right.

A wave of regret and gratitude rose from the Duchess's stomach, through her chest, into her throat, and out of her mouth.

And it brought Arthur with it.

30
THE NOVITIATE AND THE THIEF

Wally found his brother in the Throne Room. Graham sat in Lady Weirdwood's waxen throne. But he didn't sit like royalty. He was hunched over, hands clasped, as if he too felt the weight of the situation.

"I got Sekhmet out of the Manor," Wally said. "But I'm guessing you already know that."

Graham smiled, having once again dropped his puppet act. "Thank you, Wally. That can't have been easy." He gazed up at the ceiling, shaking his head in disbelief. "Complete control over Weirdwood Manor. I've been waiting for this moment since I was eight years old."

Of course. His brother had been peering into the future since he was younger than Wally. It was strange how something so inevitable could have seemed impossible only hours before. Then again, two months ago, Wally never could have guessed that he'd soon be training as a Novitiate magician. Only to abandon that position shortly after.

"So . . . what now?" he asked.

"*Now*," Graham said, slapping his knees and standing, "we

head somewhere special. A place where the threads of the Veil coalesce."

In order to bring the whole thing crashing down, Wally realized. His body was numb. He had no idea what to expect, but he knew they were about to change the world forever.

He wondered if there was some middle ground. Maybe they could try opening Rifts in small towns to see how things went before bringing the Fae howling into the Real.

"You made the right decision, Wally," Graham said, as if reading his mind. "You just can't see it yet." He stared deep into his brother's eyes. "But I can. And I swear, everything turns out better this way."

Wally stared back. "Just promise me we'll never work with the Order."

Graham offered his hand, and Wally shook it.

"First stop," Graham said, retaking the waxen throne, "take Jamie back home. Any other requests?"

Wally looked around the walls. They felt lifeless. The air empty of giggles and cheesy jokes. Before he'd come to the Throne Room, Wally had checked his room in the Moon Tower for Breeth's body. But all he found was broken glass and tufts of hair.

He didn't know what it meant, but he hoped his friend was okay.

"I miss Breeth," he told Graham.

"Who is . . . *Breeth*?" Graham asked, sounding honestly surprised.

Wally gave his brother a questioning look. Graham was an oracle. He saw *everything* . . . right?

Or did he? Wally recalled how his brother had failed to foresee what would happen to the water tower. As if he hadn't anticipated Breeth's interference with the flaming bull.

Wally's throat tightened. *Could Graham not see ghosts in his visions?*

"Um, I meant I miss *breathing*," Wally said. "I've just been going nonstop the last few days and . . . it will be nice to breathe easy again."

Graham arched an eyebrow, then shrugged it away.

Wally had no idea how all of this would turn out, but there was something reassuring in knowing Graham couldn't see everything.

"What about our parents?" Wally asked to change the subject. "I know they're only Fae-born, but . . ."

"We'll be back for them," Graham said. "When all of this is over." He straightened his posture, sitting with a bit more confidence on the waxen throne. He smiled at Wally. "Ready?"

Wally expected fear to rise up in him. But instead, he felt calm.

"Actually," he said, "I am."

Graham gripped the armrests as if taking a horse's reins for the first time. "I've only seen Lady Weirdwood do this in visions, but . . ."

He closed his eyes . . . Wally felt a floating sensation in his stomach . . .

And then the Manor slipped off through the expanse between the worlds.

❋❋❋

Arthur scrambled back across the clouds, waiting for the Duchess to swoop down and swallow him again. Was she playing with him like cats play with mice? Were dragons actually ruminants who swallowed their food twice? Had she forgotten to *chew*?

But instead of attacking, the Duchess shrieked something at her guards, who angled their wings toward the horizon. Once they were gone, she landed on a cloud bank and coiled her great neck, hiding her face beneath her wing. Golden tears dripped onto the clouds.

Arthur, heart pounding, skin sticky with digestive juices, blinked at the breathtaking sight of a weeping dragon and wondered what miracle had saved his life.

A hand clamped down on his shoulder.

"Augh!"

"I need you to tell me how you did that," Amelia said, her blue eye burning through him. "Do not leave out a single detail."

"*Hi, Arthur,*" Arthur said sarcastically as he stood. "Welcome back from the *dragon stomach*. Nice to see you didn't *die*."

Amelia waited for an answer.

"I . . . honestly don't know," he said, wringing the last of the dragon bile from his shirt. "One moment I was in a dark, wet sack, the next—"

"Not that," Amelia said. "I spotted a girl-shaped cloud of Mycopath spores fly into the dragon's throat. Breeth must have revived memories of Huamei to haunt the Duchess and make her regurgitate you."

"Oh."

Arthur stared back at the crying dragon. He was, of course, grateful not to be digested, but he wouldn't wish the Mycopath on his worst enemy. Especially one who had lost her son.

"I mean how did you do everything else," Amelia said. "The miners, the pliers, the cloud-soled shoes."

"Where do I start . . . ?" Arthur said.

He told her about comforting the grieving souls of Kingsport with a place called the *Great Elsewhere*. How he and Liza had stumbled onto a strangely familiar storm cloud city right after Arthur had been thinking about the time he'd consoled Wally following the deaths of their parents. And how a single piece of cloudy butterscotch had brought a great epiphany.

As he spoke, Amelia's expression *changed*. She stared at him with a sort of confused admiration. Like a cockroach had just cleaned her sink.

"You were so determined to heal strangers' hearts," she said, "that you spun their memories into an *entire pocket-world* for them to believe in." She gazed across the clouds. "I was wrong about you, Arthur Benton. You do have magic. You can bring others' imaginations to life."

Arthur breathed deep and took in the whole of the Great Elsewhere. "I guess I can."

Amelia arched an eyebrow. "I thought you'd be elated. Running around, *boasting* like you do."

Arthur was as surprised as she was. He had *finally* impressed someone in Weirdwood Manor. *Amelia*, no less. But Arthur felt . . . wary.

"If I can create pocket-worlds," he said, "then I'm responsible for the damage they cause."

He looked past Amelia toward Pyra and Ludwig in the distance. The giant was on his knees, his remaining hand pressed to the spot where his twin had been erased. The cook stroked his bark-crackled arm.

"You saved our lives, Arthur," Amelia said. "None of us could banish the Eraser. But you did."

Arthur couldn't take his eyes from the tragic scene. He wanted to speak Weston back to life. To use his newfound powers so the giant could see his twin again. But if Ludwig was anything like Arthur—like *Liza*—a fake ghost version of Weston would feel as empty as cloud shapes.

"How did you do it?" Amelia asked. "How did you defeat the Eraser?"

It was only then that Arthur remembered the flash of golden eyes within the Eraser's depths.

"Um . . . ," he said.

Amelia was still looking at him with admiration. He didn't want that to go away. If he told her the truth, she'd know that his actions had inadvertently killed Weston. He would never become a Novitiate and lead an honorable life. He would never see the Fae again.

"I created the Eraser," he said before he could talk himself out of it. "When I retired Garnett Lacroix."

Arthur explained, and Amelia fell deathly silent. When he finished, he tried to read her expression. She looked like she was deciding whether or not to stomp a surprisingly helpful cockroach to death.

"It seems I was wrong about something else," she finally said.

Arthur winced.

"There just might be a Gentleman Thief on every adventure you go on." She turned and swept toward the staff. "You can start making up for the damage you caused by joining the Manor as a Novitiate."

"Wait, *what*?" Arthur said, following her.

"I don't trust you back in Kingsport with magic this strong," Amelia said. "Besides, who better to help us bring down the Eraser than the person who created it?"

Arthur stumbled to keep up. "I thought you said I was a horribly selfish child."

"I did," Amelia said.

They reached Pyra and Ludwig.

"I hate to interrupt your grieving," Amelia said softly, "but we must attend to urgent matters. We shall pay tribute to our fallen comrade once we've returned to the Manor."

The giant and the chef stood at attention.

"I'm going to collect the Wardens and Fae-born from Kingsport," Amelia said, and nodded beyond the battlefield. "And then I'll seal the Rift."

"Um . . ." Arthur remembered the horrifying moment when the Eraser had entered the House of Spirits. "The Wardens are trapped in a doorless room."

"Good to know," Amelia said. "Pyra?"

Pyra handed her a black powder vial.

"You two split up and find Lady Weirdwood," Amelia told the cook and the giant. "You might want to look *lower* than usual."

Ludwig, sniffing, and Pyra, grumbling, set out across the clouds.

"Arthur?" Amelia said. "You're on Dapplewood duty. We must return the kidnapped critters to their home."

Just the name of the town broke his heart. "But how?" he asked. "It was *erased*."

Amelia sighed. "Must I really spell it out for you?"

"Um . . . *maybe*?" Arthur said. But then a light flicked on in his mind. "Oh! . . . *Oh*." He turned in a circle, glancing around the Great Elsewhere. "But where do I . . . ? How do I . . . ?"

"You'll need to speak with her," Amelia said, and nodded to the Duchess, whose face was still hidden behind her wing.

Arthur's body went cold. "You're kidding." His pants were still damp with dragon saliva.

Without another word of advice, Amelia set off toward the Rift that Wally had left open, leaving Arthur to face the Duchess all alone.

"*For the Dapplewood*," Arthur whispered.

He approached the Duchess on trembling legs.

Just over a dragon's-neck length away, he stopped and took a deep, shuddering breath. "Um, *excuse me*?" Arthur's voice cracked in fear. "Duchess?"

The dragon lowered her wing, which shimmered into a silken sleeve, sweeping over dragon skin and leaving robes behind. The Duchess unveiled not a face of scales but smooth human skin. She looked more like Huamei than ever.

"*Hi*," Arthur said, still terrified out of his mind. "Hello. I'm sorry. Um, thanks for not eating me."

The Duchess wiped away a tear with a pearl fingernail, then bowed her head to him. "I absolve you of your crimes, Arthur Benton. I don't know how you stirred those visions from my stomach. But I thank you for them."

Arthur considered explaining about Breeth and the spores, but then decided it was too complicated. "You're, um, y-you're welcome."

The Duchess gazed into the sky. "I owe my son an apology. But to confess that puts me in exile from my kingdom." Her white eyes fell to the horizon. "Perhaps I'll found a new pocket-world. *Huameia*."

She lifted her arms, and her sleeves began to expand into wings.

"*Wait*," Arthur said. "Before you leave . . . could I ask you a favor?"

The Duchess's face flashed with scales at the impropriety of a boy asking a dragon for a *favor*. But then the scales smoothed away. Her wings shrank back into sleeves.

Arthur cleared the fear from his throat. "You know how I did some *damage* in the Fae?"

After he had explained, the Duchess silently raised a fingernail and sliced open a Rift in the air. Behind it was a blank slate, waiting to be filled.

Arthur watched as the Duchess took off into the sky, opposite the direction her guards had flown. His heart was still pounding in his chest.

***

Not long after, Amelia returned with the Wardens and the Dapplewood citizens. Most of the critters scrabbled to stay atop the clouds, but the duck had no problem.

"They had already undone their chains and were wandering around the house," Amelia said. "They all know how to pick locks for some reason."

Arthur smiled at that, then raised his hands. "Gather 'round, everyone!"

The adorable critters formed a circle around him.

"I know you lost your town recently," Arthur said. "But I also know it lives on in your memories. I want you to tell me everything you can about it."

A hedgehog grandmother stepped forward. "In spring, the sun remembered the roofs, lending each and every home a bit of golden warmth."

"There were certain days in summer," a badger said with a tender voice, "when the air blew cool in the light and warm in the shade."

"I remember the way autumn leaves danced rainbows from the branches," a mole said, "reminding us it was nearly time to rest."

"Winter held a magic all its own," said a mouse. "It dressed the world in shimmery white and decked the window glass with patterns of blue. The cold always reminded me to never take food and warmth for granted."

Arthur listened and lent his own details—the purple cobbled streets, the cozy-as-cotton houses, the watercolor skies. He felt a new glow in his chest. If bringing comfort to

Kingsport's grieving had felt like stars, this felt like an entire *constellation*.

When the stories were through, Arthur led the critters to the Rift the Duchess had created. The Dapplewood was waiting for them on the other side. Every cobblestone and leaf, every house and burrow was in place. Only one thing had changed. The seamstress's shop had a new roof.

"Consider capitalizing the *W* in *DappleWood*," Arthur told the citizens as they skittered and waddled and pawed into single file. "In honor of your *newish* town."

Each of them took a deep breath as they stepped through the Rift, grateful to be back home. Arthur wished Audrey was there to see it. Where had that lovely ferret scampered off to anyway? He searched the Great Elsewhere, which blurred in his vision. He was so tired he swore he could curl up and fall asleep on the clouds right there. The feeling in his chest was starting to feel less like a glow and more like someone had punched him.

"*Over here!*" a booming voice shouted in the distance.

Arthur shook the spots from his eyes and ran toward Ludwig.

The giant held a baby wrapped in a lacy blanket. "I barely caught her," Ludwig whispered, "before she fell srough ze clouds."

"Where is her snake?" Amelia asked, looking even more concerned than usual.

Ludwig shrugged his giant shoulders.

It was only then that Arthur saw the blanket was actually a wedding dress.

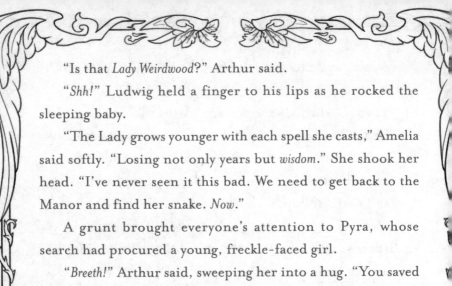

"Is that *Lady Weirdwood*?" Arthur said.

"*Shh!*" Ludwig held a finger to his lips as he rocked the sleeping baby.

"The Lady grows younger with each spell she casts," Amelia said softly. "Losing not only years but *wisdom*." She shook her head. "I've never seen it this bad. We need to get back to the Manor and find her snake. *Now*."

A grunt brought everyone's attention to Pyra, whose search had procured a young, freckle-faced girl.

"*Breeth!*" Arthur said, sweeping her into a hug. "You saved my life. *Again*."

Breeth pulled away and smiled big, red cheeks. "Yer welcome."

Ludwig covered the baby's ears and whispered, "*You saved mine too!*"

"Yer welcome," Breeth said again. It sounded like she had a cold.

"The Manor is this way," Amelia said, leading them.

Arthur took one last look at the city in the clouds. He considered saying farewell to the Fae-born who resembled his mom. But he knew it would only make him sad. Like trying to hug a woman made of wax. Instead, he would make his mother's memory proud by behaving mostly like a gentleman with just a dash of thief.

He caught up to the others, who had stopped at a large, rectangular absence in the clouds. Like the foundation where a house once stood.

"*Uh-oh!*" Baby Weirdwood had woken from her nap and was pointing a chubby finger.

"*Shh shh shh.*" Ludwig bounced the child and stroked her hair.

"They took it," Sekhmet said.

She stood nearby, staring at the empty foundation in disbelief, slowly sinking through the clouds.

Amelia clenched her teeth. "*Who* took *what*?"

"Wally and Graham," Sekhmet said. "They *took* the Manor."

"*Cooper* did this?" Arthur said. "Why?"

Sekhmet closed her eyes. "I think he's going to help his brother bring down the Veil."

"He *what*?"

Arthur thought that Wally had left his thieving days behind. In fact, the last time Arthur had seen him, Wally had seemed dedicated to the Manor's purpose. When had Wally decided to betray the Wardens? And why hadn't he talked to Arthur about it?

"Wherever the Eraser heads next," Amelia said, "we'll be powerless to stop it."

"I vould ask Lady Veirdvood how to track ze Manor," Ludwig said as the baby reached up and pinched his lips with her chubby fingers, "but I don't sink she vould understand ze question."

"You mean we're *stuck* in this place?" Sekhmet said, gazing across the barren clouds.

Arthur felt strange staying in this imitation afterlife. He didn't think he could bear running into his Fae-born mother.

"I have a better idea," he said.

He, Breeth, Sekhmet, Pyra, Amelia, and Ludwig, holding

baby Weirdwood, all walked toward the last remaining Rift. Arthur gave one look back, checking the horizon for signs of Rook Liza. When he didn't see any trace of her, they stepped through the Rift . . .

Into the DappleWood.

AFTERWEIRD

B reeth had a long journey back to herself.

Escaping the dragon duchess's memories was *hard*. Not because she didn't know the way back, but because she didn't want to leave. She had started to feel motherly feelings toward Huamei, and she wanted to stay with him. Her baby boy wouldn't be there when she returned to the world . . .

But Breeth quickly remembered her old life and responsibilities. She had to make sure Arthur was okay. And Wally. Especially Wally.

So, she extracted herself from the memories and swam through seawater arteries on little raft-like blood cells, back into the dragon's lungs and then into her throat. From there, it was just a matter of working the spores up to the dragon's nose.

The Duchess, who had already taken flight, *sneezed* . . . and Breeth found herself sailing through the sky. A little mucusy. But free.

As her spores slowly floated down toward the vast, clouded expanse of the Great Elsewhere, she searched for her friends. She had decided that the *Mycopath* was too hideous a name for the mushroom that had saved the day, and she couldn't wait to tell everyone its new nickname: *Fun Gus*.

She floated a little lower and spotted Arthur and Amelia walking across the clouds in the distance, safe and sound. She would sneak up on them and give them a scare, and then they'd all go back to the Manor. Wally would tell Audrey to free her body from that glass box. And everything would be right again.

Except Weston. She hadn't forgotten Weston.

Breeth performed several whirls through the sky, enjoying her last few floaty moments before returning to life and all of its restrictions. But as she drifted closer toward the group, she noticed they were walking with a girl. A girl with a bad haircut . . .

Breeth's spore heart sank. That was *her* body. *Without her in it.*

She tried to get herself to fall faster. But her lighter-than-air spores were at the mercy of the wind. "*That's not me!*" she screamed a hundred feet in the air. "*Danger! Imposter!* Pin her down!"

But no one could hear her. Not Arthur, not Sekhmet, and not the staff. Wally wasn't there to translate.

Breeth bundled the spores together, trying to make them heavier. But below, the group stepped through a watercolor Rift, and Amelia turned to seal it.

"*Don't leave me with the rain ghosts!*" Breeth screamed so loud she thought her spores might explode.

The Rift closed, and her friends and her body vanished.

"Come back!" Breeth called after them. "Please! *Pleeeeeaaaaassssse!*"

Join Arthur, Wally, and Breeth
on their epic, final adventure in:

NIGHTMARES OF WEIRDWOOD

Coming April 2022